PRAISE FOR RICK WILBER

"Wilber's voice (has) a kind of authority and compassion that have helped him carve out a niche identifiably his own." —Locus

"Wilber ... will exhilarate, startle, and dazzle you."
—Michael Bishop, award-winning author of *No Enemy but Time*, *Unicorn Mountain*, and *Brittle Innings*

"Rick Wilber ... tells you the truth, a quality that can be unsettling sometimes, but is never less than absolutely refreshing. Wilber knows how to do justice to the nuances of a complex story, and he deserves a huge readership." —Peter Straub, author of *Ghost Story*

"Brilliantly crafted, fiercely real ... Relentless and original, this is science fiction that matters now. Highly recommended." —Julie E. Czerneda, award-winning author of the Web Shifter's Library series

"A major collection from what it's high past time to admit is one of our major writers. Wilber writes with literate flair, compassion, and a deep understanding of human psychology. Highly recommended!"
—Robert J. Sawyer, Hugo Award-winning author of The Oppenheimer Alternative

RAMBUNCTIOUS

RAMBUNCTIOUS

Nine Tales of Determination

RICK WILBER

WFP
WORDFIRE PRESS

CONTENTS

EBook ISBN: 978-1-68057-067-0
Trade Paperback ISBN: 978-1-68057-066-3
Hardcover ISBN: 978-1-68057-068-7

Cover design by Janet McDonald
Cover artwork images by Adobe Stock
Kevin J. Anderson, Art Director

Published by
WordFire Press, LLC
PO Box 1840
Monument CO 80132

Kevin J. Anderson & Rebecca Moesta, Publishers

WordFire Press eBook Edition 2020
WordFire Press Trade Paperback Edition 2020
WordFire Press Hardcover Edition 2020

Printed in the USA

Join our WordFire Press Readers Group for
sneak previews, updates, new projects, and giveaways.
Sign up at wordfirepress.com

INTRODUCTION

These stories were first printed in magazines or anthologies over a thirty-year timespan. The earliest of the stories, "War Bride," appeared in the anthology *Alien Sex* (Dutton, edited by Ellen Datlow) in 1990 and the most recent, "Today is Today," appeared first in *Stonecoast Review* in July of 2018. Four of the other stories first appeared in various issues of *Asimov's Science Fiction* magazine, and another appeared first in the *Magazine of Fantasy & Science Fiction*. One story appeared in *Gulf Stream Review*, and another in the anthology of original stories *Adventures in the Twilight Zone* (Daw Books, 1995, edited by Carol Serling).

You will find here the Sidewise Award-winning story, "Something Real," which offers an alternate history take on famous baseball player and World War II spy Moe Berg, and you will find in "Today is Today" an alternate universe take on parenthood, professional football, and Down syndrome that was recently reprinted in *The Year's Best Science Fiction and Fantasy: 2019* (Prime Books, edited by Rich Horton).

Much of the science fiction and fantasy that I've published is about relationships, both good and bad. Often, these relationships are between two human beings, and sometimes they are relationships between humans and aliens because I am, at heart, a science fiction writer, and aliens serve as wonderful examples of the "other" in stories, allowing writers the latitude to consider all sorts of odd relationships, as you will see.

Being a science fiction writer at heart doesn't mean that I've abandoned things here on Earth. I grew up in a family immersed deeply in sports. My father played major-league baseball and was a minor-league manager and major-league coach and scout for many years. I played high school and college baseball myself, though not all that well, and I was also a football and basketball player of dubious quality in college. I sat on the bench for all three sports, but enjoyed being on the teams and practicing and playing the games. I enjoyed it all so much that I continued to play at the amateur level in those sports and soccer, too, well into my fifties. To readers new to me and to my short fiction, this will help explain how sports in general, and baseball in particular, keeps cropping up in these stories and, indeed, all my fiction and occasional poetry.

This immersion in sports has prompted my use of women characters as often as men, and this collection reflects that. My extended family includes women who played high school and college basketball, ran cross-country and starred in high school soccer and track and more. Today, several of these talented athletes are still active, running everything from 5K fun runs to ambitious marathons.

In my own immediate family, my wife is one of those athletes, running half marathons now and again just to stay in shape for the heavy-duty thinking required of a full professor of finance. Our daughter is a talented, athletic biologist and zookeeper, who runs for fun these days, enjoying the exercise just as much, I think, as she did on her high school track and soccer teams. My son, now in his fifties, is a wonderful Down syndrome person who's happily made a liar out of all the experts who told me when he was young what he wouldn't be able to accomplish, even as he was growing up to accomplish those very things. He's an avid bowler and, back in the day, found great joy playing basketball and soccer in the Special Olympics. I have dedicated this book to him and our daughter, for all that I've learned from them both.

In all cases, the characters in these stories are inventions, though I sometimes borrow historical figures for purposes of storytelling. I greatly appreciate the fine advice of my agent, Robert G. Diforio of the D4EO Literary Agency, and the support and advice from Kevin J. Anderson and Rebecca Moesta, who together founded WordFire Press. Thanks, too, to Marie Whittaker and the rest of the WordFire Press publishing team, which has done an outstanding job in all regards. All errors in editing and storytelling are mine.

—Rick Wilber, St. Petersburg, FL, June 2019

DEDICATION

This collection is for two wonderful children who grew to become outstanding adults. Samantha Wilber and Richard Wilber, Jr., thank you for teaching me so much about life, parenthood, storytelling, and the merits of being rambunctious.

There was a very long incubation period for this story, which is deeply personal for me in several ways, including my being the parent of a remarkable Down syndrome son. When an editor at Stonecoast Review, *Jess Flarity, solicited a story from me for* Stonecoast Review #9, *I took another, deeper, look at the story and finally realized what it needed and how I could get it done. With the help of Flarity and other editors at* Stonecoast, *the story clicked for us all. A couple of months later* Locus *magazine reviewer Rich Horton liked the story well enough to call it a Recommended Read, and then also selected it for inclusion in his annual* Best Science Fiction and Fantasy: 2019 *anthology (Prime Books, 2019).*

TODAY IS TODAY

"You can think of our entire universe, our reality, as one bubble surrounded by an infinite number of other bubbles, each with its own reality. Do those bubbles touch? Can you cross from one to another? That's an entertaining possibility."

—Janine Marie Larsen, PhD, Physics, University of Loyola at St. Louis

I n one tiny part of one of the new bubbles emerging from the bubble that is our particular universe, there is a place and time where you might exist and I might exist and I have a daughter named Janine.

Perhaps, in that tiny bubble, I was lucky with sports and found some success. A quarterback in high school, I'll have converted to a tight end in college at the University of Minnesota, where I'll bang heads and block like a demon and catch most of the passes they throw my way. I'll be All-Big Twelve, then a second-round draft choice, then I'll make the team in St. Louis for the Brewers and get my chance to start when Rasheed Campbell blows out his left knee. Then I'll never look back. Seven years later I'll wind down my career as a backup on the Falcons, but that will be their Super Bowl year, so I'll get my ring, mostly, by sitting on my butt.

It will be a nice way to spend my twenties. I'll stay single and have a blast, though my body will take a beating. When I lose a couple of steps and the good times come to an end I'll try to move to broadcasting, but that's a lot harder than you'd think. I won't be able to think that fast on my feet, so it won't work out.

Still, I'll feel like I have plenty of money for life as a grown-up, and you'd think I'd be happy; but it's hard to be a has-been, no matter how much money you've saved. I'll never marry, never have any kids, never grow up, really, and I'll know it. Later in life I'll be lonely and bored and broke. And thanks to all that head-banging work on the offensive line in my football career, I'll literally be losing my mind. Eventually I'll run out of money and run into trouble and only then will I have any regrets.

In another tiny part of another emerging bubble where you might exist, I'll break my collarbone in the second game of my senior year of high school and by the time I'm back the season will be over and my football career along with it. But my left-handed pitching skills will be unfazed by my fractured right clavicle and I'll pitch us to the state championship where we'll lose by one unearned run. My fastball in the high eighties and my nice, straight change will earn me a free ride to Loyola University, where I'll have four good years as a Billiken and five more in the minors before I'll hang them up and get on with real life in the business world.

I'll meet a woman who loves me and I, her. We'll marry and have two sweet kids. I'll have a good life and some nice minor-league memories from Tampa and Atlanta and Durham and Spokane. You'd think I'd be happy.

In another tiny part of another of my emerging bubbles where you might exist, the Golden Gophers will keep me at quarterback and I'll do fine as the starter, though I'll never be a star, and I won't make the NFL. I'll knock around a bit in arena football and then swim up to the surface as the quarterback of the Hamilton Tiger-Cats. Once, in my nine years there, I'll lead the Ticats to victory in the Grey Cup. In the CFL there's room to pass, and room to run, and I'll do both, often.

I'll meet a woman named Alene in my second season when we'll beat the Alouettes with a lucky rouge. We'll be celebrating at Yancy's on Hanover Street and there she'll be, dark hair and blue eyes, stunning and smart and ambitious. I'll have had a good day on the ground, gaining ninety yards before taking a stinger and coming out of the game. She'll have been there, rooting for the Alouettes, and seen that hit I took. She'll wonder how I am feeling. Just fine, I'll say, though I'll have a worrisome headache.

She'll be an actor; a smart and successful French Canadian who speaks four languages. I'll feel lucky. By my third season we'll be married. By my fifth season we'll have a child, Janine. We'll call her Jannie.

Janine Marie Larsen will be born two weeks early on July 21st, a Saturday, at four in the morning. Alene will have a rough time of it with a fifteen-hour delivery and then it will only get worse: Jannie's feet, hands, and the epicanthal folds at the eyes. Her muscles will all have a certain flaccidity, even for a newborn.

Trisomy 21, the doctor will say.

Down syndrome.

Alene will have been through ultrasound and blood tests and everything will have looked fine. But here will be Jannie, and that will be that. There's a lot these kids can do, the doctor will say as Alene and I both cry. Really, they can accomplish a lot.

Really, the doctor will emphasize.

We'll have a game that night at home, in old Ivor Wynne Stadium against the Alouettes, and Alene will insist I play. So I'll go and do that, earning my paycheck with a couple of touchdown passes and a good enough night of football. I won't remember much of the game. All I'll be able to think about is: Down syndrome.

I'll go right back to the hospital after the game and Alene will be weak but smiling and more beautiful than ever. There will be a picture the next day in the Hamilton Spectator of her with the baby—the whole city will be behind us. I'll hold that baby and kiss her cheek as the cameras whir and click.

Two years will go by when I won't play much: some knee surgery, a discectomy for a herniated disc, a couple more concussions. The docs will say it's time to hang them up and so I will. That's about the time that Alene will get the movie role she's always wanted, filming in Vancouver. Our parting will be amicable. I'll get Jannie and Alene will get visitation rights and there she'll go, heading west.

I'll have no reason whatsoever to be happy, but, holding Jannie, I will be.

There is another tiny part of a different bubble where Alene and I will stay together and things will go differently for Jannie. She'll be normal and fussy and hungry at birth and she won't stop being any of those things right through high school and college. She'll get her brains from her mother and her athleticism from me, and get a full ride to play soccer at Rice, where she'll major in physics. Then she'll choose brawn over brains and turn pro for the Washington Whippets before joining the national team in the Global Cup. She'll be a star and a household name after they beat the French on her hat trick to win it all.

By that time, I'll be coaching football at Buffalo State and happy enough with how I've reconciled myself to the paycheck and the fall from fame. But Hamilton will treat me well with a big ovation when I go there to see Jannie play a friendly against the Italians and she'll have a great day, scoring a brace. We'll have dinner afterward and she'll be polite, but distant, and we'll smile for the cameras and then I'll go my way and she'll go hers.

In a more important tiny bubble, Alene and I will do our best to raise Jannie to be everything she can be, Down syndrome be damned. After I hang them up, Alene's career will prosper and we'll do fine. We'll move to Vancouver, where most of her work is, and I'll spend a lot of time with Jannie. She'll be a sweet kid, but there are heart problems and a leg that needs straightening will create an uncertain future for her and me both, as my football past and all those helmet hits come back to haunt me: foggy mornings will turn into long, dark days, and I'll worry about just how long I'll still be me.

I'll be in the dumps a lot, but I'll need something to do, someone to be, so I'll take care of Jannie, one day at a time. Today is today. There'll be speech therapy sessions and school and all the rest. There'll be some joy in this, some deep satisfaction. She'll be my girl, my always girl.

In this bubble, even as I lose some recent memories, I'll still remember certain moments from my past that were so perfect, where I was so tuned in—so fully one with the moment—that I captured them completely in my mind in slow-motion detail. I'll remember them vividly, even when I can't find my car keys. I still feel the perfection of the pass to Elijah Depps deep in the corner of the end zone against the Argos. And I'll still watch in awe that time I swear I guided the ball in flight to bend it around Ryan Crisps's outstretched hands as he tried to intercept for the Blue Bombers, and instead the ball found Jason Wissen with no time left and we won.

And I'll feel that joy, too, when Jannie, on her twenty-second birthday, in one of her many Special Olympics soccer games, steals the ball off the player she's defending and sprints down the field with it, dribbling like mad. She'll weave her way past three defenders, come in on the goalie, fake left and shoot right, an outside of the shoe push into the upper ninety for a goal. It'll be a great goal, and everybody on both teams will come over to hug her and celebrate, because that's how it's done in Special O's. I'll beam. That's my girl.

There's another tiny bubble, one I imagine every now and then, where after my divorce I'll spend a lot of time with a woman named Emily. She won't be bothered by Jannie, she'll just want me to be me and Jannie to be Jannie and Emily to be Emily. In that bubble we'll make it work, and there'll be a new drug on the market for trisomy 21 and the sun will shine every day and the Yankees will never, ever win the pennant but the Ticats will be the powerhouse team of the CFL and my knees won't hurt and my mind will be clear and my memories all there as Jannie goes off to college and the sun will shine every day in Hamilton, Ontario.

In one particular spot in one particular tiny bubble, Alene will be a grad student when we meet, and an associate professor by the time she leaves for a post in Quebec. She can't turn it down, and the stress and strain of raising Jannie is, she'll say in distancing French, is *complètement impossible*. I'll have seen it coming for years, but we'll still do the divorce through lawyers.

As time goes by, she'll call Jannie often enough, and send her cards and cash on her birthday and Christmas. She'll even bring Jannie up for a week or two visit in the summer.

Jannie will do fine. By her sixteenth birthday she'll be doing third grade arithmetic and fourth grade reading and tearing things up in Special Olympics soccer. This will be better than the school-district psychologist thought Jannie would ever do. It will be so good, in fact, that after her birthday party, after the neighbor kids and her special pals are gone, after the cake is eaten, she'll be sitting on her bed kicking a plastic toy soccer ball off the opposite wall: shoot it, trap it with her foot, shoot it again, trap it, shoot it, trap it.

I'll come in to stop the racket and she'll look at me: that wide face, those eyes. Her language skills aren't all that great, but from the look on her face I'll be able to see something's up. "My father," she'll say, "I sixteen now."

I'll sit down next to her. "Yeah, young lady; you're growing up fast," I'll say, but what I'll be thinking about is all the things Jannie and I have learned together, often the hard way. Boyfriends, how to handle her periods, what clothes to wear and when to wear them, how to tie her hair in a ponytail and put in a different bow every day, how to ignore some people and pay attention to others, how to be so different and still be so happy. Tricky business, all of that.

"My father," she'll say, "I not be like you or Mom-mom."

I'll be the lunkhead I am in every one of these bubbles, no question, but I'll be able to see where this is going: my Jannie, my hard-working girl, is doing so well that she knows how well she isn't doing. She's been expecting to grow up, to leave Never-land. But in this bubble it doesn't work like that.

"Jannie, Jannie," I'll say, lying to her and not for the first time, struggling with how to handle this. "Look," I'll say. "We're all different, Janster, we all have different things we're good at or bad at."

She'll look at me. She'll trust me. I'll say, "I wanted to be an astronomer, Jannie; you know, look at the stars and figure out what it all means. I wanted that, Jannie, in the worst way. But I couldn't do the math."

"Bet Mom-mom could," Jannie will say, smiling, getting into it.

"Yeah, Jannie, your mom sure could. She's one smart lady," I'll say, though I'll be thinking some other, less generous, thoughts about Jannie's mother just then. To be kind, she'll have missed out on a lot of good things.

"Sure, my father. I get it," Jannie will say. And then she'll stand up to give me a hug, and I'll hug her back and then I'll leave the room. Later, out in the driveway, we'll shoot hoops and she'll seem fine. I'll join her in a game of one-on-one, make it-take it, and she'll clobber me. I'll blame it on my bad knees.

In my least favorite bubble I'll die at age fifty-two of an aneurysm. Alene won't be around and I'll have no living relatives. I won't leave much money behind. Jannie will be stranded. Alone. Unhappy. And there'll be twenty more years of her own decline into senescence before there's peace.

In another bubble Jannie will be an intellectual powerhouse. In high school she'll think calculus is fun and physics is entertaining. She'll have a perfect score on the science portion of the PSAT. Caltech will come calling, and MIT, and Yale and Stanford and Loyola and Case Western and Harvey Mudd and Duke and the University of Chicago. Astronomy in college? Physics? Biology? She'll find it hard to decide.

She'll be patient with me in this bubble. She'll be understanding that her father is a decent guy but not the sharpest tool in the shed. When she walks across the stage for that college degree, and then the next one, and then the next one, I'll there in the audience, proud as I can be.

In one particular bubble, the one that you and I share, Jannie and I will be at the Brock Theatre in Hamilton, where we both live; me in a two-bedroom condo, Jannie in a group home that she's recently moved into after years of living in her own apartment. Down syndrome people slide into early-onset Alzheimer's, almost all of them. It's unfair, but there it is.

Jannie will be thirty years old and I'll be fifty-seven. We'll be laughing and joking about old age on that January day as we walk through the parking lot's snow, go into the sudden warmth of the theater, buy our tickets and take our seats. Then we'll watch a movie, something about memory keepers and cute Down syndrome kids and the sweet and soapy ills of the world. I'll be squirming in my seat; Jannie will be quiet.

When we walk out of the place people will be staring at Jannie. She'll not be cute, and she'll be shuffling some because of some knee trouble that I probably caused her, encouraging all that Special O's soccer and getting her out on the basketball court with me for all those years. We won't have played in a while.

It will be snowing lightly as we walk away from the theater and get in the car, a beat-up little Toyota that I'm determined to keep running. You don't get rich in the CFL, and there are better uses for my retirement money than buying shiny new metal and plastic. As I start the car and get the heater going Jannie will look at me. I'll see it in her eyes. That movie was a bad idea.

"My father," she'll say. "I. Am. Me." And she'll punch herself in the chest with her right fist, hard.

"You are that, Jannie, you certainly are," I'll say, kicking myself.

"Thank you," she'll say, and sit back and relax.

There are all those different bubbles, but right then and right there, this will be the only one that matters. This is it. Reality. We are who we are, and we are where we are. We're in this bubble, the one we share, the one where we do the best we can with what we have.

We won't talk about the movie as we drive off and head for some ice cream and then, later, the group home. Instead, we'll talk hockey, father and daughter, something about the Sabres and how maybe they'll move to Hamilton and wouldn't that be great? Or we'll talk about Jannie's bowling team, where she's holding down that ninety-six average and I couldn't possibly be more proud of her. Or we'll talk about the Ticats and how much fun we had going to the games last year and soon enough the season will be back and this year, for sure, the Ticats will make their way back to the Grey Cup.

We won't talk about the path I've started walking down. Jannie wouldn't understand. But the reason she's in that group home is that they don't trust me to have her anymore. Mood swings. Anger. All those hits in all those practices and all those games. CTE my doc calls it, chronic traumatic encephalopathy, and the league agrees. I have good days and bad ones, and she's safer in that home.

I'm not happy about that.

I was counting on holding Jannie's hand as she crossed that street into the confusion and then the darkness she faces, and now it's her who'll be holding mine.

But that won't come up. We won't say much about anything. We won't need to. We'll just eat our ice cream and hang out together and enjoy this little bit of a bubble as best we can. This is our bubble, right here and right now. Today is today.

This story appeared in the June 2016 issue of Asimov's Science Fiction *magazine. I was working on my First Contact novel,* Alien Morning *(Tor, 2016), at the time and gave serious consideration to plugging it into that novel. It seemed to stand so well on its own, however, that I ultimately decided to give the protagonist her own story. One of these days I'm going to write another story about Emma when she's a little older and heading out for some new adventures.*

RAMBUNCTIOUS

It started when Grandma Edna lost her marbles again and wouldn't eat the dinner I'd made her and so I had to ask Grandpa Posey to help me get her settled down so she'd eat at least a little of the macaroni and cheese as she chattered on about how the aliens had sent her a message saying when they would arrive and take her and Grandpa back to the homeworld. I knew it was all a bunch of hooey, and there's a lot of that from Grandma Edna these days; but still, How about me, Grandma? I asked her. Don't I get to go? And she looked at me real quiet, like this thought hadn't occurred to her before, and then she shrugged and said I don't think so, Emma.

Well, that was so upsetting all the way around that the next day during recess at Barney Hill Elementary I went and punched Adam Hardy in the nose when Ms. Jacoby asked me how my grandma was doing and I said she's fine and Adam Hardy laughed out loud and made fun of how Grandma had spouted off about UFOs during bring your parents or guardians to school day last week and that got me sent to the principal's office where Ms. Candy told me for the hundredth time that she understood how hard it all is for me but I really have to stop hitting the boys.

Well. They pick the fights and I end them, that's all, I said to Ms. Candy, and she smiled and said, You're really something, Emma. Why don't you sit down here and rest a spell? I think that'd be best. And so I did that and then, later, when I walked back into the classroom Adam Hardy had a Band-Aid on his nose and wouldn't look me in the eye so I guess I made my point.

Grandma Edna will tell me about anything that crosses her mind these days. She's not much in touch with the here and now, but the stories she tells are wonderful. She's had tons of adventures, from helping Nellie Bly go through the Suez Canal to flying across the whole country one time with Amelia Earhart to being the copilot with Sally Ride on the old space shuttle. I mean, I believe almost none of all that, but you got to admit they're fun to listen to on a quiet night on the back deck, the lights turned down so they won't attract those dang mosquitoes and the stars filling the sky in the spring when the wind picks up out of the south and pushes the clouds away. Grandma Edna and Grandpa Posey and me see shooting stars about every night when that happens, and some of them go arcing across the sky and then splinter into tiny bits of lights that fall toward the water; well, you see stuff like that and you listen to the waves crinkle over the coquina and you look up at that big river of the Milky Way and you listen to Grandma's adventures and you think Adam Hardy deserved that punch in the nose for saying dumb stuff about Grandma Edna.

After the Yellowstone Eruption in '26 and then the Big Collapse, Grandpa Posey took his wife and his granddaughter (that'd be me) and headed to Pass-It-By Key in the Florida

District, where he'd had a home since way back in 1885. Built it with his own hands and a little bit of help from Grandma Edna, he says (mostly handing him nails he had to travel all the way to Arcadia to buy). He knew what he was doing, and now, one hundred fifty years later, the roof leaks here and there but only in the worst storms, and the floor sags here and there but not so much as you'd notice, and I think it's the best place to live in Florida, or maybe the whole world. We're away from all the trouble up north and we net mullet, we deep fry conch, we raise our own lettuce and tomatoes and things like that, taking the skiff over to the mainland for dry goods and cans when we have to, and we keep a dozen chickens. We eat a lot of eggs.

We are not poor, no matter what Adam Hardy and Trish Jessen and the others say. We live on our key because we want to, and I sail my skiff across the sound to get to school because I want to, not because we can't afford a boat with a motor. Grandpa Posey says we have plenty of money, but he's saving it just in case, and he and Grandma Edna don't much like engines anyway. Nothing but trouble. And, by the way, Grandpa knows right where all his marbles are so I believe what he says.

Grandpa Posey says I'm exactly like my mother was when she was a girl. Rambunctious, he says. And smart as a whip, he says. And headstrong, he says.

What Grandma Edna says is that it's about time for me to learn the truth about how We Are Not of This Earth. She did that last night again when she was tired and a little cranky, and Grandpa Posey frowned at her and said Now, Edna, and then smiled at me and shrugged and said, Let's get her to bed, Emma, and then he helped me wash her up and get her into her night-gown and into bed and after that me and Grandpa Posey walked out onto the back deck to look at the moon and the stars and he shook his head and said, We belong right here, Emma, on this little island on this little planet in this little system, all right?

Sure, I said.

But we *are* a little different, he said, I'll admit that. How? I asked him. It was about time I had some answers, I was thinking. Things had been getting more and more obvious at school.

We just are, he said. But mostly it's not so much that most people could tell. Okay, I said, then how come I can read ten times faster than any of the other kids in school? You're smart, he said, that's all.

And how come I can hold my breath for a lot longer than anyone? Good lungs, he said.

And how come I'm faster and stronger than all the boys? 'Cause you live a healthy life, he said.

And how come I'm not pretty like the other girls? Oh, you are, darlin', he said, you just can't see it yet.

And how come the only friends I have are Kaitlyn Dymetryk and Bryana Hull and no one else even likes me? Emma, that's part of being nine years old, he said, and I bet those girls are sharp as tacks in school and can climb trees like nobody's business. Am I right?

They are and they can and you're right, Grandpa, I said. How'd you know that? I'm psychic, he said, and smiled at me.

Sure you are, I said, and then I added, I'm almost ten years old, you know. He laughed and said, That's right, you're almost all grown-up, Emma.

And I said, I sure am. And then I gave him a big hug, because he'd earned it.

I mostly like the teachers at Barney Hill Elementary. Oh, Mr. Townsend isn't as smart as he thinks he is in Algebra 1 (and what could be easier than geometry and algebra anyway?), and either Ms. Ramon in American History has it all wrong about how the

Civil War got started or Grandpa Posey is misremembering things when he talks about the Dred Scott Decision. But Mr. Palmer in Social Studies is great, and Ms. Jacoby in Earth Sciences is pretty smart, and Ms. Candy, in Language Arts, is so great that she's not only a teacher but she's the principal, too. She's my favorite person, I suppose, after Grandma Edna and Grandpa Posey. Ms. Candy knows how to listen.

Last week Grandpa Posey went into his private footlocker and opened it up and got out his Library. I was astonished. I'd never seen any real tech before: Grandpa and Grandma always said we didn't want electricity at our house. It was unreliable, they said, and we'd done fine without it for a long, long time. But here was a Library! Solar powered even through a cloud cover, it held thousands of books on a single sheet of paper that you could read all day on. There were ten thousand, four hundred and sixteen books in that Library, Grandpa Posey said, and he'd read them all, mostly when he was traveling back in the old days, seeing the world. He said I'm done with that now, Emma, and all of your travels are yet to come so I thought you should have the Library. And it's not just for reading, you can dictate to it or write in it and take pictures and videos if you want.

Grandpa Posey! I said. Do you mean it? And he said he did and then he showed me how to use it and it's amazing. I read my first book from it—*Podkayne of Mars*—that night and it was simple but fun. I read *Middlemarch* the next night and it was a whole lot better. One book a night was going to take me a while. I tried telling it some diary stuff, too, but that wasn't nearly as much fun.

The other night when I was sitting in the rocker in the living room reading a novel about whales, Grandma Edna came over and said, You know, I don't have to read those books since they've all been downloaded into my brain. Sure they have, I thought when she said that, but I wanted to make her feel good so I said, Here, I'll give you a test, Grandma Edna. And then I swiped back to the first page and said, Call me Ishmael, and asked her what that was from and she said That's *Moby-Dick*, dear, but everyone knows that. Sure they do, I said.

I told Ms. Candy about it the next day because she knows all about how odd our family is and about Grandma Edna losing her marbles and she heard it and she said That's too easy, Emma, find another one to try on her and so I said, Ms. Candy, what about Everything is changed, changed utterly, a terrible beauty is born? and she said That's Yeats, and that's a little tougher so maybe that's a good one and so I got back in the skiff and sailed home after school and ran all the way across Pass-It-By Key from the dock on the Sound to the Gulf, and I asked Grandma Edna about that line from Yeats and she said That's from *Easter 1916*, Emma. That's a great poem, about revolution and independence and a whole lot more. Your grandpa was in Ireland when all that happened.

That's right, said Grandpa Posey who was right there listening to me quizzing Grandma. And he said I'm really pleased that you know that one. I said Thanks, I'm going to ask Adam Hardy if he knows it tomorrow and if he doesn't I'm going to punch him in the nose.

And if he does know it? asked Grandpa Posey, and I said, Well, then I might kiss him. Or I might not. And Grandpa Posey looked over at Grandma and said, I think we're safe enough, Edna, don't you? And Grandma just said They'll be here this Friday, right about dawn, Posey. And he said, Sure they will, Edna, and then he got up to walk into the kitchen and cut himself a slice of store-bought bread, which is all we have since Grandma Edna says making bread now is a waste of time.

I walked out there with him, and got a slice and put some butter on it and then folded it up and ate the whole slice in one big bite. Very ladylike, said Grandpa Posey.

I don't care about that, I said. What I care about is what's going on with you two. Are you leaving me?

How much do you remember of all those books you've been reading in the Library, Emma? Grandpa Posey asked me.

About everything, I said.

Word for word? he asked.

Yes, I said, word for word.

I thought so, he said. And then he put some butter on another slice of bread and said, I don't want to leave you, Emma. You're the best granddaughter a man could have. And I love this old place, too. So I don't want to go.

But you might? I asked.

Oh, Emma, he said, let's not worry about it. You know how your Grandma can be. I'm just humoring her. She'll probably forget about the whole thing inside an hour or two.

Sure, I said. But I didn't think she would. And she didn't.

When I was five years old Hurricane Petra changed our whole island around. Coming just two years after Yellowstone it was, Grandpa Posey says, just one thing after another there for a while.

I remember every second of what it was like to live through that hurricane. We stayed in our house and battened down the shutters and hoped that being raised fifteen feet in the air on our stilts would be good enough to let the storm surge go by and not wash us away and it was. I remember thinking I was in a boat, even though I was in my own bedroom with everything tightened down. The floor shook and I swear we started floating and turned sideways and then back and then settled back down on the same spot. Grandpa Posey always says I made that part up, that he was there and the house where he used a steam drill to put in the pilings and then poured the foundation himself was plenty strong enough to take anything Mother Nature could throw at him and it didn't have to turn or float or none of that to still be standing after Petra had gone on her way, moving inland after cutting a pass right through our island and shoving our village into the sound and then piling up all that sand at the far end so that some of the old abandoned houses on that side were buried in fifteen feet of white sand.

I remember the eye of the storm passing right over us. Me and Grandpa Posey and Grandma Edna unlatched things so we could walk outside and see how bad the damage was. All the palm trees were down and the beach dunes were all rearranged and there was standing water in a lot of places but the house looked good and solid.

And the blue sky! That was amazing. It's cloudy and gray here most days except in spring at night when the winds are from the south, so we don't see much sunlight. But in the eye of Petra the sky was so clear it took my breath away. You could see forever if you looked straight up. If you looked to the side there was a huge moving mass of black cloud, like a wall circling and circling around us. It was awesome and about the coolest thing I ever saw.

Then it got bad again, from the opposite direction, but Grandpa had all his marbles when he built the house and so the wind didn't tear down Grandpa Posey's work and the storm surge that came with the back half of the storm flowed right under us like it was supposed to and we came through it fine. Even better, to my mind, since it knocked down the old wooden bridge as it cut away a big hunk of the key and widened the sound and so we were like in Swiss Family Robinson or something, all by ourselves on Pass-It-By Key.

After that, whenever I went sailing in the sound, back and forth to school or sometimes just for fun, I always made sure to pass right over the top of the drowned village. The water there is only twenty feet deep and it's crystal clear so you can see the whole town as you go over the top, especially if you're smart enough to have a grandpa who loans you his polarized sunglasses.

The top of the spire from Holy Innocents Church is just a couple of feet underwater at low tide, and so lots of times I could tie off on that spire, grab my mask, and go diving down into the town. It was great, like a secret village just for me. I'd float through the buildings, sit in a pew in the church or swim through Holman's Sundries with its shelves picked clean by hungry fish and crabs and octopuses.

It's changed pretty fast since then, silting up with sand and starting to crumble away, but I still dive out there a lot, in and out of buildings and sometimes just drifting along Main Street, one block long and with half the buildings, at least, still standing. It's pretty magical the way the light shimmers against the walls and ceilings. I watch the fish watching me: skittish sheepshead and schools of mullet. Occasionally, on a very lucky day, there's a curious porpoise sharing the street with me and every now and then a barracuda or, worse, twice, a big bull shark ominous in the distance.

I can stay down there for about fifteen minutes. When I told Grandpa Posey about that for the first time he laughed and said I shouldn't exaggerate. I said No, I really can. Show me, he said, and so I held my breath while he watched the second hand on the big grandfather clock in the living room as it went round and round. It was a really boring sixteen minutes and thirty-two seconds, plus Grandpa Posey said I should keep that to myself, that it would cause all of us a lot of trouble if anyone knew I could do that.

Grandma Edna came to me two nights ago and said Emma, I need you to do something for me, dear. Sure, I said, whatever you need.

Grandma Edna reached down and took my hand. She seemed to have all her marbles right then, which was weird because what she said was crazy. I've just received a query from that ship,

Emma. The people in that ship want to know if it's safe to land, and where should they put the ship down so they can pick us up. I think it's safe, what do you think? And maybe right off our beach, out on the second sandbar? It's only a couple of feet deep there.

Well, how do you answer that? You sure you don't want to ask Grandpa Posey about this? I asked her.

Oh, not him, she said, and then put her hand to her mouth. She'd said that so loud he might have heard. Then she winked at me. You know how he is, Emma, she said. He'll say about anything to keep them from landing. He likes it here. He built all this.

I didn't know he didn't want them to land, I said. And that was true, insofar as it goes. Only in hearing this from her was I beginning to put two and two together. But you *do* want them to land, and right here, Grandma Edna, is that right?

Yes! she said, and clapped her hands. Of course! I've been waiting two hundred years for them to land, Emma, dear. Why wouldn't I be happy they finally got here?

I was starting to get real worried that maybe Grandma Edna hadn't lost any of those marbles, but I was the one who was a couple of cat's-eyes short. Well, of course you would be, I said to her.

I was wondering where Grandpa Posey was during this whole conversation. Was he outside with a flashlight, trying to wave off that ship? Or was he sending invisible psychic rays up there saying no, this isn't the right planet for you after all, just leave us here and you all turn yourselves around and go home? Or had he already been taken up by that ship and was he in there now talking to some bug-eyed aliens about what life was like on Earth? Or was he dead so he wouldn't be able to stop them? Had Grandma Edna killed him? Oh, my. There's a reason Ms. Candy says I have a vivid imagination; but I was worried and I had to know.

Grandma Edna, I got to go check on something, okay? I'll be

right back, I said, and then I lit out, opening doors and scrambling down the stairs and shoving open the bottom screen door and then onto the boardwalk and through the dunes and out onto the beach. And sure enough, there was no Grandpa Posey. Gone. No blood on the beach, just his footprints down by the water and then I followed those for maybe fifty feet or so and then they disappeared under the water that was working its way in with the tide.

Gone. I yelled for him, loud as I could. Grandpa! Grandpa Posey! Grandpa Posey!

No answer.

I ran up the beach, yelling. No answer. I ran down the beach the other way, yelling my head off. No answer. Damnation. I wanted nothing more in that moment than the smug face of Adam Hardy to show up right in front of me so I could take out my being mad with a good punch to the nose. But Adam Hardy wasn't there, either. No one was.

So I gave up. I stood there, looked all around. Nothing. I headed back toward the boardwalk and the house and Grandma Edna. When I got there, Grandpa Posey was on the back deck, sitting with Grandma Edna, the two of them holding hands. Grandma Edna was smiling. Grandpa Posey said Hi there, Emma. Sorry for worrying you. Grandma and I have been doing some thinking out loud, the two of us, and we think it's time we explained some things to you. You better sit on down, girl, and give us a listen. And so I did.

On Friday, Grandma Edna woke me up in the middle of the night, shaking my shoulder and saying, Get up, Get up, you lazy girl! And so I got my feet over the wooden side of that old bed and stood up and Grandma Edna took me by the hand and walked me down the stairs from the bedrooms and into the living room and through there into the kitchen and past the old wood-burning oven and out the screen door, all squeaky and needing some oil on the hinges, and then onto the back deck and right down off it and down some more steps to the board-walk that leads from our house out through the dunes—I helped Grandpa Posey rebuild that boardwalk after the storm of two years back broke it all up and scattered the slats all over the dunes and the beach—and onto the beach and there was Grandpa Posey himself, looking up at the stars. He pointed and I looked up that way and saw nothing but stars and planets.

That's Mars, right, Grandpa Posey? I asked him, pointing at it. I knew right where it was, of course.

Can't you see the ship up there, Emma? he asked me.

I had to shake my head. No sir, I cannot, I said.

Can you see still see it, Edna? he asked Grandma as he took her hands in his and stared into her eyes.

Oh, yes, she said, in a small little-girl voice I don't think I'd ever heard from her before, Yes, oh yes I can, Posey. And then she reached over to take Grandpa Posey's hands and they started to dance, the two of them, holding hands and looking at each other and then up at the stars and then at each other again and smiling and slowly turning. Great, I thought. They're all happy, but what about me?

Your grandmother oughta go to the loony bin is what Adam Hardy had been yelling at me on the playground on Monday past, with nine of us from the fourth grade playing the usual stupid game of tag. She isn't! I yelled at Adam Hardy and tagged him and said You're it! and he said, No I'm not you missed me! and so I stopped running and so did he and I walked over to him and I punched him right in the nose. He cried and mostly I didn't even care I was so mad about him saying Grandma Edna should go to the loony bin. And now here she was dancing around in a circle holding Grandpa Posey's hands and both of them all excited about that ship and I was looking up and I saw nothing. Not. A. Thing.

So if I was the crying sort I would've cried over that. I didn't

23

have a mom or dad since both of them died when Yellowstone blew and the only reason I didn't die with them was because I was with Grandpa Posey and Grandma Edna while my parents studied what was happening in Yellowstone. When it went, they went with it. I was three years old.

So Grandma Edna and Grandpa Posey are all I have, and I love them both to death, no matter how odd things get around here sometimes. Like Grandpa building a rickety old wooden lighthouse out at the high-tide mark. Or Grandma working on her mullet pie recipe all the time, trying to perfect it so they'd understand us. They like fish, you know, Emma, she said. They're from a water world themselves. They're sort of like porpoises only with arms and legs, and super smart, like you.

I'm not sure I'm all that smart, Grandma, I said back then, watching her roll out the dough for the pie crust. And on their world do they have mullet? That seems a little strange.

Well, she said, I was young when I was back there, so I don't recall too specifically. But they have fish, I'm sure; and I remember them being a lot like our fish. And you know I love eating smoked mullet, so I figure they'll like it too. And everything's better in a pie, Emma, don't you think?

That I do, Grandma, I said back then. And then I went back to writing in my diary while she worked on the pie; which was really good, by the way.

But all of that lost-marble kind of nonsense was fun when we were in the kitchen talking, and it's not so much fun when you're out under the stars and your grandparents are dancing with joy because some ship you can't see is coming to take them away from you.

Don't cry and whine, Grandpa Posey always said, and so even then when he was staring at the sky and acting like a fool with Grandma Edna I did not cry and I did not whine. Instead, I just walked over to my grandma and my grandpa and took one hand from each of them and slowly pulled them away from the water's edge and back to the boardwalk, both of them coming along quietly, smiling at me, and then through the dunes and up onto the back deck and then inside and I sat them down and was going to give them a good talking to about how I didn't care what Grandpa had told me, they couldn't leave me and what was I going to do and all that, when the screen door slammed and Ms. Candy came in and smiled at me and said Good morning, Emma, and then she looked at Grandma Edna and Grandpa Posey and said So I'm here, you two, but it's no fun getting up this early. Are you sure it's this morning? They're here at last? And they both nodded yes.

Ms. Candy said okay, then. Then she walked over to me and took me by the hand and said, You are going to have a wonderful life, Emma, full of adventures. I promise.

Sure I am, I said, but don't you care about Grandpa Posey and Grandma Edna leaving?

They've done their work, Emma, that's all, she said. And now it's your turn. Then she lifted me up from the chair and gave me a hug and put her arm around me as Grandpa Posey and Grandma Edna got up, too, and then we all walked, together, down the steps and onto the path and then up onto the board-walk that goes out through the dunes and then we walked out to where the water was lapping at the beach and then, together, the four us sat down to wait.

At first, they were looking up at dark sky, the three of them, but I was just looking at them. A life full of adventures, sure that sounded wonderful and awesome, and I was happy that Ms. Candy would be my guardian and all that, which Grandpa Posey had promised when he told me The Whole Story about him and Grandma Edna coming here to be in charge of keeping an eye on Earth, and then handing it over to my parents, and now me. Too soon for you, really, Emma, Grandpa had said, but you'll do fine if you listen to Ms. Candy and grow up right. And that all sounded important and exciting and I sure wanted to do that. But no Grandpa Posey and no Grandma Edna? That sounded terrible.

And now here we were waiting for them. I was not very happy. Then I thought about Adam Hardy and all the other kids in the fourth grade at Barney Hill Elementary and how Grandpa said I couldn't tell them anything which was pretty cool in itself right there, and how it would only be a few more years and I'd start traveling around and seeing things and meeting all sorts of people who would not care one jot about a tiny school in a tiny town on the West Coast of Florida. I would, I thought, remember all my friends quite fondly and I would tell them that when I came back between adventures to stay in my house with its leaky roof and saggy floors.

Then I heard something up above us and Ms. Candy reached over to hold my hand when I looked up and, sure enough, there was that ship, all fat and bubbly and coming down right out there at the second sand bar and I wondered, as I watched it land, could I do a good job for them?

You'll be great, Emma, I know it, said Grandpa Posey as he came over to give me a hug. You're rambunctious. And We believe in you, Emma, said Grandma. Your mother would be proud of you, and she kissed me on the cheek.

I'll do my very best, I said to them both as they started wading out into the warm water. But I'll miss you both! They looked back once to wave, and then they turned back around to wade out to the ship and Ms. Candy held my hand as we watched them go. And I did not cry and I did not whine but I will admit that I held on tight to Ms. Candy as they boarded that ship and then it slowly rose and drifted up into the darkness. We just watched and when it was finally gone Ms. Candy looked down at me and smiled and said Come on, Emma, it's time to get you started. And I said, Sure, Ms. Candy, and I held her hand and led the way as we headed back to the house.

This novelette appeared in The Magazine of Fantasy & Science Fiction *in December of 1992 and some years later became the novel,* The Cold Road *(Tor, 2003). It was recently republished by New Word City publishing as an ebook. The story was an Honorable Mention for the* Year's Best Science Fiction *(St. Martin's Press, 1993) edited by Gardner Dozois.*

ICE COVERS THE HOLE

It is a Saturday morning, the seventh of January, near Mankato, Minnesota. The temperature is twenty-seven degrees below zero as Melissa O'Malley tries to finish her homework. She has a basketball game coming up in the afternoon, her Crusaders against the Eagles from New Ulm. Melissa is a forward, and a starter as a freshman. A rugged defender; she's tall, muscular, fearless. She's all elbows and hips under the rim and so she rebounds like a fiend. She's hoping to play college someday, but needs to get her grades up.

The farmhouse where she lives is a once-proud, old two-story frame with white siding and faded brown trim. It was, for decades, a handsome home; but time and weather have worn it down.

A frozen deer carcass hangs from an upstairs window. Melissa's father, Melchior, hung it there four days before. Mel killed it out of season, but the farm is isolated, the window faces north, looking away from the unpaved road, and so he isn't worried about the kill being discovered.

The O'Malleys, just the father and daughter for some years now, have a freezer to hold the meat, but Mel has hung the deer outside until he can find the time to dress it. The cold will preserve anything when Minnesota is in the depths of another interminable winter.

The carcass hangs from a rope that is tied to Melissa's mother's bed. Melissa was five when Mother Mary walked off into another frozen January night. She headed south toward Lake Minnetoksak, and Melissa never saw her again.

Melchior keeps Mary's room ready for her, as if she might return home at any time. The general consensus, though, is that she found a hole in the lake's thick cover of ice and climbed in. They dragged the lake's deep glacial bottom, but found nothing. She hadn't been happy.

The rope snakes out through the insulation on an attic window and is then wrapped tightly around the front legs of the deer. The back legs, seven feet farther down, tap against Melissa's window when the winter wind sends the carcass swaying. The quick scrape against the window reminds her of something, something hidden deep that disturbs her, and it has nearly driven her crazy.

Two days before, to solve the problem without offending her father, Melissa opened her window and wrapped the hooves in an extra pair of mittens, thinking to quiet the metallic crack. On this cold, quiet morning, Melissa has her headphones on, listening to Lord Huron sing about the Great Lakes, but through the music she can almost feel the rasp of the mittened hooves against the glass, the sound now more of a strange muffled tap and scrape then the earlier sharp snap. She looks up from her algebra and stares into the bright, cold sunshine that darkens as the huge shadow sways by.

It is all too much. Melissa yanks off the headphones and rises from her desk. She loves her father dearly; he's been everything to her, especially since Mother Mary left. But this is just too much.

She walks over to the window, tugs down on the old wooden frame until it gives, then reaches out into the bitter cold to grab the legs as they go by. All she wants to do is stop them, keep them still and silent.

And as she makes that hard grab, the bitter wind blowing past her, the sunshine blinding off the clean, white snow that surrounds the house, Melissa feels an electric shock, a hard, erotic pulse in her stomach that travels down into her hips in a muscle-tightening spasm. She gasps in pleasure and pain and thinks, for a moment, that she is falling, but is, instead, pawing away at the hardened snow to reach the grass beneath, when she smells the Man and looks up to see him there.

She knows what that stick is that he holds. She tries to bolt, to dodge the death, but not in time. There is a bright bark of thunder and a flame and her legs don't work as she tries to spring into the underbrush and away. She stumbles and falls and breathes a shallow, quick breath that seems almost nothing at all, and then there is puzzlement, and then there is one final dull ache of pain, and then there is darkness and nothing at all.

Five years later, to the day. Melissa is a beautiful, sacred nineteen, long black hair soft against her sweatered shoulders as she cries softly and wonders how this could be, how Danny could possibly be dead. Her Danny, her touchdown quarterback, her handsome, kind Danny Finnegan, home now from the desert in a body bag, home a medaled hero of the low, simmering struggle that steadily takes lives from the heat of a desert a million miles away from the clean, understandable winter of southern Minnesota.

They were happy, the football king and the basketball queen. Sports talent, good enough grades, true love. They had it all. She went off to college and played games. He went off to war, her hero, and this is what happened. She stands in the front pew of the funeral home's small chapel. She thinks of how it was when she and Danny first kissed, fumbling around in the front seat of his Toyota pickup.

They never made love. Sex is not at the top of Melissa's list of favorite things and Danny honored that. All her friends have done it, and she does wonder sometimes if she's frigid. Now, with Danny gone, a part of her wishes she'd allowed him, at least once.

Poor Danny. Melissa rises, walks over to her hero, and reaches down to touch the waxy face that looks so wrong, so falsely serious. She reaches down to touch him one last, final time. He is cold, she thinks as she strokes her hero's cheek, thinking about what was and might have been.

Then, in a wave of emotion, comes again that convulsive electric shock—that hard throb that washes through her as she is suddenly terrified: the sheets are coming over their trenches just a few hundred meters away while the gas is rolling ahead of them right toward him. It's been ninety-seven days of terror and boredom and hell and fear in this sweat and stink. He looks between the slits of the sandbags, reaches down to grasp his mask again, discovers it isn't there.

It isn't there! He scrambles around for it and can't find it. He's seen the mucous pink death that retches up from the lungs of too many friends, and he can't find the mask, the damn mask! He stands, turns once to fire a witless burst toward the roiling smoke, and then vaults back out of the trench to run from the sheets, to run from the smoke, the fear and the coughing death, the blistered skin that falls away to the bone. He hears, distantly, an order to halt, but can't; he can't stop at all. He feels a slap in his back, a punch, and then warmth, a pleasant glow. His legs give way, and he falls onto the sand that is oddly cool and comforting. He tries to look up. He is quite calm. He wonders why he ran as it gets perversely dark around him, and then, slow fade, there is nothing.

Detective Robert Finnegan is standing at the left of the casket as

Melissa touches his dead son's cheek. He sees her freeze, watches her eyes go glassy. She seems ready to faint. He takes three steps around the edge of the casket and reaches toward her elbow to give her support. Poor kid: Danny's girl and now this. Damn.

Finnegan grasps her elbow, and there is a quick flash of something, an image: of blazing sun overwhelming him, and then of sand, heat, and fear. He suddenly knows his hero son died a coward, was shot in the back. The image, in an instant, tells him that, and then it is gone, nothing, as if never there.

He shakes his head slightly, clears the cobwebs. Danny ran? His Danny? Christ, the kid never ran from a fight in his life. What was that? What just happened?

He looks at Melissa, Danny's girl.

She looks at him, speaks softly: "You saw it, too. At least part of it. You know."

He can only nod.

Later, in his office downtown, they talk. The detective has his son's death spread out in front of him on the desk: the letter from the company commander, the official word from the Army, the pieces of paper, pieces of metal, pieces of cloth that say his son died a hero's death, defending democracy somehow.

"But it isn't true; at least, I don't think it is," says Melissa. "You saw it, too. He ran. Danny ran."

And Detective Finnegan—Jesus, Mary, and Joseph—knows it, too.

It is the fifth of January, and very warm in Georgetown. Melissa at twenty-five is beautiful, smart, and determined to never be cold again. She has been on this tiny island for two years now and hasn't tired of it a bit, has no intention of ever leaving. She works for a charter company that's run by her boyfriend's father. She met the boy her senior year in college and when they graduated she fled south, away from Minnesota and those cold memories. He wants to marry her, but she won't. She's not sure why. He's handsome, bright, and kind, and the charter company is hugely successful. But Melissa dodges those final commitments. They've never made love.

She handles most of the PR for the company, sitting in the office with Ziggy Marley on the sound system talking about conscious parties as she writes press releases and brochures and, in her spare time, poetry. She has long black hair, her mother's Celtic blue eyes, and that athletic body that she's kept strong, lifting weights, running on the beach, staying tough.

The phone rings and it is Robert Finnegan. She hasn't seen him since a few days after the funeral, when they talked about what had happened.

Finnegan hasn't called to chat. There's been a murder in Mankato, a nasty one. A mother and her young daughter were raped and then knifed repeatedly and then left out in the subzero night for their blood to freeze as it oozed from their wounds.

Finnegan wants to know if Melissa will come up and try to help. The department—hell, everyone, including the FBI—is lost on this one. The guy is good, very good, about cleaning up his act; he uses bleach at the scene to obliterate evidence and he's careful about all the rest. Finnegan will try anything, even a vision from a touch on the dead. Melissa can fly in, visit with her father, spend a day or two in town seeing old friends, and then head back to the sun—Finnegan will pick up the tab just on the odd chance that it might help.

See her father? She'd like that, she has to admit. Saying goodbye to Melchior was the only hard part about leaving cold, frozen Mankato. He's a good, strong, no-nonsense man—hardworking, simple, straightforward. Those big, rough hands of his have helped lead her toward adulthood. Melissa has always loved her daddy, been grateful for his guidance. It was just the two of them for all those years.

Finnegan goes on, talking about the murders, about how horrible it all is, but Melissa doesn't need any more cajoling. She hates the cold with a passion, and fears what the touch might bring, but she agrees. She'll stay only one night, though, she tells him. Fly in, try for the touch, see her father, and fly back out, that's it. He agrees.

A bit later she calls her father, tells him she'll be home for a day or two, makes plans to see him. The next day there are kisses in the morning from the boyfriend, the little prop plane over to Antigua, the big jet from there to the Twin Cities nonstop. Weird, from eighty above to forty below in about six hours. Now, here she is in Mankato again: frozen town with hard, dirty ice in the streets and a thin sun in that pale blue sky and the steam rising from everywhere, from car exhausts to homes to faces— vapor everywhere in the cold.

Finnegan has aged some, Melissa thinks. There's more gray hair and a thicker paunch. He met her in Minneapolis, drove her the eighty miles down to Mankato, got her checked in at the hotel and gave her a couple of hours to get settled, and now he's driving her to the morgue for the big touch, a glimpse maybe, of the murderer.

They pull into the small parking lot, tires crunching over the frozen ice and snow. They get out, walk over to the entrance and go right in. They're expected. An autopsy techni- cian walks with them back to the main room where there are two rows of drawers. Finnegan goes directly to the top row, far right drawer and asks the technician to open it. Melissa watches as the big drawer is pulled back and Finnegan zips back the thick plastic. The poor woman's gray skin has one slash on the right arm, and then six orderly, precise puncture wounds that start near the navel and end at the neck. It's horrible, unbear- able, nothing prettied up like at the funeral home. Gray lips. Gray face.

Melissa takes a deep breath, the smell of formaldehyde every- where, and reaches down to the skin. Touches it, expecting that jolt again after all these years, expecting that pulse and electric shock.

But gets nothing. A soft give, that's all. Nothing. No vision, no hard pulse, nothing.

She tries the body in the next drawer, the poor little girl. The corpse is perfect; the only mars are dark bruises around the throat. But the body seems deflated, pathetic. Melissa touches the cheek, the shoulder. Nothing.

"It was worth the try," Finnegan says a few minutes later as he walks her back to the car in the dying afternoon sunlight. "Maybe it was something you've grown out of, or something that would happen only once or twice in a lifetime. Something like that. It was worth a shot. I'm glad we tried."

"Sure," she says, but knows better. He's disappointed in her; he's put his own career on the line just getting her here. She wishes she could do something for him, but it just wasn't there.

He drops her off at her hotel, a new, plastic Holiday Inn just across from the mall at the south edge of town.

"Pick you up about ten tomorrow," he says as they pull up to the main entrance. "That'll get you to the airport by noon. By this time tomorrow, you'll be back in the sunshine, and you can forget about all this."

Melissa watches as Detective Finnegan wipes his brow. He's sweating despite the cold; the car's heater and his own nervous energy or something are overheating him. She knows he'd hoped that this might help. She knows he wants to figure out a way to stop this guy before he does it again.

He looks at pretty Melissa, thinks of his son again by looking at her. "You've come a long way, Melissa," he says, "and not just to get here. You had a rough start in life, with your mom's disappearance and all. And now look at you, an island girl." Then he smiles thinly, says, "Hey, look, we tried, okay? It was worth it. Have a good time with your dad tonight; tell him hi for me. I'll see you in the morning."

"Sure," she says, opening the door, feeling the heat ooze out from the car as she swings her legs over, steps out. She feels awful about this. She shakes his hand, then waves as he drives off.

Damn, it's cold. She wraps her coat tighter, the old down jacket a holdover from her high school days, the only thing she could find in her closet in Georgetown that might measure up to this weather. It's a quarter to five in the afternoon, and pitch-black out already. God, she hates this bitter wind. She has hours before Melchior will come to meet her for dinner at the Roundhouse. She goes to her room and showers, the water as hot as she can stand it.

At nine on the dot, Melchior is there, wheeling the same old Ford truck into the parking lot, climbing out stiffly on that bad left leg, walking in the main entrance and then through the swinging doors into the restaurant and bar. Melissa watches all this out the window from her little table with the silly red glass candle and the silly checkerboard tablecloth and the corny farm implements hanging on the wall.

She waves at him. He smiles, strides over to her with that slight hop the bad leg gives him.

"Mellie, Mellie. Good to see you, sweetie. I'm so glad you're here." He hugs her, almost picks her up from her chair, crushing her in those strong, wiry arms.

"Hi, Dad," is all she can manage. He looks happy, happier than she's seen him since as far back as she can remember.

He takes off his gloves and the thick coat and piles them onto the empty chair next to his and then sits down. They order some coffee, go through some perfunctory apologies. She's sorry she hasn't called more, but the island phones aren't that good. He's sorry he hasn't written more often, but he didn't know what to say, how to talk about how much he's missed having her around. He's not good at putting stuff like that down on paper.

He hits her with questions. How is it down there? Island fever yet! Ready to come home?

"Dad, I'm happy there," she says. "Billy and I get along fine, and the island is just heaven. You'll have to come and visit. There's a live volcano you can walk down into, and a waterfall that you can stand under, and the sailing is ..."

He shakes his head. "I couldn't stand that heat. I need the cold, Mellie; need winter. It's honest, clean. The best time of year. Besides," he adds as an afterthought, "someone's got to look after the farm."

"In the dead of winter, Dad? There's nothing for you to do. Get Old Man Svenson to look in on the place every now and then. Unless you've gone and got some more cows or something, that's all it would take."

"No, you know I gave up on that. Gave up on most of it, really. Just plant some corn down by the stream, and soybeans up in the top twenty. Spend most of my time hunting and ice fishing. I've still got that little shack down on Minnetoksak where I drop a line, and that's about it."

He smiles at the thought of leaving all that behind, even for a few days. "No," he says, shaking his head. "No, it's just that I can't leave it; that's all. I get up early, get a few chores done, drive into town for scrambled eggs and hash browns and bacon at the Little House, buy some supplies, and come back to the farm and put in some time working on things out in the barn. It's a good life, Mellie. Dependable, you know?"

Melissa looks at him; his clean, plaid work shirt buttoned to the top, his cap covering that every-week haircut right to the trim line, his nails cut and cleaned despite all the dirt they go through every day. He's always been tidy.

Before she left for the Islands she tried again to talk to him about that, about how maybe it was time to sell the farm, move forward a little bit in life. He wouldn't listen, just shrugged it off as he had the other times she'd tried. Melissa wonders if she should ask him if he still keeps Mom's room ready for her return, the lace dusted on the top of the old chest of drawers; the bed made with the sheets and comforter cleaned every week, the windows cleaned every Saturday—all of it for Mom, poor missing Mary O'Malley.

She doesn't ask him anything like that. She just smiles; agrees with him, keeps the peace. "I'm glad you could come tonight, Dad. It's good to see you."

He pauses, gets very serious. "I'm glad you asked me, Mellie. Gives me the chance to say something."

He puts his hands on the table, folds them together, looks at his daughter. "Things are better now, Mellie, I don't drink much anymore, and I try not to get so mad about things."

He's struggling with this, working hard to admit these weaknesses. Melissa hurts for him. He's always been so strong, so dependable. Hard, cold land. Hard drink. Some anger. She has always just accepted it, embraced it really as a part of him; a strong, important part,

"Hell, I know how bad I was, honey. It was awful for you. I'm not surprised you left. I understand all that. Took me a long time, that's all—a long time."

"Dad, Daddy, that's not why I left. It was the cold, and this town ..."

He brushes her thoughts aside; he has a lot to say here, and means to get it out in the open.

He sips his coffee, collects these hard thoughts. "I know you're not ready for this yet, Mellie. I know you think I'll just go on forever. But the farm is out of debt, and when I'm gone, it's yours. I'd like you to settle on it, find the right guy worth spending time with, make the place really yours."

She starts to speak again, to slow him down. She doesn't want to hear this. But he raises his hand to shush her.

"I know I did a lot of bad things, Mellie. Awful things. Your poor mother. Hell, it was my drinking that caused all that; I'm sure of that now."

He stares right at his daughter, and she can only look back, wondering why he's doing this.

"I just want to say I'm sorry for all that. It's different now: I know you don't want to come back yet, but when you do, well, things are different. I'm a better man."

He sits back, smiles again. "There, I've said it, okay?"

"Okay, Dad. You've said it," says Melissa, and she smiles back at him, reaches across the table to take those huge, rough, gnarled hands into hers. So strong. Kept that farm going all these years.

She looks outside for a moment; a gust of wind steals a thin haze of snow from the frozen drifts the plows have edged around the parking lot. It's a long way from Georgetown.

Dinner is hamburgers done up fancy, and then there's more coffee and more talk. Mel talks about the farm, about ice fishing on Minnetoksak, about hunting, about the weather and the drought and the soybeans and the prices. The evening flows along nicely.

Eventually it's all pretty much been said. It's midnight and they're the only ones at a table, though the bar is still busy. Mel, though, is an early riser, gets up at dawn, so he's going to head home. Melissa walks him to the truck.

The aurora dances across the northern horizon, and they stop to watch for a minute in the parking lot.

"None of that down on that island," Melchior says.

"You're right, Dad," Melissa agrees, and then pulls the collar of her coat up tight against the cold.

They reach the truck, and damned if there isn't a deer carcass in the back bed of the pickup.

"Found it on the highway on the way here," Melchior says with a shrug. "Broken neck, I think. Still warm when I stopped. Just put it here to get it off the road, but now I'm thinking I might as well take it on home and dress it. No sense in letting good meat go to waste."

Melissa just shakes her head, smiles at her father. Some

things don't change. He's still neat and tidy with everything in its place and nothing going to waste.

She looks at the deer, dark eyes filmed over in the harsh light from the parking lot. Poor thing. She reaches down to give it a pat, express a little sympathy.

She flashes; that pulse grabs her. There is frozen ground beneath her in the moonless dark, then gravel, a smooth, hard surface, sudden lights, horns, screeching noises, a huge Man thing bearing down; turning its side to her, slamming into her as she is tossed across the smooth, hard surface to its far side, where she lies for a moment, struggles to rise but cannot, tries to move her head but cannot, tries to see but cannot as the darkness grows and overwhelms her until there is nothing.

Melissa jerks her hand back. She saw it, saw the end.

Melchior is talking: "It's been great, Mellie. Thanks, honey, for giving me this chance to say some things I needed to say."

He hugs her hard and then, not looking back, climbs into the Ford, slams the door shut, jams it into reverse, pulls back, and then drives off. He hadn't noticed her shock at the touch of the deer, was too occupied with his own changes, his efforts to put a couple of lives back together.

Melissa watches him drive off, the red taillights shrinking into cold and then gone. Overhead, the aurora grows brighter, half the sky in muted reds and yellows, shattered waves of it moving across the dark dome over Melissa's head.

She goes inside. She calls Finnegan, wakes him up at home with the number he left her, tells him what happened, waits for him to arrive.

Finnegan doesn't question the 12:30 AM call. He just gets up, whispers to his wife where he's headed, and goes. She's used to it, he knows with a certain regret. Comes with the territory. It's left her lonely, though, and that's too bad. Another child might have helped.

It's only ten minutes to the Little House. Fifteen more to the morgue. They don't say much as they drive over the flat once-prairie, now housing tracts and strip malls.

They pull up to the morgue, neither having said much. Melissa wants this to be over. Finnegan wants to stop this damn butcher before it happens again.

A locked door, a buzzer, a technician, a long walk into the cold room redolent of formaldehyde. The drawer needs to be oiled; it squeaks as it opens. It is the mother, gray.

Melissa touches her; Finnegan puts his hand on Melissa's shoulder and together they are jolted, a spasm in the loins, a surge: There is a blade, rising and dropping, held by gnarled hands. A red baseball cap with a large bill covers the top half of a face that flashes by. Splattered blood, droplets of it in the air; she knows it is her own.

Cary, her sweet little girl, is in the other room crying. Cary wants her mommy, but Mommy's busy right now, raising her right hand to ward off that blade, and seeing the slash open from the palm down past the wrist so more spurts out. There is a certain curious pressure on her chest. She looks, and sees the blade, in a horrid kind of forever slow penetration, punch its way through her, then rise for more. There is no pain. There is no feeling. There is the distant cry of Cary as the scene fades, darkens, is black, and then there is nothing.

"My God," says Finnegan, taking his hand off Melissa's shoulder. He turns away, walks away from the smell, the touch, the awful reality.

"I couldn't see a face. Just a mouth, and that cap. And I'm sure it was a man," Melissa says, quite calm now as she stands her ground. This has to be done.

Finnegan walks back, pale, and helps the guard pull out the next drawer. This one runs smoother, no squeals from it as it opens. It is the daughter, Cary.

Finnegan puts his hand on Melissa's shoulder as she reaches down to touch the girl's cheek. It is even worse, though far less violent; Cary doesn't understand the man with the blade, what he's doing to her, and why those rough hands are holding her there on the neck, and why Mommy won't help stop it, and why is this happening, where is Mommy, when will this stop?

It does stop, mercifully, and Melissa pulls back. Finnegan keeps his hand on her shoulder, for support now. He should never have asked poor Mellie here for this. It isn't giving him anything much he can work with, and the toll is enormous. He feels tired, very tired. She must be near collapse.

But it is over. They leave. On the way back to the hotel, nearly two in the morning now, no aurora in the darkness, Finnegan apologizes, sums up what they've learned in one sentence.

"Well, at least we've got that red cap to work on."

"And that's it," Melissa says. "I'm sorry. I wish I could have helped more." She wants to sleep, climb into that hard bed at the hotel and sleep.

"Listen, Melissa, you going to be okay? You still want that noon flight? I'll change it for you to something later."

"No, no. I want that flight; I need to get out of here now. God, that poor little girl, that poor woman."

Melissa will have this to trouble her forever. That blade, those strong hands, the way the little one couldn't understand the hurt or why Mommy wouldn't come help.

Finnegan drops her off. "See you at nine, right?"

"Right," she says. "Nine o'clock." She smiles at him. "I'm sorry I didn't help more."

He smiles back, reaches out to touch her shoulder, give it a squeeze.

In her room, five minutes later, she can barely get out of her clothes, but once she does and gets under the sheets and warm blanket, in seconds she is fast asleep. Her dreams are not good.

An incessant, annoying telephone ring brings Melissa up from the depths. She slaps at it, knocks the receiver off the hook, fumbles around to find it on the night table, brings it to her ear. Finnegan?

"Hello," she manages. What could he want at—what time is it, five in the morning?

"Mellie, it's Dad. I'm sorry to wake you up, but I have something I have to show you, sweetie."

"Dad!" She shakes her head a bit to throw off a few cobwebs. Melchior calling her now? "Dad, what's the matter? What are you doing calling now?"

"Sorry, sweetie, but this is something I just have to show you. I've been up all night thinking about this."

"Dad, I have a plane to catch at noon in Minneapolis."

"This won't take long, Mellie. Please. You'll still make your plane, I promise."

"All right, all right," she says. "Are you coming by here to show me this thing?"

"I'm here now, Mellie. Down in the lobby. Just get down here as soon as you can, and I'll take you there, all right? Please, sweetie."

God, it must be important. She takes a deep breath, tries to come up fully from the depths of her sleep, from those new, cold dreams, says, "Okay, Dad. Give me a few minutes, and I'll get down there. And get me a cup of coffee, okay?"

"You got it, sweetie. One cup of coffee, no sugar, two creams."

"Okay, okay," she says, and hangs up, struggles to get her legs over the side, rises, stumbles into the bathroom and splashes water on her face, brushes her teeth.

In ten minutes she's down in the lobby. Melchior hands her a go-cup of hotel coffee and says they can talk on the way. He has to show her something; it's really important, so they leave.

Father and daughter, heading toward frozen Lake Minnetoksak and holes in the thick ice.

Finnegan has been up all night, too, thinking about what he saw. There was something about the face that rings a bell, something about that cap. The more he thinks about it, the more he thinks he knows the murderer, but he can't quite put two and two together. That red baseball cap. Those rough hands. He's been wrestling with it all night.

His mind drifts to thoughts of breakfast finally, giving up the struggle with his subconscious and its hazy memory.

Two or three times a week, Finnegan gets up early so he can stop in at the Little House diner and have a western omelet, hash browns, sausage patties, rye toast, and scalding coffee. Now, the thought of the coffee gets him up out of the bed. He likes the Little House. It's warm, comfortable, and cheap.

It hits him. The Little House, that red baseball cap. Up at the counter, usually with his back to the table where Finnegan sits. Damn. Always with that friendly smile, those big ham hands wrapped around a mug of coffee. Melchior O'Malley. Old lonely, silent Melchior. Christ.

Melissa. Sweet mother, Finnegan thinks, how will he tell her about this, tell her that he thinks her dad is the murderer, the vicious butcher who could do that to a kid?

He shoves on his pants, shrugs his way into a bulky knit sweater, pads barefoot into the kitchen, dials the hotel, asks for her room, waits for her to pick up. Hell, he'll tell her he's got news, something important, and then drive over there and explain it to her face-to-face, tell her what he thinks, get it over with.

There's no answer. He lets it ring: still no answer. He calls back to the front desk. The girl there, too damn cheerful for this time of the morning, tells him that Melissa left with a man just a few minutes before. Her father, the girl thinks; she thought she heard Melissa say that as the two of them walked out the door.

Oh God. With Melchior.

Finnegan runs back up the stairs to the bedroom, shoves his feet into socks and shoes, grabs his coat, whispers to his wife that he'll be back later, and goes back down the stairs, out to the garage and the tired old departmental Dodge that he drives.

The farm; that's where he'll go. Maybe Finnegan can get there in time to stop things from happening. If what he fears is what Melchior has planned ... Finnegan doesn't want to think about that. Just drive. Fast.

But Mel and Melissa aren't at the farm. They're a few miles north of Lake Minnetoksak. Melchior is talking, explaining things to his daughter. "It's been strange, Mellie, really strange since you moved away. After I left tonight, I thought about it, about what I'd said, and I thought it was time to show you something. I think you'll understand, honey."

"Understand what, Dad?"

"Just bear with me for a few more minutes, okay sweetie?"

And Melissa shrugs her shoulders, hunches down some into the hard seat to ward off the bitterness of the predawn cold.

There's a thin streak of pale gray on the eastern horizon as they drive up the access road to the lake. A right turn past the old oaks, a quick left and they drive right onto the ice. The lake is four miles around; the ice is two feet thick or more. The surface is dotted with ice shacks and parked cars. Lights shine from some of the shacks, people up fishing already.

Melchior drives the old pickup to his shack, over near the southern shore, maybe forty yards out onto the surface of the ice.

He parks; they get out and walk into the shack. There's a gas heater in there, already lit so the edge is off the cold. There's an ice auger over in the corner for drilling holes, a hammer for cracking them open each morning after they start to freeze, and two gas lamps, one of them lit, its mantle glowing to throw shadows into the corner of the shack

Melchior takes some steaming water from a pan on top of the heater and pours it into a thick mug. He pulls a small jar of instant coffee out of a cardboard shoe box, carefully spoons out some of the coffee, drops it into the mug, stirs it a moment or two, then hands the coffee to Melissa while she stares out the door at the predawn darkness. What is this all about?

Her father smiles disarmingly at her. "Come here," he says. "Please. I want you to see this."

He takes her by the hand, pulls her to the back of the shack, away from the hole out front that she'd noticed as they walked in.

There's another hole there, a huge one, four or five times as big around as the normal twelve-inch-diameter hole used for fishing. He must have used the auger several times and then pounded away with the hammer to clear a hole this big. There's a thick rope coiled by the side of the hole. One end of it leads down into the black water.

"I came out here a while ago, Mellie, and got the heater started up, hammered open the holes to sort of get things ready for you," he says, walking over to the rope and grabbing it where it emerges from the water. "Now help me pull this up, and you'll see why, sweetie."

She does, wondering what's going on as they start to pull. The effort takes a while, and Melissa starts to think after a few minutes that she maybe doesn't want to know what's at the other end of the rope. It feels heavy. Too damn heavy. Tugging it in is hard work. What's he got in mind here?

She stops. "Dad, what's going on? I don't like this."

He turns to stare at her, hard, the old anger showing. "Just pull, Melissa. Just do it." He turns back to the task.

Melissa helps; there doesn't seem to be anything else to do.

They pull for a good ten minutes more. The rope is cold and hard and stiff. The water down at the bottom never gets much above freezing year-round, but things live down there; the rope is covered with green slime, tiny snails, long, stringy plants.

Something bumps against the bottom of the ice, just a few feet away from the hole. They tug more slowly.

Melissa can't take her eyes off the hole as the rope pulls the thing clear.

It's a tarpaulin, wrapped around something and then sewn shut, a concrete block tied to the bottom of it. No wonder it was so hard to pull up.

They get the tarp out from the hole and onto the ice. Melchior turns to smile reassuringly at his daughter, takes his deer knife, and cuts the fishing line that has sewn the thing tight. It parts with precise little pops as he takes his time opening things up.

As he cuts, Melissa can see inside. There is a piece of worn blue cloth, torn and shredded. There is a body, gray but preserved in the depths of the lake. A face. Melissa can't turn away. Wants to, but can't.

It's Mary. It's her mother.

Melissa drops the rope, backs away. She turns to leave. She notices a red baseball cap sitting on the top of the upturned crate that serves as Melchior's table in the shack. Jesus. She freezes.

"Help me finish this, Mellie. It's so cold that my fingers go numb."

She turns back and goes to help him. She's part of this now, she tells herself; she has to finish it. She's starting to remember something, gets little flashes of it as she helps her father pull the tarp away from the body. "That's good," Melchior says at last as he straightens the body a bit. He turns to look at his daughter.

"I thought you'd want to know about this, see her one more time. I found her like this in the tarp last November, still perfect, after all these years."

Oh God. Melissa struggles to keep herself sane, to not just scream and run. She looks down at the body, shakes her head, shivers, starts to lose it. "You're insane, Daddy. You're sick. You need help. Let me drive you back to town. We'll get this all taken care of; everything will be fine, just fine."

She's babbling, talking too damn fast. This is all way beyond belief.

Her father has a puzzled expression on his face. "I just thought you'd want to know that she's been okay, down in the cold. I thought you'd want to know that before you headed back south to that island," he says.

Melissa tries to be calm, tries to slowly back away. She can get out that door and run, get to another shack, get some help. She is thinking very clearly now, seeing it all with crystalline clarity. She knows she has to run, get away from him, get help somehow.

She takes one step to the left, another, but then Melchior moves right and blocks her path to the door, says, "I can't let you leave just yet, sweetie. You have to stay for just a few more minutes. I have one more thing we have to do; that's all." So she tries to get past him, tries to elbow her way past him and out the door.

They struggle, and Melchior is strong, wiry and quick no matter his age. Still, she pushes him away, hard, and he stumbles and slips on the ice, falling hard on his side. He turns and looks at his daughter in disbelief. "Mellie?" he asks her, and then again, "Mellie?"

He grabs her foot and pulls it hard and she slips, too, and puts her hand down to break the fall, and places it right on her mother's arm. The flesh is gray, icy and cold, incredibly cold.

That pulse, that throb hits her. She is watching a much younger Melchior, a strong young man in his prime, angry, drunk, brutal, who holds a knife, the one he uses to gut and dress the deer he kills.

He is shoving her around the room; he slaps and then hits

her with a fist—hard. There are throbbing waves of pain in her jaw, her cheekbone, her eye. Her face is wet from tears and blood. She wipes her eyes, and her hands are covered in red. She prays that he'll leave little Melissa alone. That's what started this fight, her saying he shouldn't be touching their daughter like that, in those places, talking all the time about doing more. It's just not right.

There is a raised hand, that knife, a bright flash of reflected sunlight from the window of her bedroom that bursts off the blade to blind her for a moment. She shuts her eyes, opens them, and sees a final maniacal smile on Melchior's face as the blade goes up and down and up and down until there is nothing.

Robert Finnegan makes it to the farmhouse in twenty-seven minutes. It is obvious immediately that no one is there; no truck in the yard, no lights, no activity. He gives the place a quick once-over anyway; the door is unlocked when he tries it. Then he stops to think it through. Where else? What makes sense from Melchior's perspective?

The lake, of course. Minnetoksak. Where Mel's wife was thought to have drowned. Where he keeps that fishing shack. Where he wears that damned red cap as he sits out in front of the shack and waits patiently for the fish to bite.

Finnegan runs back to his car, cranks it, floors it, spins on the ice-covered gravel of the drive, roars away toward the lake, another three miles down the road.

"I had to do that to her, you understand? I just had to stop her, Mellie. She said she was going to go to the police about it, about us, sweetie, about how much I loved you. I'm not saying it was right, what I did to her. But she just got on me so much about it."

That smile again, as he remembers it. That cold smile. "I was just touching you; that's all. She just didn't understand, sweetie. You were always so pretty. And you liked it, Mellie, you really did. You told me so." He shook his head. "She pushed and pushed at me until I had to take her up to her room and shut her up, I had to do it to protect you, Mellie. I loved her so, sweetie, but I just couldn't stand it when she got like that. I don't know, I just loved you even more, I guess. That's all, I just loved you more."

He is waving the knife around as he explains all this. Melissa sits there, on the ice, next to her mother's frozen gray body, and listens to him. Water from the hole has splashed onto the ice where she is sitting and soaked through her blue jeans. Her rear and her crotch are very cold. The chill seems to soak all the way through her.

Melissa shivers. She's starting to remember things that she had put away forever. Memories frozen away for twenty years crack loose and climb out of the dark hole where they've been hidden. She remembers a face above hers, smiling and kissing her cheek. She remembers him touching her, the way it felt so rough.

"It just happened, that's all," he explains, breaking into her past. "It was her birthday. It started out so happy, and then ... nothing on purpose, Mellie. It just happened. She just egged me on until it happened." He looks at the knife.

Melissa remembers: noise, shouts and thumps from her mother's room then silence. Melissa remembers waiting a few minutes, cautiously opening the door to her own room and looking out. No one there. The back door slammed; her father's heavy footsteps crunched through the old, hard snow as he walked out toward the barn. Quickly then, knowing he might come right back, she ran up the stairs, anxious to comfort Mommy.

Little Mellie knocked on her mother's door. No answer. Knocked again, a bit louder, afraid to bring Daddy back if she was too loud. No answer. She opened the door, peeked in. Mommy was on the bed, sprawled, arms wide. And there was blood everywhere, like when Daddy killed the chickens. Blood on the curtains, even splattered on the window glass.

Mellie wondered what this all meant. "Mommy?" she finally got up the nerve to ask. "Mommy, are you all right?"

No answer. Mellie walked over to look at Mommy's face. She loved her mother's smile, that happy laugh. But this was a nothing face: no smile, no laugh.

Mellie turned to leave, and there was Daddy.

He sighed, disappointed. "She had to learn, Mellie, and now look what's happened. She just had to learn." And then he reached out to hold his daughter by the shoulders.

"Did you hurt her, Daddy?"

"She made me, sweetie. She was going to tell on us, and we couldn't have that, could we?"

Mellie shook her head no. This was all so very hard to understand. She turned to look at Mommy, turned back to see Daddy's smile. Daddy's cold smile.

She wanted to cry, but Daddy shook his head no, shushed her, and moved her over so he could sit next to her on the side of the bed. He leaned over. Melissa tried to move away, felt Mommy's cold left arm against her bottom, and screamed, hard, once, before Daddy started.

After a while, Melissa lay next to her mother's body and pretended to sleep while Daddy cleaned the room. Melissa listened to the quiet rub and tap of his towel against the bloody windowpane as he cleaned the splattered glass. In the morning, Mommy was gone, and Melissa believed Daddy's story of how Mommy had woken up and been okay, but then just walked away. Melissa couldn't remember it any other way.

All this at age five. All of this closed off, sealed off a whole part of her life that her mind wouldn't let her recall.

Where was her early childhood? Where was reality? She'd thought it happy enough, Mommy's smiling face and Daddy's hard work on the farm. There were hazy memories, brief snatches of snowmen, of sleds, of hot chocolate and marshmallows. How much of that was real? How much was blocked off in an icy part of her mind that hid the horror, the pain of what he'd done?

Now, here, the ice that surrounds those memories is beginning to crack, to break apart. Melissa can see her past in all its jolting, horrific reality.

Melchior is very calm. "January seventh," he says, "I celebrate it every year. January seventh. Her birthday. God it was cold, worse than this. Twenty years ago to the day."

He lowers the knife, smiles. "That was the time we finally did it, Mellie, you and me, remember? That time with her, and never again. I stopped everything after that, for the longest time, and you forgot all about it. I stopped just for her, but God, I wanted to, sweetie. You grew up so beautiful."

He's proud of himself, proud of the self-control he had practiced starting twenty years before. "And now that I found her, I started making her presents. Good presents."

His smile broadens. "You came back, too, Mellie. Right on time. So I know things are going to be all right."

Melissa sees it all. January seventh. That's why she can do this, see these visions; but only on this day, this horrible day, January seventh. God, he's a monster.

"Presents, Daddy? Oh Christ. The woman? The little girl?"

"Woman? Little girl?" He frowns. "I don't know what you're talking about, sweetie."

"I think you do, Daddy. I think you know."

He shakes his head, trying to put it all together, concentrating. "Maybe," he says. "Maybe the presents weren't right. That girl wouldn't be quiet, Mellie. I had to shush her. It wasn't perfect, like with you and me."

"God, Daddy. Jesus. You killed them, those poor people."

Her voice unsteady, shaking. She stares at her father. "You killed Mom; you raped me." Her voice is rising, near hysteria. She forces herself to calm down, talk her way out of this, end it. "Dad, you've got to stop. This has all got to stop."

"No, it doesn't," he says. "You're back, Mellie. You came back to me."

He starts moving toward her, actually putting the knife away in his belt and then unbuckling the brass belt buckle. His Melissa has come back to him.

Melissa scrambles on all fours to get by him, to get outside of this frozen hell that she's in with him. He grabs her left arm to pull her toward him, but this is Melissa O'Malley, the all-state basketball player, the one who lifts weights and runs and played college ball and is tough. Very tough. She punches and elbows and kicks him hard in the chest and with a loud *oomph* he loses his grip on her.

Melissa clambers outside the shack, rises to her feet, and runs, slipping badly on the ice. It is light out now; she can see where she's going. She heads for the shoreline.

"Mellie! Sweetie, wait!" Her father comes out behind her. "You don't understand. Wait a minute!"

She runs on, still slipping, falling with every third or fourth frenzied stride. She should have gone to a nearby shack, even if it was farther out on the ice, she realizes. She could have gotten help that way. Somebody to stop Melchior. She hears a car engine behind her, thinks it must be him in that damn truck, turns to look.

Melchior is trotting along behind her, taking his time on the ice, not slipping so badly despite his bad leg, walking calmly toward her.

She scrambles onto the shoreline, then up into the frozen snow that lines the lake. She turns once to see how far back he is.

That engine noise was a car that's roaring toward them on the ice. It's aimed at Daddy.

Melchior turns to look, then dodges to the side as the car narrowly misses him, then skids and turns completely around on the ice.

It bumps onto the shoreline, not ten yards away from Melissa. Finnegan is behind the wheel, his side window down despite the cold. "Get in," he says.

"No. We don't need to, Mr. Finnegan. Look," Melissa says.

Melchior has his arms raised. He is walking toward them, limping now on that bad leg. As they watch, he takes out the knife, throws it so it skitters across the ice.

"Mellie," he says loudly as he walks closer. "You don't understand. I'd never hurt you, Mellie. Never."

And then, "Hi, Bob," he says when he gets to them, smiling in the cold, vapor from that friendly grin. "Maybe you can help me explain things to Mellie. Tell her I love her."

Finnegan gets out, walks over toward Melchior, takes Mel's right hand and brings it around behind. Does the same with the left. Cuffs him.

And then, while Melissa watches in stunned silence as though it were a movie, not real at all, Melchior pulls free from Finnegan, shoulders the detective down onto the ice, and starts trotting back toward the shack, running as fast as the slick surface and his bad left leg will let him.

Finnegan scrambles to his feet, runs after him, Melissa after them both. Finnegan can't quite catch him, and Melchior makes it first to the shack. Finnegan gets there a few long seconds later, and Melissa a few seconds after that. As she enters, there is only Finnegan, hands thrust down into the black hole in the ice.

The body is gone, her father is gone, there's only Finnegan grasping something, hanging on for all he's worth, almost going in himself until he loses it, falls back onto the ice, holds his freezing hands out in supplication.

Mary is gone, back into her grave. Melchior has kicked her in, and then followed, and Finnegan couldn't hang onto him, couldn't bring Mel back from that deep cold, that perpetual preserving chill of the bottom of Lake Minnetoksak.

Melissa finds a tattered blanket in a corner, wraps it around Finnegan's arms and makes sure he's next to the heater. The two of them watch for a good five minutes, say nothing. There's no chance of diving in there to rescue anybody. Melchior is gone, down into the cold that he loves so much.

In the distance, they hear a siren. The backup that Finnegan radioed for while on his way to the lake is finally arriving.

It is very cold. Melissa, hugging Finnegan, thinks about her island boyfriend Billy, about warm seas and charter sailing. She wonders if she'll ever really escape the cold.

By the next day, ice covers the hole. There is nobody to break it clear and in another two days, it is smooth, as though the hole had never existed.

It's two months later before Melissa flies up for the funeral. She stands with Finnegan and his wife as the bodies are lowered into the earth, first her mother and then Melchior.

An early spring chinook has blown in and there's a light drizzle but temperature in the sixties as the coffins are lowered and then Melissa walks up to throw a handful of dirt onto each coffin.

It's done. She walks over to Finnegan and his wife, and stands there next to the two of them for a quiet few moments. Then she takes a deep breath, releases it, unbuttons her coat, turns to Finnegan and says, "It's warm out," and he nods, says, "It sure is," and they walk away.

This story appeared in Asimov's Science Fiction *magazine. The alternate history story is set in the 1980s and the 1940s and was a* Locus *magazine Recommended Read. The* Locus *reviewer said the story showed that when it comes to alternate history from the World War II era, I was "a master of the form." A novel length telling of this story is a work in progress.*

WALKING TO BOSTON

D riving the new Buick Riviera to the nursing home, Harry is thinking about the war years. That's where Niamh's head has been for the last month or two, back in the 1940s, back when they first met. She was a colleen in County Galway, and Harry was flight engineer and top turret gunner on a Mitchell, a B-25 on Lend-Lease to the Brits. A crash landing on a narrow strand of rocky beach, a beautiful local girl, a year of internment in neutral Ireland. One thing and then another and then she was his and vice versa. Back in the States, back in St. Louis, shoes and booze and the Cardinals and the Brownies. Those were great days.

They'd flown out of Gander, the RAF Ferry Command base there in Newfoundland, and the idea was to land in Northern Ireland, refuel, and then hop over to England. Take a boat back.

It worked out otherwise, that's all. Things went a little off course. Better in a lot of ways. Not so hot in others. It's all been on his mind a lot these past few months, calling it all up from way back when, remembering it all for Niamh's sake.

Harry turns the corner onto Essex Avenue, and heads toward

Kirkwood Haven, where they are doing their best for Niamh. It all started a couple of years ago. A little forgetfulness, some confusion. More. And then the steady slide into the gray haze. That bright, wonderful woman—gone.

He's all cried out about it. Eventually, you adjust. You have to, you have to deal with it, get on with things, with your own life. And now, at least, she seems to be pretty stable, living in the past for the most part; a better past, really, than the one that really was. And hell, Harry figures, she can live anytime she wants. He owes her that much, more, after all the stuff that went on back then. Harry shakes his head. That was a long time ago, a whole different world. A different him.

He pulls into the parking lot of Kirkwood Haven and sits in the car for a few seconds. He loves this Riviera. Leather seats, front-wheel drive, power windows, the sunroof, all the bells and whistles. So damn perfect, so solid and safe and perfect, that he marvels at what Detroit can offer these days. Best cars in the world. Best country, too. Cable television in every home, gas stations where you can pump your own gas, automatic teller machines at the banks so you can get some cash when you need it, supersonic passenger jets. Wonderful stuff.

But with all these marvels, no one can help Niamh. Making her comfortable, that's the most they promise, and it doesn't seem like much. He sighs, opens the door, looks up, shading his eyes. It's a beautiful spring day, puffy clouds in a blue sky, a few contrails up there, jets heading back and forth from coast to coast. Life goes on.

Inside, at the front desk, he signs in and the one nurse he really likes walks over. Rochelle, large and black and friendly. She seems to know her stuff.

"Hello, Mr. Mack," she says, "Niamh"—she pronounces it "Neeve," like you're supposed to—"is doing just fine. In and out, you know, like it's been, but she's happy."

Harry nods. The long, slow slide. "Is she awake?"

"She is, and all bright-eyed. Said she's been talking to her sisters lately. Said they've asked her to visit with them, up in Boston. You know anything about that?"

"Sisters?" He shakes his head. Poor Niamh. "No, she doesn't have any sisters. She has a brother back in Ireland. I met him once, ten years ago when we went for their mother's funeral. Nice guy. A fisherman, like their father had been before him. He took us to a local pub where they had some music, all fiddles and tin whistles. Good craic, the Irish say."

She smiles at that, knows the term. "But no sisters? She's talking a lot about those sisters." And then she shrugs. "She's a real sweetheart, Mr. Mack, a really nice lady. And, you know, strange things crop up for them when they go more and more into their own worlds. These sisters? Maybe they're friends she had when she was young? You know, a sisterhood thing?"

"I don't know," he says. "Last week it was her mother, God bless her soul, and the week before that she thought I was her brother Michael."

Rochelle smiles sympathetically and nods. "Yes, that's how it goes sometimes."

"But she's happy, Rochelle? That's what matters, right?"

Rochelle nods again, pats his hand. "Yes, sir, Mr. Mack. She's happy. Come on, let's go see her. It's a nice day. You can take her for a walk in the garden. She loves those butterflies."

And so that's what they'll do. And Niamh does love the butterflies. Big orange monarchs, on their migration, just passing through St. Louis, headed somewhere.

JULY 1, 1940

The rear tire on her bicycle was flat and Niamh Sayers had neither a patch nor the money to buy one, so she was on foot again, chasing after her grandmother Máire who for the second time in a month had decided to leave her home in Kinvara and walk to Boston in far off Massachusetts to visit her sisters.

The weather, at least, was perfect, a sunstruck morning that began with dawn at 4:00 AM and now was full and bright at 6:30 AM—as perfect a day as the year had seen on this rainy west coast of Ireland. The sky looked endless; a pale, perfect blue that held a few puffy clouds, a handful of fat puffins out searching for a meal, and a single cawing seagull on its way to steal a new chick from the puffins' nests on the cliffs.

Maybe, she thought, smiling, this was the start of a long stretch of summer weather, good for drying the turf and warming the soul. Then she laughed at that thought the moment she had it. She was far too worldly-wise to hope for such weather; they'd be lucky if the dry sunshine lasted into the afternoon.

For the moment, though, the day was blessed; perfect for a walk down the narrow boreens that led into Kinvara and from there to the rocks and strands of beach that looked out to the water. In the distance was Dunguaire Castle and beyond that the wide expanse of Galway Bay and if one went out on the bay and headed west, well, next parish Boston everyone said with a dry laugh that supposed you knew how many had gone to just that place in recent years, leaving behind mostly the women, the boys, and the old men. It was a sad state of affairs, the way Ireland bled away her young, as the men in O'Brien's bar regularly said over their thoughtful pints of Guinness while she waited tables and cleaned up the place.

At least those young men who'd left had gone by train and boat, Niamh thought as she reached the top of the grandly named Market Street that ran through town and down to the stone quay. As for grandmother Máire, as she slid ever deeper into her private world she seemed firmly to believe that she could manage the trip on her own two feet; and she was growing braver each try.

The first few times the shock of the cold water against her bare feet had brought her to a stop, if not completely to her senses, in six inches of tidal pool. But those early efforts had been in winter. In more recent months, as the water had warmed, Grandmother had gotten bolder, and the last time, just a fortnight ago, she'd been knee-deep and still struggling to walk west when Niamh finally caught up to her in Spanish Cove.

The cove was just past the quay, where a spit of land jutted out into the water, helping sailors mark the rocks of the shallows. Fifteen minutes' walk now, ten if she hurried, and Niamh would be there. Grandmother, with a bit of luck, would be there, too, no doubt staring west, her teeth chattering even in this warm summer sun as the cold water nipped at her ankles, her calves, maybe this time up to her waist. Then would come some gentle coaxing, that was all, and things would be set to rights again. For a while. Niamh sighed and picked up the pace.

There was a distant throb of aeroplane engines. She glanced at the sky but couldn't spot anything through the sun's glare. No matter, she knew what it was. Until the hostilities in Europe had slowed the number of flights, the flying boats from America and Europe had thundered overhead on their way into Foynes every day, just thirty miles away on the Kerry side of the River Shannon. Niamh felt herself quite worldly when it came to matters of air travel. No mere aeroplane on its way from sunny Portugal to America would bring her to a stop anymore, eyes wide in wonderment as they'd been when she was young and amazed at the thought of where that plane had come from and where it was going.

No more than a hundred yards down from where she stood, a long seawall fronted with huge round boulders held back the tide. She walked on down to that seawall, climbed up and headed out to the west on it, all the while that steady hum from the plane going along with her. She looked again and spotted it finally in the distance, an odd-shaped speck in the blue. It must be circling, she thought, before it came in for that final splash onto the smooth Shannon.

Grandmother, as Niamh had guessed, wasn't on the first beach, which meant another hard walk through the loose sand and out to the point, getting her own feet wet in the bargain as she scrambled around the rocks, cutting off the corner to save ten more minutes of walk on the inland side.

She climbed and descended in good time, all the while hearing that noisy plane in the background, its clatter penetrating even the roar of the surf as it pounded against the western side of the headlands, great white plumes of spray rising from the rocks as wide, thick combers rolled in to end a journey they'd begun thousands of miles west.

There, on the thin strand of beach that faced west at Spanish Cove, she saw Grandmother in the distance, nearly at the far end, surely enough wading into the cold Atlantic, heading west herself. Niamh shook her head, happy enough to have known just where to look, and headed that way.

And the engines changed behind her.

Subtle at first, a missing beat somewhere in the steady clatter, then a loud bang like a bomb going off. Niamh turned to look and the plane had circled closer. There, so low she could see its markings, flew a kind of craft she hadn't seen before. Big, with two engines, the one on the right side smoking badly. Not a flying boat at all. At the back, an odd twin tail, two tall upright sections, one on each side of the fuselage. It was silver, with windows all over the front nose so the pilots, she guessed, could see what they were doing. A German bomber far off course? She'd heard of that happening in County Cork and over in Waterford and Wexford. But here, in the West?

She raised her hand to shield her eyes from the sun's glare off that sheen of silver and then watched, amazed, as men started jumping out from the underside. She opened her mouth to speak, to yell, to tell someone, anyone, what she was seeing, but nothing came out and so she simply stood there, mouth open, watching as one, two, then three men fell to their deaths in the bay.

But then a parachute opened for the first, and then the others, and in a flash she understood that they had parachuted out from the plane, that it was crashing and they'd saved themselves.

They were landing back behind her, in the town or near it, and she started to run that way in excitement, actually made ten good yards of a sprint when she remembered her grandmother, waist-deep in the Atlantic, heading to America. Oh, my.

She turned and saw Grandmother there in the distance, wading back toward the beach, waving at the sky, yelling something unintelligible. She must have seen the men, the plane, the parachutes, and they'd lured her back to shore with the excitement.

But Grandmother still needed help, surely, and the men falling from the sky beneath those silky white parachutes—nylon! That thought hit her in a flash. It was said those parachutes were made of nylon! She'd seen a bit of it a year ago—before rationing—in the shops in Galway and hadn't quite believed it, the miracle of it, a kind of fabric like silk only not so impossible to afford. But then, overnight it seemed, it was gone, a miracle taken away so it could be used for war, for parachutes, and now here it was, falling into her lap.

She turned back toward town. Caught herself. No. It had to be her grandmother first. She turned back again and ran down the beach to rescue Grandmother Máire from the clutches of the ocean. With any luck, she thought, she'd be able to get to her in just a few minutes and then they both could get back to town before all the nylon, and the men who'd dropped from the sky beneath it, were gone. Oh, sweet mother of Jesus. Nylon!

MAY 7, 1984

Rochelle unlocks the door to the quiet wing and they go through and down the hall and turn left and there, in the reading area, Niamh is waiting for him, rocking in her favorite chair, a book open in her lap. Harry thanks Rochelle and walks over to Niamh on his own.

She looks brighter, more energetic than he's seen her in a while, though still too thin, too frail. Her gray hair is nicely combed. She's wearing a little makeup. She looks a lot older than sixty-two. She remembers him today.

"Hello, Harry," she says. "I'm glad you're finally here. Let's get going."

Get going? Oh, Christ, what now, he wonders.

"I hope you're ready for that long drive, Harry," she says, rising from the rocker and offering her hand, the motion a girlish reflection, coquettish. It's been, God, forty years since he's seen that little flick of the wrist, the offered hand, and it all comes back to him in a second.

He takes the hand. He will not, absolutely will not, cry, he thinks to himself. Damn. "Long drive, Irish?" he asks, using his favorite nickname for her, the one they got started with in 1940, walking along the cliffs near Doolin and looking west. "I don't think we'll need that for a walk in the garden."

"Oh, Harry, you haven't forgotten, have you?" She smiles at him. "We said we'd leave today, so we'd have plenty of time to make the drive and be in our hotel by the ninth. Our anniversary, Harry. Have you forgotten? And after just five years? A honeymoon at last!"

Anniversary? Long drive? A honeymoon?

Oh, God. Harry thinks he knows what's going on in her mind. They were married in a hurry in 1942, just before he shipped out to Pearl and then, later, to do some island-hopping in the Mitchell. Scary damn stuff, that, the props almost touching the waves as the B-25 came in over the beach and dropped the bombs onto the Japanese lines, Smitty pulling back on the stick just as the bombs left the bay, so Stinky seemed to hop up into the air and make her getaway.

Harry had been no angel, God knows, since he'd first met Niamh on that Irish beach. A whole string of women during the war. The uniform, maybe? The war? The sense of doom? All of that. And through it all he was in touch with Niamh, letters back and forth. Love letters, eventually. Pretty damn passionate.

And then she'd sent him the note saying she'd been accepted for training as a stenographer for Dev's government and after six weeks of secretarial school in Dublin she'd be off to the embassy in DC, and that's where he was stationed, so it all seemed like fate. He got a two-day pass and met her at the pier when the flying boat with the Irish delegation came into New York harbor and oh, hell, she was so damn pretty stepping onto the pier that his stomach tied right up into a knot and his knees got wobbly. He knew then that he loved her and they both knew he was leaving in a week or less for the Pacific and might not see her for six months or even a year or two. So they found a priest, a Jesuit at Georgetown, who would marry them, doing the banns in a couple of days, understanding the situation, wishing them well. And that was it, they were hitched. But no time for a honeymoon, not then, so they promised themselves that trip to Boston that she wanted so much. She'd heard so much about it from relations who'd gone there that it mattered more than New York or Chicago to her. A honeymoon there would be wonderful. Someday, they agreed, someday.

And now, for Niamh, it's 1947 and the war is over and her flyboy is home and it's time for that honeymoon. She squeezes his hand. "I'm ready, Harry. I'm all packed," she says and waves her hand toward her room and he looks in. Sure enough, two suitcases by the bed. Oh, Christ.

Well, hell, their anniversary was two months ago, for starters, and he took her out to Stan and Biggies for a steak. Nice evening, now forgotten. But she's right about the honeymoon that never happened and there's no reason not to humor her a bit, poor Irish. She'll probably forget all about it in a few minutes anyway. He walks over to the coat rack, grabs her favorite old wool overcoat. She seems cold all the time these days. "Sure, Irish, I remembered," he says. "Let's go, Honey. It's a long drive."

"I wondered, Harry," she says with a worried look on her face. "You know how you are, dear. So forgetful sometimes."

She slips easily into the coat, too easily, all that lost weight. She takes his hand and pulls him toward the front door of the place. "Oh, Harry, I've been looking forward to this day for weeks. We can make it to Chicago by tonight, don't you think?"

"Sure, Niamh," he says. "Sure. Chicago." On the way out he tells Rochelle what he has in mind and she smiles. A nice outing. Drive around a bit in the great weather, maybe a walk in Forest Park. Get an ice cream.

Niamh is quiet as they drive through the residential streets toward Interstate 44. Harry begins to think she's forgotten the wedding, the anniversary, and the honeymoon already. Maybe, he figures, he'll just take her to the art museum or the zoo. She'd like that.

He looks at her as they drive down Lockwood Avenue. So innocent, so sweet. This terrible thing that has happened to her has returned her to her childhood.

She notices his glance. "You keep your eyes on the road, Harry Mack, and not on your bride," she says, laughing. "These roads are dangerous enough without you staring over at me instead of paying attention to your driving."

He smiles, shakes his head. Ten minutes later, he isn't sure why, he decides not to get on the interstate and instead drives on down Berry to Gravois, old Route 66. He goes east on that, and figures by the time they cross the Mississippi and get into Illinois she'll be over this thing and maybe they can get a bite to eat over there somewhere and then head home.

But she doesn't get over it. Instead, they take the old Chain of Rocks Bridge across the river, ignore I-64 and then I-55 and get back on old Route 66, the two-lane road that heads north and east toward Chicago. They slip on through Edwardsville and Hamel and keep on going and somewhere on that road, maybe around Staunton, Harry realizes he's passed the point of no return. As long as Niamh is going to be like this he is going to play along.

She's been sleeping, but when they stop for some gas at a Shell station in Lincoln she wakes up, straightens herself in the seat, looks around the interior of the Riviera. "I love this car," she says, her Irish accent returning after years of being gone. "It's a marvel, isn't it, so? This fancy wireless in it." She reads the name in script. "Sonomatic, that sounds magical, does it not, Harry? It's like Jo Stafford and Tommy Dorsey are next to us here in the car, so. Our car, Harry, and it's grand, with all these dials and knobs. Well. My," she says, and sits back, smiling.

Harry takes a breath. So it's not over yet. It's worse, in fact, since he could swear himself that they're in that great old '47 Buick he bought after the war. Damndest thing.

But he smiles and pats her hand. It's a great car for sure, he's thinking, as there's a polite tap on his side window. A guy in a white uniform is there, smiling. Harry rolls down the window and the guy says, "Welcome to Soulsby's Shell. Gas her up for you?"

"Sure," he says, "fill her up with high-test," and smiles mostly to himself as the guy does just that. Gas is nineteen cents a gallon.

As they pull away from the station Harry looks straight ahead down the road. "You know," he says, "the *Post* said it's nice weather on the East Coast, up in the sixties in Boston, I think."

"Well," she says, "it sounds wonderful to me. We'll stay in that guesthouse in Marblehead, remember that?"

"The Seagull Inn," he laughs. "Funny I remember that. In Marblehead Neck. Nice place."

"*Ah*, Harry. Surely we promised ourselves that we'd honeymoon there and now we are. It's a little late, that's all."

He nods. She's thinking a few years late. He's thinking decades. Still, "Yeah, a little late, Irish," he says. "I'm so sorry about that. I really am."

"It will be so beautiful there, Harry, I just know it. The shore, the sea."

One thing St. Louis doesn't have, Harry thinks, is much in the way of oceans. Big Muddy is it when it comes to big water in St. Louis. The Mississippi, a mile wide and brown with silt. So what the hell, a few days at the shore, watch those waves roll in, walk along the beach. It might be nice.

"It will be terrific, Niamh," he says. "I'm sure of it. We'll relax, go for walks, eat a lot of seafood, get all the fresh air."

"Oh," she says, and then "Oh," again. "The sea. So long since we've been to the sea. Years and years, Harry."

Should he ask her about those sisters of hers? The ones she was talking about with Rochelle, back at Kirkwood Haven. What the hell was that about?

He turns to look at her and her eyes are closed. She's back asleep in a heartbeat, does that a lot lately, quick little catnaps. He turns back to keep his eyes on the narrow road, looks up at the sky. Yeah, it has clouded over. It was a long, gray winter in St. Louis, all that cold rain. She says she's tired of all that gray. So she wants some sunshine and seashore. Well, fair enough, he won't argue with that.

They're almost to Bloomington. Those clouds have built up and it's starting to rain. He turns on the windshield wipers.

JULY 1, 1940

Sweet Christ, they were going to crash and die. Right from the start, Harry hadn't believed they'd make it all the way across from the RAF Ferry Command base at Gander, and now, right at the end, it turned out he was right.

God almighty, the flight was over nineteen hundred miles of open water, well past the normal range of the B-25. But no one listened to all his worry. They laughed, instead, saying he was their official worrywart and every crew needed one. Instead of taking him seriously, they'd filled up the bomb bay and the rest of the fuselage with gas tanks and run all the numbers and decided two things: One, that they had enough gas to make it, especially—and he loved this phrase—"in light of the prevailing tailwinds at this time of year." Two, that all the extra weight from the additional fuel wouldn't pin them to the ground when they tried to take off from Gander.

On the second point they'd been right, the Mitchell had cleared the trees and phone lines at the end of the runway with maybe a foot to spare—a real Lindbergh of a takeoff, Harry had thought as they'd struggled up off the wet runway, spray flying from the prop wash and from the wheels. He'd looked down through the Plexiglas of the ventral turret to watch the leaves whip by inches below. It was, until now, the most scared he'd been in his life.

On the first point, they'd damn near been right, too. Just after sunup Bobby Smith—Smitty—had called out from his pilot's seat that he could see Ireland up there and they were going to make it, right on schedule and with enough fuel left to find the field, get things lined up and then bring her on in.

But not enough fuel, as it turned out, to handle being one hundred miles off course. They were supposed to land in Londonderry, for Christ's sake, where they could refuel before taking the B-25 on over to England so the RAF could put her through some real action and see how she did. She was the first of thirty of the bombers the Brits had taken on Lend-Lease from Roosevelt, and she was going to show off, starting with the long flight across the North Atlantic to Northern Ireland.

Instead, they were south, way south, of where they should be. That wasn't Malin Head and Lough Foyle down below, Digger told them as he worked on his charts. Instead it was the Aran Islands and the mouth of Galway Bay. That tailwind must have shoved them south, and that wasn't good, since this part of Ireland was its own country and a neutral one at that. It was only in the North that they could land and refuel. In the south, they'd been told back at Gander, belligerents from both sides were interned in camps for the duration of the war, and while the US wasn't in it, these Lend-Lease flights might mean the Irish would make the obvious connection between England and the US flyers and throw their butts into a camp. Which was just terrific. Goddamn Army Air Corps at it again, screwing the crews.

It was way too late to worry about that now, though. No problem, boys, Smitty had said, we'll just take her in at Shannon and let the politicians figure out what to do with her, and with us. And then he'd wrestled her around some, circling once and heading toward Shannon field. No problem, boys, he said again, we'll be fine.

And then the starboard engine disagreed, with a loud bang that had to be that number nine cylinder head cracking loose, followed by smoke and flame and fire extinguisher handles getting pulled and that weird controlled chaos that just happens sometimes and you deal with it.

Harry, with nothing to do in the crisis but stay out of the way, could only watch as Smitty and Digger fought the controls and tried to douse the flames. For a few moments, it looked like they'd done it, but then the flames came back again, and their airspeed was too damn slow, and they didn't have enough damn altitude, and so Smitty told them all to get the hell out and he'd be right behind them.

And Harry wanted to, he really did. He wanted to get over there and tumble out through the belly hatch and then pull the cord and float serenely down through this beautiful Irish summer sky.

But he couldn't. He couldn't move. Petrified with fear: he'd heard that phrase and never understood it until this moment, crouching there by his turret. One part of his brain seemed perfectly normal, registering all the events going on around him, taking it in so quickly and clearly that it was almost like he was watching it all in the front row of the Osage Theater back home in Kirkwood, some really great movie full of all the right details, including a guy named Harry Mack standing there by the top turret guns, his left hand on the firing trigger, his right hand held out straight in front of him, trembling, the palm up so he could see how badly it shook.

All he had to do was take three steps that way and let himself go. Easy as pie. Slick as oleo. Nothing to it.

But the other part of his brain, the part that controlled his muscles, his motion, maybe his courage, couldn't do a damn thing. It was locked shut, tight. He watched as Sam Ewell, then Digger Hargis, then Danny Morrow all did what they had to do, committing themselves to the nothing. It was the right thing to do, it was the only thing that could save his life, to do that very thing himself.

But he couldn't. It was asking more of him than he had to give, that was all. All night long he'd listened to those twin 1650-horsepower Wright Cyclone engines thundering out that steady roar just knowing one of them would eventually fail. That number nine piston had been a problem all along, the valve guides warping and then the piston cracking in there probably and finally the whole thing breaking apart. Just like that, blown.

Smitty was yelling at him. He wondered if he could turn and see what the guy wanted. One hell of a pilot, that Smitty. Harry and the rest of the crew believed firmly that Smitty could set this thing down on a baseball diamond if he had to. Hell, pull it right in at Ebbets Field. Come barreling in over Brooklyn and touch it down at home plate, gentle as a feather, then run it out to that short right-field wall, just 297 down the line. That'd be a sight.

Harry managed to turn sideways and face Smitty, who was still yelling, "Get the hell out of this plane, Harry! And right now!"

Harry just shook his head. "Sorry, Smitty. I can't do it."

"Can't do it!? Can't do what? Jump? Jesus Christ, Harry, we're heading in, man. You got to jump!"

He just shook his head again, clung tighter to the twin fifties.

Smitty shook his head right back, yelled, "Well, hang on

then, Harry, this ain't going to be pretty!" and turned back around to wrestle with the stick.

Harry managed a look down through the open belly hatch, the wind whistling by. The water looked close, real close. They couldn't be more than a hundred feet up.

He remembered, in great detail, what they'd told them back in flight school about a water landing. There'd be a hard thump when the tail hit, and then another thump, harder, when the belly hit. It was important not to think the first thump was it because the second one was even harder and you had to stay braced. Then they'd come to a pretty quick halt and then they had seven minutes, not much more, to get out before she went under.

He remembered distinctly how a Captain Wellman had told them about how these techniques would save their lives. Sure, save their lives: he chewed on that thought for a moment, took another look down through the belly hatch. Fifty feet now, maybe less. The water was beautiful, blues and a little green to it, and nearly calm. Smitty could do it. Smitty could bring this thing in on its belly and they'd both walk away.

Harry had all the time in the world to watch the water come closer, forty feet now, the water's clarity surprising; he could see right to the bottom, underneath the waves. Amazing. Sand down there, some seaweed growing. A big fish or two, and was that a seal? Hell, five or six of them, all looking up at him as he looked down to see them pass by. Did Ireland have seals?

Blue, very blue now, twenty feet away and the port engine's prop stirring up the water and the clarity was gone and when the hell would they hit? A quick sign of the cross, suddenly Catholic again, a true believer as the water was right below him and then here it was here it was here it was.

Niamh stood on one side of the half-moon of narrow strand and looked across to see her grandmother there in the distance, walking to Boston, knee-deep in the water already and struggling to go farther, her arms out to the side, paddling with them as the water slowly deepened. It's a long way to Massachusetts.

The waves were famous here, focused and compressed by the mouth of the bay and the beach strand facing straight west as the combers rolled in, horsetails flying back across their top as the breeze blew out to sea. But they were quiet today, praise the saints, and it was low tide, so there was another fifty meters or more before Grandma would be grabbed by the rushing water.

Hurry then. And Niamh did, bare feet on the wet, firm sand near the water's edge, running and running and then hearing again the roar of that aeroplane.

She stopped and turned to see that it hadn't left at all but had only described a great, huge circle and now, one engine smoking and the propeller still, was coming in toward the shallow water in front of the rocks and the narrow beach at the far end of the half-mooned shoreline where the rocks were fewest and the water smoothest and Grandma, Máire Caitlin O'Mahoney herself, was coming to a halt in her long walk west and turning to stare at the great, huge thing that was about to land on her.

Turning back to run, pulling up the great huge wet skirt that slowed her down, grabbing it up in great handfuls so her legs could churn along the beach, Niamh ran and in rhythm to her stride was chanting, sisters, sisters, sisters, sisters, oh sisters, and then again, repeating the chant and then again and then again, pleading for help, for intervention, as a huge roller emerged out there, big and wide and tall, coming in to meet grandmother Máire and that plane all at once; sisters, sisters, sisters.

They'd hit once, hard, just like that Captain Wellman had promised back in San Antonio, and then, sure enough, they'd hit again, harder. The first one had torn Harry's hands free from the grip of the fifty-caliber machine gun and then thrown him down against the hard edges of the bomb door crankshaft. It hurt like hell, but the pain woke him up somehow, made things understandable. Suddenly everything was in slow-motion and he was thinking more clearly than he'd ever thought in his life, more clearly than he'd ever guessed he could be capable of thinking, seeing it all in a way he'd never seen it before. And in that clarity he knew that the pain in his side where the crankshaft handle had ripped into him was a good thing: it meant he was alive.

He'd heard Smitty talking as the tail section hit and they felt that first thump: "Goddamnit, goddamnit, goddamnit, goddamnit, goddamnit," Smitty had been saying, nice and calm, repeating it, cool and flat as they slid along for a few seconds and then, with a huge thump, twice as hard as the first one, a bone-rattling, steel-rending pounding, the fuselage finally slammed down onto the water and they were fully down.

And, like Wellman had promised, they were still alive. Harry was bounced back hard against the copilot's seat again by the second impact and then rebounded back into the jump seat, his forehead cracking hard into the edge of the warm air duct.

For a second, there was a weird calm as they slid along and Harry thought they might just dodge all those shoreline rocks and slide right up by the beach and come to a gentle stop and wouldn't that be nice?

Then things started to happen. He could feel the whole plane rise, some huge wave grabbing it and tipping it to the right, so they must be winging over into the water or maybe even the bottom if it was shallow enough. He twisted around with the momentum of that shift and could see Smitty lying, still, on the stick, his head forward, blood everywhere.

They tilted even more to the right and Harry slipped back along the folding step of the navigator's compartment and found himself kneeling there looking right out the belly hatch to the water and the bouldered beach. And there, on the beach, stood the Virgin Mary, staring at him.

He must be already be dead. Through the belly hatch he could see her, tall and thin with jet-black hair down to her shoulders, dressed in a long, blue skirt that she'd gathered and pulled up with her left hand, a blue hood over her head, her right hand raised to shield her eyes as she looked right at him. She couldn't be more than twenty or thirty yards away.

Harry was Catholic, from a long line of old Highland Scots Catholics that his mother told him with pride went back past Culloden to Bannockburn and beyond. Hell, he'd been an altar boy at Holy Innocents and been a real believer back then.

But he'd lost that faith in high school, had it beaten out of him by the Jesuits at the University High who told him he had to think for himself. He had, and ditched the whole damn nonsense; forever he'd thought for the past five years since he'd quit going to Mass.

But damned if that wasn't Her, the Mother of God, a vision, standing there looking right at him, right through him. He felt like waving to her, but then the plane tilted even more, the wing rising on a wave so that it passed right over the biggest of the rocks in the shallow water—a miracle for sure—and the Mother of God disappeared as the open hatch looked out now to low, stony mountains and then, the rocks cleared, the big B nosed down hard into the bottom, the tail came up and he was flying through the fuselage, somehow missing everything that should have stopped him, soaring along like Superman right into the instrument panel and the Plexiglas front nose where, face pressed hard against the glass, he watched rocks and sand come right up at him and crash into the glass and crack it and water, a lot of it, started squirting in.

Niamh could not believe what she was seeing: the sisters out there in the water watching as the great huge beast of an aeroplane bore down on her grandmother and then the frightened, lonely face of that pilot inside the belly of the beast as it tipped up and he was looking right at her and she at him through that small open door. Then the aeroplane twisted more to its side as that one great wave reached and lifted and twisted it—her sisters, her lovely sisters doing this—so that the front of it, the nose, rose right over grandmother and settled on the far side of her and then the whole huge thing settled with a splash and there was, for a moment, water rising and spouting everywhere, great geysers of it on all sides as Niamh came alive, thinking of her grandmother, and running again the last twenty yards to where the aeroplane had settled.

As she approached, the spray subsided, a rainfall of cold Atlantic splashing against the sand on the shore and the gleaming silver of the aeroplane. For a moment there was a bright, partial rainbow as the sun glinted through the falling mist.

Then it was over. She stood there for a long moment, trying to figure out what to do. Where was grandmother? What of the man she'd seen in the belly of the beast?

In the sudden silence she could hear herself breathing hard from the run, could feel her heart pounding. There was a creak and moan from the aircraft as it settled and then a sharp crack as something gave way and the plane settled deeper into the water, nose down. She felt distant from this all somehow, a spectator in some cinema show like she'd seen that time in Galway at the Odeon; figures on a screen, safely up there so the bullets didn't fly into the audience and the American gangster—that James Cagney fellow, what a look on that face!—couldn't climb right down into the audience and start shooting away, willy-nilly, slaying the lot of them as they sat there watching.

Her mind was going too fast, in a panic, and some small, calm part of her somewhere knew it. She ran around to the other side of the wreckage where the wing, snapped in half, tilted at an angle against the aeroplane's hulk. Where was grandmother? She called for her as she ran "Grandma! Grandma!"

Nothing. No one. Her grandmother had disappeared into the wreckage somehow, the great beast swallowing her up. And that man? The pilot? Nowhere to be seen.

She yelled again. "Grandmother, are you there?"

But there was nothing.

Harry was trapped. The cockpit was underwater and the Plexiglas shattered in a half-dozen spots so that tiny streams of cold Atlantic were splashing against his chest. His right leg was jammed down into the few inches of space next to the copilot's seat and his foot was trapped there. A piece of torn metal cut into his ankle. It hurt like hell. His face felt warm. He reached up to touch his forehead and came away with blood. Oh, Christ.

He tugged again and there was more pain, a lot of it, but then the foot came free. All right, then: he pulled the leg out of that tight spot and glanced at it, pants torn, bloody as hell around the ankle. Jesus H. Christ, he had to get out of here, and fast.

He turned around, thinking to get back to the belly hatch, which might be above the waterline. Smitty was lying in the way, unconscious, maybe dead. Shit, he'd have to climb over the body, or push it out of the way. Poor damn Smitty.

He reached down to grab him by the shoulders and Smitty moaned. Still alive, then. Harry pushed him to the side, stepped over him with his left leg, shoving aside a big piece of metal and there, a bright answer to his panic, was the open hatch, sunlight streaming in. He headed that way, trying to bring the bad leg over Smitty; but, Jesus, it hurt like hell and the leg didn't seem to want to do what he needed it to do. He tugged on it with both hands and the pain, great bolts of it, jagged edged sharp knives of it, stabbed at him.

Smitty moaned again. Harry couldn't stop to help him, damnit, he had his own problems right now, the water rising as he felt the plane settle deeper into the sand with a loud moan. The water pushed hard into the cockpit.

He looked toward the hatch. A face peered in, a little old lady. *"An bhfuil tu ceart go leor ansin?"*

What the hell language was that? He thought the Irish spoke English. Maybe they weren't in Ireland after all, maybe in France? Was that French she'd used? Dutch? Oh, hell, he didn't know. Smitty moaned again.

The pain had subsided, but the leg felt stuck. He looked down there to tug on it and damned if Smitty hadn't grabbed it in a death grip. He still seemed unconscious, but he had both arms wrapped around the stupid leg that wouldn't do what Harry wanted it to do.

Oh, Christ. He started crawling toward the hatch, pulling the leg behind with Smitty still hanging onto it. It was comical. Ten feet away was that bright opening of the hatch and sunshine and air and safety, but it was a long damn ten feet when you were pulling someone along with your leg. Goddamn Laurel and Hardy, it was. Some Three Stooges gag, *whoop whoop whoop*. He tugged hard and gained a couple of feet. He looked at the hatch and the woman was smiling. *"Fáilte,"* she said. That's great. Very helpful. Smitty moaned again, then mumbled something. He was coming awake.

Harry looked back, tugged again, and the plane shifted in the water, something pushing against it, some shape out that window, seals again, curious? Then some wave maybe or some stray current rocked them a bit, something was pushing him from behind and damned if they didn't move pretty good, the whole damn package of them sliding along, two feet, another four.

He looked forward and they were there, at the hatch. He reached it, pulled himself through and dangled there for a second, then felt a push from behind: Smitty, awake, helping to shove. They fell through and landed in the water, a couple of feet deep, and onto some rocks and sand. Alive. Jesus, at least that, alive.

He looked up. The old lady just stood there, smiling.

MAY 7, 1984

By suppertime they are in Chicago, taking Route 66 right to its end near Lake Michigan and then heading up the road a bit to the Piccadilly Hotel in Hyde Park. All of this is happening in the brand-new 1947 Buick Super Sedan, which Harry really likes, from the smell of it to the feel of the big steering wheel with "Buick Eight" written across it, and the fancy Sonomatic radio, and the jump seats in the back. Gauges everywhere, oil pressure and battery, the works.

They could really build them in 1947, all those guys back to work in assembly plants, happy to build cars instead of tanks. And it is, in fact, one hell of a car; painted a deep sky blue, like they were flying, he and Niamh, flying north out of all the troubled years in St. Louis; all that trouble he caused, all the pain and, let's admit it, the torment.

But Harry and Niamh don't dwell on that. Instead, Harry's listening to the *Jack Benny Show* on the radio, with Frank Sinatra as a guest, and Abbott and Costello doing "Who's on First?" Funny stuff. Easy to forget how funny that was. But how in the hell? No, Harry thinks, don't go there. Just drive along. Be happy. Like Niamh over there, wonderful Niamh. A saint, putting up with him all those years. A saint.

They spend the night in the Piccadilly, a great hotel with that famous large movie house on the first floor, complete with a big vaudeville stage for the occasional live act. Damn, the hotel is really something. Harry's been on plenty of business trips to Chicago over the years and he knows the place quit being a hotel and became student dorms in the 1960s when the University of Chicago took it over. But that was now and this is then, so he chooses not to worry about it as they check in, registering at the front desk, chatting with the bellboy and the elevator operator as they take their bags up the elevator with them. It all seems so damn normal that he just doesn't even want to think about how it has all come to pass.

Truth is, he thinks, he even feels better physically. Stronger, younger. He takes a look in the bathroom mirror as they are getting settled in the room and he can't see much different; but, God, he feels good. Maybe it's Niamh, rubbing off on him. She is as alive, as bright as he's seen her in years. That, alone, makes this whole madcap thing worthwhile.

They eat dinner at the hotel restaurant, Schoenstadt's, where they each have the prime rib, baked potato, beans. The whole thing is under ten dollars, including the glass of wine for Niamh. Harry doesn't drink anymore, not since the big blowup twenty years ago—damn, he almost lost everything then: his job, Niamh, the house. And all for the booze. But, like everything else, they got through it. He got dried out, hasn't touched the hard stuff since.

He wishes he could say the same about the women, old and new.

He's thinking about that. He's sorry about it, damn it, as they finish their dinner and then go for a walk to buy a few things. On the way out Harry uses the phone at the front desk to call back to Kirkwood Haven. Rotary dial and the charge added to the room and somehow it all works fine. He tells them he's taking Niamh on a little vacation and he'll have her back in a few days. Then, as they walk along Hyde Park Boulevard Harry tries not to gawk as they pass by the storefronts, ads everywhere for Frigidaires and DeSotos and Maytag washing machines. The war is over and the boys are home and business is booming.

As they walk past the Sears with the big display in the window there's a nasty crack in the sidewalk and Niamh stumbles as her heel catches. She and Harry are arm in arm, and he holds on tight as she stops, then looks around, puzzled, and asks, "Where are we, Harry?" She's in the Now for a moment and

Harry's about to tell her and expecting this all to dissolve when she turns to him and smiles and says, "It's a lovely night, isn't it?"

And he smiles back, says it is, sure, and they walk on into the Sears and buy a suitcase and some clothes for him. Two pairs of nice slacks are four dollars, three shirts at two dollars each, socks, underwear. It all doesn't break the bank, that's for sure.

And then an hour later they're lying in bed together, on their backs, Harry reading a *Life* magazine that he picked up at the newsstand outside, a picture of Ted Williams on the cover, when Niamh reaches over to take one hand and says, "Harry. Aren't you going to, you know ...?"

He looks at her and smiles as she goes on. "Harry, I worried so much about you during the war. About us. Was it real? Were we in love? We were, weren't we? We are, aren't we?"

"Sure," he says, thinking about the war again and that girl in Pearl. God, what a beauty she'd been. Irresistible.

It's the damnedest thing, thinking about those days. It's like there were two of him. The one that pined for his Irish girl from County Galway, and the one that didn't pine so much and thought about the missions he'd been on and the ones to come and how short life was, really.

"Sure," he says again firmly, "sure we were. We are, Irish," and he rolls on his side to look at her. She's beautiful.

JULY 1, 1940

There was blood everywhere, the belly of the aeroplane looked bruised with it—red splotches on the edges of an open hatch and then more bright splashes of red against the silver of the aeroplane's skin. And there were two men there, not just the one she'd seen through the hatch. Both of them were bloody and awful, near death she guessed. They sat there numb in the shallow chill of the seawater while her grandmother, God bless her in her madness, was herself untouched by all the chaos and stood over them chatting away in Irish, the two poor pilots not understanding a word of it, just staring up at her as she rattled on.

Niamh had struggled to get to this spot. The crash of the aeroplane had seemed to swallow them up at first. She'd cried out for her grandmother, yelling "Grandma! Grandma! Grandma!" as a litany, a prayer, while she'd clambered over a torn part of the wing, then slid down the other side and splashed into knee-deep water—so cold it took her breath away—and then she'd pushed aside a huge flap of silvery metal that had torn almost free from the side of the aeroplane so that it hung there, barely attached.

She'd been afraid that the metal might fall off in her hands as she shoved at it and, concentrating on avoiding that, she wasn't really looking beyond the metal until she'd shoved it aside and slipped by. And there, sitting in the shallow water, their backs against the side of the aeroplane, staring up at her grandmother, saying nothing, were the two pilots. Above them, sermonizing, was Grandmother, babbling on in Irish about selkies and the Tuatha De Danaan and the Children of Lir come back from the Sea of Moyle. God bless her, but thank God, too, that they couldn't understand her. Selkies, indeed.

Niamh splashed across to her grandmother and took her into her arms, then stood back for a second to take a look at her. "Are you all right, then, Grandma?" she asked, speaking in English for the sake of the men. "You're not hurt too badly, so?"

Grandmother Máire smiled brightly. "Oh, hello, Niamh," she said in English. "Yes, I'm right as rain, dear, right as rain." Her eyes were bright, cheeks flushed. It was the healthiest, the most aware, that she'd looked in months. "Did you see it coming down, Niamh? Did you see the great, huge thing come swooping so?"

"I did, I watched every moment of it. God and Mary, I thought it was going to swoop right down on top of you." She shook her head. "I thought I'd find you flattened here."

Her grandmother laughed, throwing her head back in joy, the

excitement of it all too much to hold in. "*Ah!*" she cried, "It was wonderful, Niamh. It was grand!"

Niamh didn't want to admit what she'd done, but if Grandmother found out later—and she most certainly would—then it was best that Niamh had told her this first: "I asked the sisters for help, Grandma."

Grandmother's eyes widened. She reached up to take Niamh's hand. "O, mo stor Niamh, you asked them for help?"

"I did. I surely did, Grandma."

"And they helped, did they?"

"They did. That great wave saved you, Grandma, and these poor men, too."

Grandma smiled, patted that hand of Niamh's. "*Go raibh maith agat*, dear Niamh. Thank you, thank you." And they hugged, though both knew there'd be a debt with a price to pay.

After a moment, Niamh pulled back and turned to look at the pilots, poor men, broken and half-drowned. "There'll be help on the way, you two. For now, let's get you out of here and onto the beach, all right?"

And the one in better shape, handsome he was with that nice smile and those eyes that told stories, nodded his head and reached out toward her. "Hey, Irish," he said, "that's the best idea I've come across all day."

And that was how they met.

MAY 8, 1984

In the morning, after a breakfast of bacon and eggs and coffee, they drive a few blocks east to catch Route 20 and make a right to get on it, the Buick Super purring along the old highway once they clear the traffic of Chicago and Gary and head across Indiana. Route 20 will take them all the way to Boston, through Indiana and Michigan and along the Erie shoreline through Ohio and that slice of Pennsylvania and then into New York State and on into Massachusetts. Two days, Harry thinks, maybe stopping in Buffalo or Rochester along the way. Two days and then they'll slide on into Marblehead Neck and the Seahorse Inn and have their honeymoon at last.

Will this whole long dream last through all that drive and any time after they get there? Is he losing it, maybe, the way Niamh is? Are they both lying in a mortuary somewhere, dead and cold, and this is some kind of afterlife? Has time been changed somehow, so he can do better for her this time around? Jesus, would that even work? Could he be better, do better, given the chance?

He doesn't know. He just doesn't know. He looks over at Niamh and she's napping again; a slight, calm smile on her face. That's how this awful thing goes, Rochelle told him a couple of months ago. The ones with the disease don't really know about it, can't sense their own decline. Sometimes, Rochelle said, they're very happy.

Sometimes they're very happy. Harry shakes his head in wonder at that, and drives on.

DECEMBER 15, 1941

The thin December sun was shining through the wide window of Car B of the Great Southern Railways's noon train from Dublin Kingsbridge to Cobh station. Harry and the rest of the crew were on their way home at last. Dublin to Cobh and then a ship home across the worrisome North Atlantic and into training for flying a B-25 into the real thing.

The midday train was not busy, and Harry sat in the window seat, his back to the engine, with an empty aisle seat to his right. Across from him was a very pretty young lady in her mid-20s, a redhead in a white blouse and an A-line green skirt, wearing pumps and a nice smile as she looked up to see him staring at her.

He looked away, out the window, as they crossed a river, the Barrow, the sign said. Should he look back at her again? Should he say something? Irish girls in general were very pretty, but she was really something.

The Great Southern Railways steam engine jolted and struggled as it moved up an incline on the south side of the river. He did look at her. Again, she smiled. "It's the coal," she said.

"Sorry?" he said.

"The reason the engine struggles so up this small incline," she said, leaning forward a bit and smiling at him. "England is keeping all her coal for the war, and we're making do with our own coal, which is not very good."

"*Ah*, I wondered," though he hadn't wondered at all. Her smile was really something to see, those dimples lighting up the room wherever she went, he was sure.

"You're American," she said. "And not here on holiday, there's none of that these days."

"I am," he said. "It's a long story, but I was stranded here and now, at last, I'm heading home."

"So all the way to Cobh? You'll be changing in Cork, you know."

"Yes. And you?"

"I believe I'm going to Cobh, as well. Seaside and fresh air and all that."

He smiled. She was, indeed, very pretty. Thing was, he could still taste Niamh's lipstick on his own lips. A waxy taste, not at all unpleasant.

She'd come to Kingsbridge Station to say goodbye and the parting had been difficult. Harry and Digger Hargis and Sam Ewell and Danny Morrow and Captain Bobby Smith were all about to board the train that would take them to Cobh and a fast liner home across the Atlantic.

The crew had spent more than a year in the K-Lines Curragh internment camp, where the officially neutral Irish kept all the Brits and the Germans who crash-landed or washed up on the beaches of Éire. All of them, a hundred or more, and the five American flyers.

Life wasn't bad, really, in the camp. Over the course of the year the rules had gotten looser and looser and for the past few months they'd been able to leave the camp pretty much whenever they wanted to as long as they came back the same day and checked back in. The camp was near a few small towns and not far from Dublin, and when Niamh got her job at Clerys she moved to a small flat near the Grand Canal and so the two of them, the interned flyboy and the beauty from County Galway, had plenty of time to fall in love and make plans for a future together, one way or another.

And so when the word finally came that after the terrible events at Pearl Harbor the two governments had worked things out and the Yanks were released and sent home, Harry had mixed feelings about it. He'd miss her terribly and told her so. He loved her, he told her that, too. And sure, Niamh was wonderful and he knew he was one lucky guy. But he was ready to get the hell out of Ireland, get back to America and back into the war, even if it meant that Atlantic crossing and all those damn U-boats.

At least they were going on a passenger liner refitted for wartime, the SS *City of Birmingham*. Everyone said she was so fast the U-boats couldn't torpedo her. He hoped everyone was right about that. He wanted to get into this war, but he wanted to be in a B-25 to do it, comfortable behind those twin fifties in the top turret. You couldn't shoot back at a torpedo when you were stuffed into a small cabin on a big ship. Home, and back into the air, and the sooner the better.

He'd held her close; lost in that thick, black hair, those blue eyes, the way she laughed, the way she cried, her jokes, her lovemaking. He was, damnit, one very lucky guy.

"You'll stay safe for me, Harry?" she'd said as they parted at the station.

"Of course, Irish," he'd said. "Comfy ocean liner home, a train to San Antonio and Alamo Field, get ourselves a new Mitchell and train in it. That will all take months and we'll be safe as clams." He laughed. "War might be over before we get all that done."

She didn't laugh. They both knew that wasn't true; Hitler wasn't losing anywhere and the Japanese seemed to be everywhere in the Pacific. It was going to be a long slog turning all that around.

"All aboard, there, Harry," Smitty had said as he walked by, heading toward platform five and the train to Cork and Cobh. "Time to go, buddy."

And so he'd boarded and found that seat, making sure to sit across from that very pretty girl, whose name turned out to be Kathleen, who was a student in the teacher's college in Cork, and who had a few days to spare before returning to class. She was wonderful.

MAY 8, 1984

They're on Route 20 along the Lake Erie shore and it's beautiful. The clouds have disappeared from around the lakeshore, some reverse lake-effect thing, and the sun is so bright the water flashes with silver sparks that remind Harry of how the Pacific looked from thirty feet up in their big B-25 that strafed the Japs before the Marines landed at Iwo and Peleliu. Scary times, horrible times, but wonderful, too, looking back.

Windows down, Harry and Niamh are enjoying the cool lake breeze in the Buick Super. The road has a few curves and a few hills here and there, but basically it's smooth and effortless, vineyards to the right up the slopes, the lake to the left. It's peaceful as hell.

Niamh has been quiet since they got past Cleveland and started driving the lakeshore. It's the first big water she's seen in a long, long time. They did fly to Ireland that one time to bury her mother and meet with her brother, but even then she sat on the aisle and didn't look to see the Atlantic going over or coming back.

Now, here, she's awash in it, drinking it in, watching the lake go by for mile after mile, not saying much, napping for a few minutes every now and again then, without warning, sitting up to stare.

They stop once, taking a left off Route 20 when Niamh says they must, they have to, there's someone to meet. They drive down a back road for half a mile to the lakeshore and there's a beach there, beautiful sand. If this is really 1947 the lakes are a mess, polluted as hell, maybe dying; but you couldn't tell it here. Clear water over smooth sand, then some big boulders twenty or thirty yards out and there, on the boulders, sunbathing, a couple of seals.

No way, Harry thinks. Couldn't be. But then this couldn't be 1947 either, could it? What the hell.

Niamh waves to the seals and laughs, and there's a bark from both of them out on the boulders and that's it. No big deal. Harry rolls up his trouser legs and Niamh lifts her skirt and they wade in the water. It's icy cold, and then they dry off in the warm sun and get back in the Buick Super and off they go.

An hour more and they go through some small towns, stopping once for gas and a soft drink as the afternoon wears on. Then, after they pull away from the lake and head into New York State, they're driving by some low mountains and forests and then farms and then they skirt by Buffalo and head due east again before deciding to stop for the night in Alden at the Whistle Stop hotel. It's a nice place; clean rooms the sign says on the big porch, and sure enough, their room is clean and roomy. There's even a restaurant just off the lobby. They eat there.

"You've been awful quiet all day, Irish," Harry says to her after they order their meatloaf and mashed potatoes. She just smiles.

All day long he humored her, poor Niamh. He'd reach over now and again to pat her on the knee. Each time she would look at him and smile. Then she would turn her face away from him to look out to the lake.

"You liked seeing those seals out there today, didn't you, Irish?" he asks.

She smiles, blinks, shakes her head a bit, and Harry can feel something happen, something change. He looks out the window and it's a Ford Mustang going by out on Main Street, and then a Volksie bus. It's now. It's today.

He sits back, shocked. The whole thing is now more unfathomable than it was before. He looks around, the restaurant hasn't changed all that much. Blue paint and different tables, different pictures on the wall; but, mostly, it's a lot like it was a few seconds ago. He pulls the menu from behind the ketchup bottle and glances at that, laughs; now *there* are some changes.

"You all right, Irish?" he asks.

"Yes, Harry, I am," she answers. "I'm fine. That water today, it was so icy cold. It was wonderful. It's time now, I'm sure of it."

"Time? Time for what?"

"Oh, Harry. Tomorrow the Atlantic, right? In Marblehead?"

He nods. "Yep, Irish. Our honeymoon, now or back then or whatever you want. This is for you, Irish." And he reaches out to take her left hand.

She leaves her hand in his. She's thinking. She smiles, finally, and reaches out with her right hand to cover their clasped hands. "Thank you, Harry." And she pulls her hands back.

The girl in San Antonio, Miss Alamo Training Center 1941. The nurse in Pearl, the nurse in Guam, the secretary in Dubuque. The boss's wife in St. Louis; that was the one that ended badly. The wonderful one in Chicago; a lawyer, by God, strong and independent but in love with Harry Mack. All of them, a dozen or even more. He quit drinking but he couldn't quit them. Wanted to, tried to, but couldn't quit.

The next morning they're back onto Route 20 and driving across Upstate New York. The scenery is great and it's back to being 1947 and Harry is enjoying the ride, enjoying how it was back then. To the best of his memory, he was faithful that entire year. He was working for the Auto Club and had a promotion to assistant manager of the St. Louis County Triple-A Division. Pay went up to four thousand dollars, which seemed like a lot of money. He and Niamh made a real effort to make some babies, but that didn't happen. He wonders how it all might have gone if she had gotten pregnant somewhere along the line? Would he have been a good father? A better husband?

Niamh has been napping. She was chatty early on and then drifted off into a nap and missed a lot of the morning scenery, those long views of the road ahead as they crest one hill and there's a valley down below and the road going up the other side there in the distance. Everything green from the spring rains and the welcome May sunshine.

She wakes up, yawning and stretching and looking around.

"Oh, Harry," she says. "This reminds me of home. Better roads, mind you, but this could be Ireland. Do you remember Connemara, Harry? We saw those mountains when we went for mother's funeral."

"Yes," he says. "They were beautiful. I know I said back then that I wanted to get back to St. Louis, but you know what, Irish? I wish we'd stayed longer. Hell, we should have stayed all summer. You were awfully happy there."

She smiles over at him, reaches out to touch his arm, and smoothly, no transition, no jarring, nothing but suddenly it's 1984 and they're on Interstate 90, the New York Thruway, and the big sign says Albany and they're barreling along toward the bottom of the valley and the ride back up and then onward to Boston.

Harry looks over at Niamh. "You okay, Irish?"

She yawns again. "I know, Harry. It's hard to understand."

"What's hard, Irish?"

"Us, Harry. You. It's hard."

He nods. Doesn't want to touch this with a ten-foot pole. It won't all come spilling out now, will it?

And she smiles, leans back in her seat and easy as pie it's 1947 again and Harry has a grip on the big white steering wheel of the Super and the radio is playing *The Lone Ranger*, with that long, long introduction, a full two minutes of the "William Tell Overture," which he loved back then. They ruined that show when they took it to television.

MARCH 1941

The rain was slowly clearing from the west, the hard shower down to a mist as the day turned soft. In the distance Niamh could see Inis Mór, the largest of the Aran Islands. Somewhere on the far side of the island not far from the Seven Churches, was Seal Beach, where the sisters spent most of their time.

But today, surely, knowing what they must know, they would come here, to Spanish Point, to Niamh. There were goodbyes that had to be said. Promises that had to be made. Debts to be understood. They can be patient. They'll have what she needs when she needs it, and then, together, they'll laugh and play and life will go on and on.

Tomorrow she'll be off to Dublin and the new job with the government and then she'll get to spend more time with her Yank, her Harry Mack. He's a wonderful man. She loves him, for better and for worse. Truly.

MAY 8, 1984

They stop for lunch at the Westerly Hotel in Pittsfield, Massachusetts, where it's firmly 1947 and the food is good and the service excellent. They drive by a ballpark on the way and the sign out front says the Pittsfield Electrics are playing, but Harry doesn't stop. Niamh doesn't really like baseball, though she's spent decades in St. Louis.

Harry has a ham sandwich on rye and Niamh an egg salad on white. He's aching for a beer but Niamh thinks he's completely dry these days and he likes it that way, so he has a Coca-Cola. She drinks sweet iced tea. They're back on the road by 1:30 PM and two and a half hours later they're circling around the west and north of Boston and getting close to Marblehead.

Niamh is looking at a map she picked up in Pittsfield when they filled up the tank after lunch and she says they need to leave Route 20 around Waltham and take Bacon Street to Lexington and from there through Woburn and Stoneham, all of them back roads because that's what she wants. They're almost there, she says.

They drive right past a dog track and the parking lot is full. A different Harry, that other Harry, would have offered Niamh a meal in there and then would have made some money on the dogs. But that Harry isn't here now, it's a newer or older one, a better one, and so, proud of himself, he doesn't say a word and drives on by.

And then they reach an interstate and Harry realizes things have changed again. It's I-95 and the big sign says "Marblehead" and there's crappy music on the radio and at least it's the big Riviera they're driving in with all the bells and whistles. He doesn't mind the changes.

Niamh touches his arm and he takes a glance her way. "The Lynn exit," she says, firmly in the here and now. And then, when he exits and heads east she says this: "Harry, I understand. I've always understood. Men are men and there was a war on and then, after, you *are* a good-looking man, Harry Mack. I didn't expect you to be anything other than who you are."

Where was she going with this? Which time is she in?

"Harry?" she asks him and there's a kind of dizzy moment and they're back in 1947, driving along in that Buick Super, all calm and serene. "Harry?" she asks. "Where are we now?"

"Lynn, Massachusetts, Irish, and Marblehead just up the road. This is how you wanted to go. You wanted to take the ferry out to the island."

"Oh," she says, in a small voice. "Yes, I suppose I did say that. All the water. And the sisters so."

They're driving along on Paradise Road, Route 1A, when Niamh tells him to take a left. He does that and they're on Banks Road and they drive along that until it curves to the right and changes names to Redington Street and then they crest the hill and Harry pulls over. Man, that's a steep downhill in front of them, all the way down to the water. He'll have to take it in second gear all the way down.

"Nahant Bay," Niamh says. "Sure and that's perfect, Harry. Let's go."

He looks in the mirror and a local city bus is coming, so he waits for that to pass and when it does he puts the Buick Super into first gear and pulls out onto Redington and they follow the bus downhill, a half mile or so to the water. Steep, straight road down to Humphrey Street and just the other side of that the water.

The bus is making stops and Harry doesn't want to wait each time, so at the second stop he checks in the mirror, waves his left arm out the window to warn any traffic, and pulls around the bus.

"Harry," Niamh says. "I promised them so."

He looks at her. "Promised who, Irish?"

"Them," she says. "The sisters. I made a promise."

Oh, my. He shakes his head. This terrible thing that's stealing her mind.

"Okay," he says. "If you promised them, that's okay, Niamh. Whatever you want, Irish. Whatever you say." He owes her, God knows. He truly does.

Harry looks in the mirror and the bus is behind him but it's fading away, disappearing, fading away.

They're moving fast, too. Way too fast. Harry reaches up to

the gear shift to check and it's in third and they're really moving now down the hill. What the hell?

The bus is gone. They go over one cross street and that small flat spot sends the Buick Super into the air for a few feet and then it thumps to the ground.

"Hang on, Irish," Harry says, gripping the steering wheel tightly and stepping hard on the clutch and working hard to pull the gear shift back into second. No luck. He slams on the brakes. No luck; they're damn near flying. Another crossroad, this one right near the bottom of the hill, and now they really are soaring.

Time slows down. Harry looks around from his vantage point, way up in the air, the Buick sailing along at a good thirty feet, right over Humphrey Street. To the left there's a church with a big statue of Mother Mary out front, her arms out, palms up, welcoming the faithful. To the right is Niamh, and she's looking ahead toward the water, smiling. In front, in the water, are some black shapes, some heads, no, faces, no, women or something and they're treading water there, floating there, waiting for the Buick, waiting for Harry and, more likely, for Niamh.

Harry can see it all in slow-motion, see every second, see every regret, every broken vow, as the sisters in the clear blue water call to Niamh, pull her home, where the sisters are waiting.

The Buick Super, or perhaps it's the LeSabre, or perhaps it doesn't matter as it hits tail first and Harry remembers that Captain Wellman promised two bumps, the second one a lot harder, and so he's ready when the second bump hits and the car splashes into Nahant Bay and floats there. Seven minutes, Captain Wellman promised, before she'll sink. But it's seconds, not minutes, as the car starts to go under right away, the front end going down first and then pulling the rest along with it as it goes. How deep is it here? Maybe it will settle and they'll be all right.

But no, they aren't all right. Harry reaches down to unclick his seat belt but there isn't one. He turns to look at Niamh and she's rolled down her window and she's starting to climb out as the car sinks deeper and the windows are underwater now and she swims, easily and smoothly, not looking back, out to her sisters who are waiting for her.

Harry needs help. His window won't roll down and his legs are trapped under that big steering wheel and he'd like to get the hell out of here, get out of here and swim away into whatever time and place this is. But the car seems to want him. The water seems to want him. The cold water. The cold, clear water. And the last thing he sees is Niamh, poor Niamh, floating there, serene, holding up her hand to wave goodbye as the Buick slips on down deeper, and then deeper, and then deeper still.

This alternate history story appeared in Asimov's Science Fiction *magazine. It follows the exploits of famous baseball player/spy Moe Berg as he attempts to stop the German A-bomb program in World War II. The story won the Sidewise Award in 2012 as Best Alternate History– Short Form. The story has been reprinted by a number of publications, including the* Tampa Bay Times *as part of its Newspapers in Education (NIE) program, in Russian by the Russian magazine* Esli, *and in its own Kindle version and elsewhere.*

SOMETHING REAL

Baseball is a game of constant disappointment. You swing and you mostly miss. You think it's an easy grounder and it bad hops you. You're called out at third trying to advance on a single. The pop foul to end the game drifts away from your glove as you reach over the rail. One thing after another, one game after another, one season after another; all of this in an endless progression of childish mediocrity.

No wonder he was depressed. Surely there were better things to do with one's life than catch and throw and swing a stick at baseballs.

Moe Berg, MS, MA, PhD, LLD, was a well-educated man, a scholar, a man of great promise. Yet here he sat, a baseball player, in the dugout at Comiskey Park watching the rain fall and gather into puddles atop the tarp that covered the infield. The puddles rippled in the wind, tiny oceans getting wider by the second. It had been raining steadily for a half hour and then moments ago there'd been a bright bolt of lightning and an immediate and massive crack of thunder. And now it was really pouring. Surely the game would be called in the next few minutes.

Moe had two hits on the day, a very nice opposite field homer to right, thank you very much, and a rare triple into the gap in left. The Sox were in front by six runs after three innings, but now none of that would matter; the would-be victory would disappear into the hiss of the rain and Moe's home run and triple wouldn't exist past today.

Perfect, just perfect. Like his season, like his whole career, like his life; the occasional good days were always washed away by a gray, cold rain. Now, instead of this one good day at the plate, there'd be a double-header tomorrow and he'd probably go zero for the day or something close to that.

Every now and again it occurred to Moe that perhaps his father was right, perhaps it was time to retire from this child's game and get started on real life. Perhaps it was time to do something that mattered, something real.

DECEMBER 12TH, 1944

Moe Berg looked around the room. The thick wool drapes, so purple as to be nearly black, were tied back to allow the sunshine to spill through the narrow, tall windows that marched along the left side of the small lecture hall at the Physics Institute at the Eidgenössische Technische Hochschule, the ETH. The bright warmth of the room was a welcome luxury for a cold, December day in neutral Zurich.

Berg had heard just an hour ago that a few hundred miles away from this very spot Patton's Fifth Army was out of gas for the Shermans. This meant von Rundstedt didn't need to worry about an Allied relief column and so, short of a miracle like the clouds and fog clearing out unexpectedly so the P-47s could get back into business, the Nazi's Sixth SS Panzer under Dietrich was going to break through Bastogne at any moment and from there it would be easy going as the tanks headed toward the fuel depot in Antwerp. Christ, the war might go on for another year or two.

A narrow lectern stood at the front of the room. A black-board on wheels was behind the lectern, and there were two dozen wooden chairs in tight, perfect rows in front of the lectern. There were no empty seats and an extra dozen people stood against the radiators at the back of the room. Paul Scherrer was there, of course, and nodded and smiled when he saw Berg. Markus Fierz was there, too, and Gregor Wentzel, Wolfgang Pauli, Ernst Stueckelberg. And up in the front row, at the corner, Carl Friedrich von Weizsäcker.

Berg sat in the second row, where he was close enough to get the job done. He'd scored a marksman rating with a service revolver at this kind of distance. That was one reason he was here.

His pal, Paul Scherrer, had managed to get him the invitation to this speech, listing him as an Italian physicist working with Fermi in Rome. Berg felt bad about that; if he did do the job here it would get out soon that Scherrer had been involved. That would be messy; there were Nazis everywhere in Zurich. Berg had told Piet Gugelot, the Dutch Jew physicist, how to follow up on the arrangements to get Scherrer and his family out of Switzerland and down into Italy. From there, with Fermi's help, they all could get to the States. Berg didn't expect he'd be able to help with any of that, since he wouldn't survive more than a few seconds after taking action against Heisenberg. Too many Nazis in the room, all of them armed. Once they realized that the Italian physicist named Antonacci was, in fact, an American assassin they'd act quickly.

Berg did look like he belonged in this crowd: brown shoes, slacks, tweed jacket. He'd thought about smoking a pipe but decided he wouldn't look natural enough doing that; but other-wise he fit right in.

He'd earned a little credit, he hoped, by working his way into a couple of the interesting conversations on S-matrix theory that had been going on in the hallway outside before the door opened to the room. Berg liked the elegance of the math and had said so to several people, citing examples. They'd nodded and agreed, the several men then bouncing ideas off one another for a few minutes until the classroom door opened and, along with the others, Berg had walked in and taken a seat.

He crossed his right leg over the left and sat back, relaxed, as the last few stragglers came in, looking for a little space in which to join the others who stood at the back. The last to come through was a tall, very attractive woman. Stueckelberg rose and offered her his seat and she took it.

Berg knew this woman. He was sure it was her; a real looker, tall, thin, black hair, red lips, wearing a very businesslike dress with padded shoulders and a vest. He wondered if there wasn't a gun hidden somewhere in all that fabric.

He'd seen her now several different times over the past couple of years. He was certain of it; he had a very good memory for such things. The first time, back in '41, she'd been sitting in the box seats, front row, behind the home dugout in Comiskey as the White Sox did battle with the Browns on a Sunday in June. Not much of a crowd there, the Sox being all right but the Brownies miserable. Berg had played first that day and had himself an RBI double and then scored on an Alex Irvine single. He'd tipped his cap to the few fans who were cheering after he'd crossed home and was heading toward the dugout. She'd smiled at him. He'd winked back and then had the batboy take a note up to her saying he was staying at the Piccadilly Hotel on Wabash, and he'd be pleased to celebrate the day's win by taking her out to dinner. He'd look for her at eight o'clock in the lobby. The chophouse had great steaks, but she didn't show.

The second time, a year later, he'd been in London, at the Claridge, working on Alsos. She'd been sitting in the lobby reading the Times and had lowered it to watch him walk by, smiling at him knowingly. He'd smiled back, but he was already late for the meeting with Carvelli to make the final arrangements for Italy and Fermi, and so he didn't have the time to do more than smile and nod. She'd nodded back, still smiling. An hour later, when he walked back out through the lobby, she was gone.

The next time, in Paris just a couple of months later, he felt a friendly tap on his shoulder then heard her say, "Bonjour, Monsieur Berg," as she'd walked by him one evening on the Pont Neuf, where he'd been leaning on the railing, watching a barge go by on the Seine below. He'd turned, embarrassed that he hadn't noticed her until after she'd touched him, but she was already walking away, half-turning to wave goodbye. He was waiting for a contact and couldn't leave the spot and had to watch her go. He felt dizzy and nauseous for a moment and when that passed he turned back toward the Seine and the same barge from before was somehow upstream and starting its way down again to go under the bridge, again, as he watched. There was no explaining that and he was afraid to mention it to anyone; they'd pull him out of there and bring him home as a head case, probably, and he didn't want that.

The last time, six months ago in Rome, he'd been sitting outside under the awning at the Trattoria Monti on Via di San Vito, with Fermi, talking about what Italy had been like under Mussolini before the assassination in '38. A dirigible, a fast little Enzo on sentry duty, chugged by overhead. Fifty miles north was the Lateran Line and north of that there were Germans, a lot of them. Here, in Roma, though, the sun was shining and Italy was Italian again.

Enrico was talking when she walked by: "Yes, Moe, all of Italy was ours, but the price was so very high. Spies everywhere (as though there weren't any now, Berg thought to himself), and one feared for one's soul." Enrico smiled. "When the coup d'état was successful, we all thought the nightmare had ended; but, of course, it wasn't so simple."

She'd been hard to miss in that outfit; blue shorts and a white blouse with a blue scarf and a sailor cap. Her hair was different, red, and she seemed taller somehow, but it was definitely her. And she was stunning.

Enrico had turned to look at her, said *"Buongiorno."*

She buongiornoed right back to Enrico, then looked straight at Berg, smiled, said, *"Ciao, Signor Berg,"* and walked away. Moe winked at Enrico, then rose from the table to follow her, caught up with her by the time they reached the Trevi Fountain, reached out and grabbed her arm so he could finally talk to her and find out what the hell was going on. But then he stumbled, went down to his knees, sick to his stomach for a few moments, and when that passed he looked up and she was gone. As was the Trevi Fountain. He was standing next to the Colle Oppio gardens and there, a few blocks away, was the Colosseum. Jesus Christ. He shook his head and started walking back to Enrico. Good thing it was close.

So he wasn't surprised to see her here, though she was a major complication, and Berg didn't like complications. He had a job to do here, dangerous work, and if she had been in Chicago, and London, and Paris, and Rome, and now was here, then she was in on it somehow. One side? The other? Some other side completely? He didn't know. He didn't like not knowing. He had to ask himself why he hadn't brought her up with John Shaheen, his handler.

Moe shifted in his chair, putting both feet back on the floor. He could feel the uncomfortable tug of the athletic tape that held the tiny Beretta tightly against his groin. Well, there was nothing he could do about her right now. He was here, and today was today, and that was all there was to it. He had a job to do.

The door at the side of the room opened again and in walked Werner Heisenberg. There was a smattering of polite applause from the gathered scientists. How do you greet a colleague and friend, and one of the world's great minds, when he's brilliant but working for the Nazis? Heisenberg was in charge of *Uranverein*, the Uranium Club, which is to say, Hitler's A-bomb program.

But this wasn't about that, at least for everyone but Berg, so when Paul Scherrer walked to the podium to introduce Heisenberg, Berg sat back in his chair and made sure to look calm and relaxed. Time to listen. Very carefully.

SEPTEMBER 5TH, 1943

A dismal season was winding down. Moe Berg had played first base again and gone 0-for-5 as the Sox lost to the Yankees. Berg's contribution to the humiliation had been three strikeouts and an error on a groundball.

In the clubhouse after the game, the air was thick with cigar smoke, grumbling, and Monarch beer to drown the various sorrows. Moe sat, disappointed, on a folding chair in front of his open wooden locker. He was contemplating what an 0-for-5 day can do to your psyche and your season and your career when you're in your thirties. He heard a throat clear behind him. Damn sportswriters.

He turned and instead of the rumpled old suit and beat-up fedora that he expected, it was a man dressed in trousers with a tight crease, a vest, an expensive coat and a bowtie; no hat, glasses, smoking a Camel.

"Mr. Berg? Moe?"

Berg shook his head. "I'm not speaking to the press, friend. I made that clear last week. No quotes, no off-the-record, nothing, till this slump is over. Got it?"

The man smiled and was nice enough to not get into whether a .210 season batting average is still a "slump" or not. "I'm not with the press, Mr. Berg. My name is Huntington, Ellery Huntington. I'm here at the request of a man named William Donovan. He'd like to meet with you."

Berg frowned. "The Donovan who was a war hero in the Meuse-Argonne? And then the district attorney up in Buffalo? I believe I met him once, a few years ago. We shook hands and I autographed a ball for him."

"You have an excellent memory, Mr. Berg."

He did, in fact, have that excellent memory. And an IQ of

180. And a doctorate in classical languages from Princeton and a law degree from Yale. And yet here he was, playing baseball in Chicago and, mostly, going 0-for-the-day. So: "What would the district attorney and war hero want with a baseball player, Mr. Huntington?"

"Mr. Donovan is no longer a district attorney, Mr. Berg. He now works for the government in another capacity. He's more interested in your language skills than your batting average."

Berg allowed himself a sad chuckle. "That's a good thing. Have you seen my batting average?"

Huntington smiled back. "Mr. Donovan has looked at those photos you took in Japan during the Sox tour back in '37. Those snaps are very good. And he knows you speak French and German. He understands that you are something of a science buff, as well."

"And Italian. And Spanish. And Hebrew. And a few more. And I read a lot, Mr. Huntington. Science is one of the things I read, along with the sports pages in the newspapers."

"And the front pages?"

"Yes, and the front pages."

"We felt certain of that, Mr. Berg. And we feel certain, too, about your patriotism. Mr. Donovan would like to talk to you about that, about your patriotism. He knows you've tried to enlist, but the Army wouldn't take you."

"Or the Navy, Mr. Huntington. They don't like the shape of my feet. But if your Mr. Donovan has found a way I can take part, I'm all for it. Do I have time to take a shower and comb my hair?"

Huntington smiled again, and nodded. "Of course, Mr. Berg, take your time. And then we'll head over to our hotel and you and Mr. Donovan can have that conversation. Does that sound all right?"

Moe thought about his slump. The season wasn't young anymore and neither was he. And there were guys fighting and dying in Europe and he'd been thinking a lot about how he ought to be involved in that, flat feet or not.

He looked up at Huntington. "Give me ten minutes."

And that was all it took. Ten minutes, a taxi ride and a five-minute conversation with Wild Bill Donovan.

DECEMBER 12, 1944

Berg watched Heisenberg smile weakly. He spoke in German: "Hello, everyone, it is good to be here, and to see so many of my friends and colleagues from better days. May those days return soon. And for those of you who are students at this fine university, I greet you warmly and celebrate your learning. I will leave time enough at the end of this discussion to answer questions."

He paused, smiled again slightly. "Please, friends, colleagues: let us step away from the war for just this brief time and focus our attention on the matter at hand, scattering-matrix maths. I will gladly take questions on that afterward, but outside the scope of that discussion I can take no questions. I am sure you understand."

Berg understood. The Gestapo was here in one guise or another; and there were others in the room, too, no doubt, who would report back to Berlin on what Professor Heisenberg had said, starting with that weasel von Weizsäcker. The Professor was smart enough to stay out of trouble and focus on S-matrix theory, as advertised.

AUGUST 12, 1944

Lake Maggiore was warm in the shallows and then colder, much colder, the farther out Moe Berg swam with his new pal, Enrico Fermi. They were headed out to the raft anchored near the marker buoys for the swimmers.

It was a muggy day, and after a long bicycle ride together along the Via Roma the two men—Italy's finest physicist and the American baseball player—had pedaled through the village of Pino and out to the narrow strand of beach along the lake. Just a half mile away the Via Roma changed names and became the Dufourstrasse on the Swiss side of the border. In a couple of hours they'd be having lunch over there with Paul Scherrer, who had asked for the meeting.

They'd risked coming here because the meeting with Scherrer was important to the whole project, though it was fraught with risk. A ferry ride up from Rimini to Venice, skirting the Nazi-occupied portions of Italy, then a long, harrowing flight up to and then through the southern edge of the Dolomites in an Enzo Massimo dirigible that finally got them to Maccagno and the lakeshore. A real nail-biter, that blimp ride, but then it was done and they'd walked into town from the field and found their *pensione*, had a good meal, rented the bikes for today, shared a bottle of wine and then hit the sack. Now, here they were, within a couple of easy miles by bike of the meeting and with a few hours to kill. A cool swim seemed like a good idea, and then they'd get up to town, cross the border into Switzerland, and hear what Scherrer had to say.

Berg wasn't himself, palling around here with Fermi, a guy he really liked. Here, for now, Berg was Mario Antonacci, a wealthy industrialist and shipbuilder from Brindisi, a man of substance who had stopped building warships for Mussolini after the coup and had then gone back to building freighters for the Matteotti government, which ran things south and east of the Lateran Line. Strictly neutral, Matteotti and his pals, the only way to stay alive with the Germans in control of the northwest portions of Italy.

Fermi climbed up the ladder of the wooden raft and sat down next to Berg. "It's beautiful here," he said in Italian, leaning backward to get his face to the mountain sun.

"*Ed è tranquillo*," Berg said, "a separate world, away from the war."

Fermi shook his head. "Not separate enough, I think. Look

there," and he pointed east. Tiny dots marched across the sky in formation. "Your American bombers aiming for Munich, perhaps?"

"Wiener-Neustadt, I think, near Vienna. There's a Messerschmitt factory there."

"Ah." Fermi stood. He was slightly built, thin, about five foot eight. Unprepossessing. But he was a towering figure where it mattered, in physics. Fermi was one of the handful of scientists who could stand next to Heisenberg in matters of intellect. Fermi, Bohr, Oppenheimer, Weizsäcker, Hahn. The list was a short one, and with Einstein's macabre death in '38 had lost its titular head. Now it was up to Heisenberg, or Oppy, to see who'd be the one to change the world. Berg wondered if Fermi realized this. Well, if he didn't realize it yet he would in a couple of hours. Time to go meet with Scherrer and see about saving the world.

DECEMBER 12, 1944

Trouble was, as the afternoon lecture wore on, when it came to S-matrix theory, or the scattering matrix as Herr Professor called it, Heisenberg didn't seem to have anything new to say.

Berg had done his homework, reading up on John Archibald Weaver's paper from 1937, which coined the "scattering matrix" term as it described coefficients that connected the asymptotic behavior of an arbitrary particular solution with the set of solutions of a standard form. What Heisenberg had done was taken it farther; using the S-matrix idea to mathematically pick out the most important features of the theory, the ones that he tried to prove wouldn't change over time. He published this work in the German journals. The OSS had a copy of every article. Berg had read, and understood, them all. There was a reason Moe Berg was the agent who was here, listening, assessing, making a decision, a choice. That reason had nothing to do with being a light-hitting infielder for the Chicago White Sox.

But the sunlit room was warm with everyone packed in, even

with the radiators shut off as Switzerland dealt with its coal shortage. And despite the months of preparation, despite the Beretta taped to his groin, despite the lives that had been put at risk to get him here: despite all of that Moe Berg began to drift off, the S-matrix discussion so ordinary that it was lulling, his eyelids growing heavy as he jerked awake sharply once, cursing himself for his foolishness, and then again, before resorting to pinching, hard, the skin between his right thumb and the forefinger.

That worked, and he was focused again on the S-matrix, at least long enough to get to the question period, where he might learn what he needed to know. Was Heisenberg and his team on the right track for an atom bomb? Would the Germans get the bomb before the Allies did? If he thought that was the case, Berg would excuse himself, go to the men's room and get into a stall, unbutton his pants and drop them, pull the Beretta loose from where it was taped to the groin, re-button the trousers and then walk back into the room, the Beretta in his pocket. There, with no hesitation, before anyone could act to stop him, he would kill Werner Heisenberg, cut off the head of the snake that was the great bomb. A lot of lives, hundreds of thousands of them, maybe millions, would depend on Berg's aim.

He was awake now, and sharp, thinking it through. Ten minutes more, maybe fifteen, and the moment might come as the speech ended and the questions started.

Then there was a quick rap at the lecture room door and everyone watched as the door opened and a man in a suit entered, a blond German missing his right arm so he was, no doubt, a veteran of one front or another who'd found something useful to do for the local Gestapo or the embassy.

They were all watching, thirty-six of the brightest minds in European physics outside of the missing, and brilliant, Jews, as the man walked over and handed Heisenberg a note then clicked his heels officiously, spun around and walked briskly back out the door.

Heisenberg was expressionless, the blank look on his face something he must have mastered after years in the service of Hitler. "Excuse me, please," he said and turned his back to the room to read the note.

Did his shoulders sag a bit as he finished? Berg thought maybe so, but Heisenberg was smiling thinly as he turned back to face his audience.

"Colleagues, I have received information to the effect that Baron von Rundstedt's Sixth Panzer has broken through at Bastogne and is racing toward Antwerp. I have been asked to relay this information to you. There is more I would like to say about this turn of events, but this is, of course, neither the time nor the place."

And he turned his back to the room again and walked over to the chalkboard. There was no *Heil* Hitler, and, instead, he started furiously writing formulae for the S-matrix discussion, scribbling on the chalkboard in Zurich while von Rundstedt's tanks rumbled toward Antwerp and the oil tanks filled with fuel that sat there, nearly defenseless, ready to be milked. If this news was right, the war might go on for years, giving Germany time to finish a bomb, and build the rockets to deliver it. Well, all the more reason to listen closely for some hint. Any hint.

Heisenberg finished and put the chalk onto the narrow tray at the bottom of the board before walking back to the podium and asking for questions. This, Berg hoped, would tell the tale.

But it didn't. Paul Scherrer wanted to know about AdS/CFT correspondence and Heisenberg went into a long, rambling response that amounted to "We'd all like to know the answer to that." Then Wentzel got into a question about the analyticity of the first, and Heisenberg went back to the chalkboard to erase the previous formulae and put up some new ones, talking as he jotted them down, explaining things. There were lots of nods and murmurs.

This went on, but never in the direction that Berg was hoping for. It wasn't going to be that easy. There was, ultimately, no hint of anything else, anything that mattered. Berg left the Beretta taped where it was and was left, in the end, to wonder if von Rundstedt's success was enough on its own to require the death of Heisenberg? Maybe, just maybe.

When the questions ended Heisenberg looked tired but relieved. He thanked everyone and then Scherrer returned to the podium and thanked them all for coming. There would be a reception at 7:00 PM at Scherrer's house tonight, #27 Versterstrasse, in District 2 on the west side of the lake. They were all invited.

The audience stood and gave Heisenberg another polite round of applause as he exited, and then, slowly, chatting with one another all the while, started heading for the one open door. It was a slow process.

Berg was lost in thought as he ambled slowly in line. He'd heard nothing that had given him a definitive reason to pull the trigger; but the question had changed, really, and now he had to factor in a longer war. He needed a little time to think it through. Heisenberg would be at Scherrer's party later tonight, and then another reception tomorrow at the German embassy. Heisenberg liked long, contemplative walks and he'd be coming and going on foot to these social occasions. Berg had two opportunities to kill him, then. The first one was tonight, probably in Backer Park on Hohlstrasse, which stood between the Baur au Lac hotel and Scherrer's home. It would be dark. It would be very easy.

And if not there and then, tomorrow would do, but that was trickier, in the daylight. That would have to be a sidewalk encounter, one shot, very clean, and then try to disappear into the crowd.

But, first, in either case he had to decide, and he needed a little time to puzzle it through. It would be good to talk to Heisenberg first somehow, perhaps at tonight's party, get a feel for things, all of it very sociable. And then, maybe, kill him. Berg had never killed a man, but that was what most of the training had been for. That moment. Pull the trigger. Save the world. Maybe.

He was just out the door and into the hallways when he felt a touch on his left shoulder, heard a deep, warm female voice speaking very quietly in German: "Yes, you must decide, Moe—may I call you Moe?—and very soon. So much hangs in the balance, yes?"

He turned to look at her. She was nearly his height and even more attractive up close, perhaps in her mid-thirties, black hair, not a lot of makeup, some real strength of character showing in how she looked right back at him, assessing him just as he did the same to her.

He steered them both out of the queue and down a side hallway. No use pretending: "I saw you in Chicago. And then in London, Paris, Rome. And now here. What gives?"

She smiled. "And the answer better be a good one or you'll use that Beretta on me, right, Moe? But only after you've dropped your pants and untaped it." She laughed. "Sometimes you do better, you know, Moe. Sometimes you *have* untaped it and you're ready to go."

So she knew about the Beretta. What the hell?

They walked back into the main hall and then, quietly, with everyone else, out of the building and onto the Zweierstrasse. She chatted briefly about the weather; colder than last year, no?

Berg could be patient. She knew way too much, but he was about to find things out, and there was nothing he liked better than learning.

Finally, at the far end of the Hottingen bridge, near the dark park, they'd left the crowd behind and, alone, they stopped to lean on the railing and look at the cold water below, ice just starting to form on the rocks that rose above the stream.

"I have something to tell you, Moe," she said. "It is very important."

"Sure," he said, "it's important," but they both knew he

wasn't about to believe anything she said, not without establishing who she was and who she worked for.

"I work for a firm that you don't know anything about yet, Moe," she said, reading his mind again. "Later tonight I'm going to tell you about the firm. You won't believe me, of course, but then I'll prove it to you. I'll also prove to you that Werner Heisenberg has to die, and soon.

"Tonight, after the little party at Scherrer's house. You must walk with Heisenberg through the park, chatting about the S-matrix and, perhaps, the weather. There will be no talk of the war, or the super-bomb. There in the park, at a spot I will take you by in a few minutes, you must use your Beretta to shoot Heisenberg. It must take three shots to make certain he is dead. The first shot has to be above the left ear. The second, as he begins to crumple, has to be to the back of the head. The third, as he lies there, face up, must be to the forehead. You will be wearing your gloves in the cold, so there will be no need to wipe the weapon. You will simply toss it into the nearby bushes and walk away."

Berg stared at her for a few moments. He wished like hell he'd put the Beretta in his pocket. "You know a lot. Too damn much, in fact."

"I *do* know a lot, Moe. I know everything in this line, in fact, from this point forward. You, me, Heisenberg, the Bomb, lives saved and lives lost. It's all right there in front of me, like reading a newspaper, as long as you stay here. You like reading the newspaper, don't you, Moe?"

He did, in fact, like reading the newspaper, liked it so much he bought two or three each day and read them slowly over coffee in the morning, savoring the easy enjoyment of reading the paper, where everything was solidly black and white, clear-cut, sharp-edges, clean. Very clean.

She stared at him, dead serious. "Problem is, Moe, there are a lot of pages in those newspapers, and different things are happening on different pages. It's all on the same day, it's all the news that's fit to print, you know? But certain things have to go in a certain order, Moe, or I won't be able to help."

He moved to her, pressed himself against her, reaching down to put his right hand over her left one on the bridge railing. A moment of dizziness and he thought he might go to his knees, but he steadied. Then he thought he could kill her now if he had to. Knock her back over the railing and into the water. Get the Beretta as she lay there. Walk down, fire once or twice, then walk away.

She smiled, pressed back with her hips, looked at him closely. "Look up, Moe, and toward the south, back across the bridge."

He stared at her.

"It's all right, Moe. You're the one with the gun taped to his balls. Me, I'm just one of the girls. Go ahead, look up."

So he did, and saw, in the night sky, a half dozen planes of some kind, nearly silent, swift, rushing over Zurich.

"Whose are they?"

"German fighters, Moe. Jet fighters, a whole new kind of airplane."

"Yeah. So?"

"You know, Moe, you know very well. Those fighters are better than anything the Allies have. And there's a jet bomber that's in trials right now. A month, maybe less, and it will be in production. It has a range of six thousand miles, Moe. You know what that means."

He did know. "How'd you know those fighters would be there?" She was, perhaps, a Nazi, a double agent of some kind. Christ, this was complicated.

"I've seen them before, Moe. Several times. And I've seen the bomber in action, too. I've seen it carry a super-bomb, Moe. For six thousand miles."

It was ridiculous, sure. But those fighters. And the stuff she seemed to know. "Look, I don't get it. Who the hell are you?"

"I'm someone like you, Moe. Someone who believes in a

world that can be better than this one. Someone willing to do what I must to stop this evil before it ruins everything."

He pushed against her, harder, squeezed that hand against the railing. Jesus, he was getting worked up by doing this, by pressing against her. Women didn't usually get this kind of rise out of him.

He felt her hips push back against him. She smiled. "There's a lot I can't tell you yet, Moe. There's a lot you're going to have to find out for yourself. But we're on the same side, you and me, and I can tell you this. There was a freighter in Lorient two months ago, the *Bremen*."

"I know about the *Bremen* and the deuterium."

"But you've been told there was a commando raid and the *Bremen* was sunk, Moe."

How the hell? "Yeah," he admitted, "that's what I've been told. So no heavy water means no plutonium means no super-bomb, at least not anytime soon. It would take another year for them to isolate more."

He paused. "But if this von Rundstedt thing is true and there's more time to isolate more deuterium ..."

Now she wasn't smiling. She pushed him back off her and he let it happen, releasing her hand from the bridge rail, pulling back. "It's worse than that, Moe. They'd offloaded more than twenty tons of the heavy water before the raid. The Germans were happy the *Bremen* was sunk, it lets the Allies think the *Uranverein* can't make the super-bomb. But the Allies are wrong, Moe. Terribly wrong."

"So they can make enough plutonium for a bomb," he said, flatly.

"Yes. Maybe two bombs, Moe. Two of them! Maybe the first for London, and the second for who knows where, New York?"

"It's too late already?" He believed her now, but if this was true why kill Heisenberg?

"Certain matters are at a critical point, Moe. At the moment, the bomb they are building is too big to be useful: it's the size of a boxcar, maybe bigger. And to keep it hidden it's been built in caves in Zugspitze. You know where that is, in Bavaria."

She said that with certainty. He nodded.

"Heisenberg is personally working on ways around the problem, Moe. He can't be allowed to succeed."

Did Heisenberg even want to succeed? That was really the question, thought Berg, but he didn't voice it.

"And if I kill Heisenberg this will end it? The bomb won't be used? The Nazis will finally lose this war?"

"It will slow things down, Moe. And in the world as it is right now, right here, there's a chance. If Rommel doesn't take Cairo, and if Patton wheels west and turns for Amsterdam. Yes, there's a chance that might end it here. But for you, Moe, no, this is not the end of it."

He looked at her. "I don't know what you mean. What's next?"

"I have to go now, Moe. See," she said, pointing at nothing, a park bench maybe over at the edge of the grass, "there's a door. I have a deadline and I can't possibly be late."

She turned to face him, reached up with both hands to hold his face, brought him to her, so close, so very close. "You're going to like this, Moe. You're going to do important work." And then she finally kissed him, hard and long, before pulling away and turning to leave him.

"Sure," he said to her back as her heels clicked against the stone path. "Sure, it's important work." He raised his voice. "Hey, what the hell does that mean? And who the hell are you? I don't even know your name."

She stopped, turned around. "You'll know everything sometime soon, Moe, I promise you. You're important. Know that, Moe Berg. Know that you're important."

"I'll see you again?"

"Oh, yes, in a way. After all, we have a lot to do, you and I."

She turned back again and stepped off the stone path to walk through the brown, winter grass and into the darkness of the park and then she wasn't there.

Berg undid his belt and reached down to his groin to pull free the Beretta. There was a brief moment of pain as the athletic tape came free and then he had the gun and was buttoning up again and putting it into his pocket. The smart thing to do was get to Scherrer's house and get back on the job: find Heisenberg, talk to the man, make a damn decision.

But where the hell had that woman gone? He wanted to know. He needed to know, in fact, and so he pulled the Beretta back out of his pocket and began walking after her, across the cold, winter grass and along the route he'd seen her take through some bushes and next to that plane tree.

There was a tingle, that dizziness, that moment of nausea, a sense of something—electricity?—in the air, but nothing else. She was gone. No footprints in the grass, no way to guess how she'd gone. Hell.

It was cloudy, dark, with snow starting to fall. But Scherrer's house had to be that way, through this little park and down onto the Seestrasse and on toward the lake. Hadn't the sky been clear a moment ago? Oh, hell. He pulled up his coat collar, shoved the Beretta back into the coat pocket, and started walking.

AUGUST 12, 1944

Moe Berg and his two pals, Enrico Fermi and Paul Scherrer, sat in slat wooden folding chairs at a very shaky wooden table at the Café Maggiore in the Swiss village of Dinella. About five hundred meters away, to the west, was the border with Italy, where Moe and Enrico had left their bikes. The act of their leaving the bikes behind had pleased both the Italian Carabinieri and the Swiss Border Guards, who had each barely glanced at Fermi's and Berg's passports before waving them through. It was hard to believe there was a war on.

Berg smiled a bit and allowed himself a moment's satisfaction. Here they were, all three with beer steins in front of them and Scherrer smoking a cigarette, calm and serene as they could be, looking out over Lake Maggiore with Locarno visible in the distance across the lake. Blue skies and sunshine; a light, cool breeze off the lake to cut the summer heat as the three men— two of them among the world's finest physicists and one of them a mediocre baseball player—discussed how to save the world.

They were the only patrons at the little café, and the owner who was the waiter and also the cook had brought them their beer and gone in to make their sandwiches, so they felt free to talk almost openly.

"Thank you both for coming. I know it was a difficult journey. But I have news of a certain opportunity."

"Something involving Heisenberg?" Moe asked. This must be good or Scherrer wouldn't have gone to all this trouble.

"Yes, my old friend, Werner. He's being allowed to visit with us in a few months."

"You're joking," said Fermi. "Germany would never allow such a thing. Hitler himself would have to know and he would never allow Werner to travel."

"I thought so myself, Enrico, for the longest time. But then one of my students, a brilliant young woman, of all things, pointed out that we could play to Hitler's vanity. And so we concocted a seminar series and asked Werner to come be our first speaker at the ETH."

"And this worked?" Berg asked, incredulous.

Scherrer smiled. "I brought you something to see," he said as he took a final drag on his cigarette, stubbed it out in the clay ashtray, and reached into the front inside pocket of his jacket.

For a second, Berg thought Scherrer might be reaching for a weapon; but that was silly, they were all friends here, right? And, indeed, it was simply a letter, still in its envelope though that had been opened.

Scherrer handed it to Berg, said "Open it, my friend. It's from Werner Heisenberg."

Well, well. Berg pulled the cut top of the envelope wide and pulled out the letter. It was written in ink, in a very nice hand. In German, of course.

Berg read it aloud, in German, so Fermi could hear. Fermi spoke German, of course.

"My Dear Paul,

"I hope this finds you well, and safe and healthy, in your comfortable surroundings in Zurich.

"Life here is sometimes difficult, as you might imagine, with the war dragging on and the occasional worries over Allied bombing. We are safe enough here at the moment, away from anything that might be thought a worthy target of Mr. Churchill's or Mr. Truman's aircraft, but I do worry over the family's safety. We all must make our sacrifices for the Fatherland, but I would happily risk my own life to save those of my wife and children. I am grateful that Herr Hitler has, twice now, allowed me to keep my family with me as we have moved our facilities from place to place to find a secure facility where we can work.

"It is grueling work, as you must know, and demands a great deal of my thought and energy. But I have, from time to time, done some interesting maths to advance the S-matrix work and so I am delighted to report to you that not only do I have something interesting to say at your little gathering, but Herr Hitler has personally endorsed my speaking to your group in Zurich in December.

"So I thank you most deeply for the invitation and am happy to report that I shall be able to attend. I am looking forward to seeing you and all my old friends in Switzerland at the Eidgenössische Technische Hochschule where, I am sure, much interesting work has been done even during these unfortunate times. I look forward to hearing from you and your colleagues and I hope that you will find what I have to say of some small interest.

"Elisabeth and the children were delighted to be invited but will be unable to attend. They do say hello and wish you and your family the best. Christine, especially, hopes to see your little Lisia sometime soon in a better, more peaceful world.

"I will see you in a few months, my friend, and I will look forward to that meeting with the greatest anticipation."

Berg looked up. "And he signs it, 'Werner.'"

He sat back and looked at Fermi, who was shaking his head in disbelief, and then they both looked at Scherrer, who was smiling broadly.

"How did you do this, Paul?" Berg wanted to know. "Heisenberg? In Zurich? In the middle of a war? How did you even manage to contact him to make such a request?"

"Paul," Fermi added, leaning over the table, "you know Werner every bit as well as I do. You must know what this means. He must have intended the implications of this letter. Surely you agree?"

Scherrer's smiled faded. "Yes, Enrico, of course. And so we must take advantage of this opportunity, as Werner no doubt would wish us to do."

"Take advantage?" asked Berg. "He's got a target on his back, gentlemen, and it's been there since the start of the war. You think he means to offer himself up at this get-together you have planned? Why would he do such a thing?"

"To tell us, to make it clear to us, that Germany does not have the super-bomb and will not build it. That could be Werner's motive," said Fermi. He leaned forward, his hands open, expressive. *"Spero che sia così."* I hope it is so.

Berg nodded. "Yes, that might be it." There was a rumbling in the distance, the low sound of engines, several of them working in unison, slowly drawing closer. "That would make sense if he's doing what you two think he is doing, finding ways to stall the creation of that super-bomb, pushing the development of it in the wrong direction."

The rumbling grew closer, the vibrations from it rattling the crockery on the table, the plates vibrating, the silverware jiggling in place. A tank column rumbling down the road? That's what it sounded like.

The proprietor, Gianluca, came out and looked up, pointed, said in German, "Once a day lately, three in the afternoon, like clockwork."

They looked up and a bulbous nose appeared over the hill behind them and then grew to include the entire zeppelin, flying low, an enormous thing, a giant when seen this close. It was the *Hindenburg*.

Safely interned in neutral Switzerland and renamed the *Wilhelm Tell*, she was still the pride of the German people, the mighty airship that had found safety here on the very day the Americans and English declared war on Germany.

My God, it was an enormous airship. Berg knew the basics; it was capable of carrying a payload of half a million pounds, double that if one wanted to risk the dangers of using hydrogen instead of helium. It was more than eight hundred feet long, had a cruising speed of seventy-five miles per hour and a range of an incredible ten thousand miles. Beginning in 1936 it made regular two-day crossings of the Atlantic between Frankfurt and New York, less than half the time the best ocean liners could manage and in greater comfort.

He wasn't surprised to see her flying so low, the *Hindenburg* was known for flying just a few hundred feet up. It made for a great view for the passengers and impressed the hell out of those on the ground as they watched the huge thing go by with its giant *swatztikas* on the side and on the tail.

Or at least that's how it had been for her before the war. Since she'd been interned in neutral Switzerland, she no longer carried the Nazi banner. Now she was flying with giant red crosses on her, the deal with Hitler being that the Swiss would let her fly, and with her German crew, as long as the paint job was Swiss.

By God, she was really something. He gaped, along with

Fermi and Scherrer, as she passed overhead and made her way across the lake toward Locarno.

And then, once she was gone, the three of them got down to making some plans for December in Zurich.

Before the afternoon ended and Moe and Enrico wandered back to the Italian Republic and their bicycles, the three of them had an idea of what to do. And, more importantly, how to do it.

DECEMBER 12, 1944

Paul Scherrer's home was a lakefront, two-story chalet, across the Seestrasse Boulevard from Rieterpark, with its woods and playing fields. Berg had spent a couple of weeks with Scherrer and his family back in mid-October and came to very much like Ilse, Scherrer's wife and the real master of the house. He also liked the three children, all girls ranging from eight to fourteen. By the end of those two weeks he'd put the family onto his mental list of people he would have to save from Hitler's anger if push came to shove on this Heisenberg thing. Fermi and his family were already on the list so, with a deep internal smile, Berg was starting to think of the list as his Phavorite Physicists list.

Heisenberg was not a phavorite.

Moe walked up the long driveway. It was snowing hard now, an inch or two on the ground already and a lot more to come, looked like. There were half a dozen cars parked on the grass to the side, showing off Zurich's relative wealth even during this war. A couple of Bugattis and a Mercedes spoke to the presence of some local politicians and leading businessmen. Some lesser Renaults and Citroëns probably belonged to professors.

Berg was about to knock on the door when Jeanine, the eight-year-old, beat him to it. "Mr. Berg!" she said with delight, and came to him for a hug. She was the most delightful of the three charming daughters, so "How wonderful to see you,

Jeanine," he said, hugging her back. "How are your sisters? And your mother?"

She laughed. "You're so silly, Mr. Berg. Amelie is fine, but she's the only sister I have and she's nearly eleven, so there's no talking with her, really. And Mother is fine, too. And Father. They're so happy you're here, and so am I!"

She prattled on a little longer, taking him by the hand and leading him into the house, presumably to meet the hosts before she would let go of him. Well, that was fine, but what was this thing about having just one sister? He knew, firmly, there were three. Was his memory wrong? He'd seen his father slip away into dementia and he didn't like considering the implications of these doubts about himself. Just nerves, perhaps, and that, he decided, he could handle.

Firmly in tow behind Jeanine, he rounded a corner and there was Paul Scherrer and beside him, Ilse. Hellos and handshakes and hugs and polite kisses on the cheek all around and soon Jeanine was back with her sister and the adults were talking, mostly about the weather and the children, since most topics of interest were off-limits in a group like this, where there was certainly a Gestapo agent or two in the crowd, along with several admitted Nazi sympathizers like Weizsäcker.

"By the way, our mutual friend is here," was all Scherrer had to say after the small talk ended. "I do believe he's out in the back room, the one with the view of the lake."

Berg nodded, shook his friend's hand again, very knowingly, since they both knew it might be the last time they'd see each other, and then left the Scherrers and walked past the likes of Gregor Wentzel and Ernst Stueckelberg, nodding and saying hello but moving, moving toward the far room, the one with the view of the lake, the one with Heisenberg.

AUGUST 23RD, 1943

William, "Wild Bill" Donovan was setting up a special kind of operation, a unit filled with people who would risk their lives for their country, working behind enemy lines, finding out things, causing trouble for the enemy.

What he had in mind for Moe Berg was work in Europe, dangerous work. He needed someone who could speak all those damn languages, someone with nerve, someone smart, someone with some physical skills and the willingness to do what had to be done. Was Moe Berg that man, Donovan wanted to know?

Sure he was. Sign me up, he said to Donovan after a half-hour conversation. And when do I start?

But it wasn't that simple. It would be best to finish the baseball season and then disappear into the woodwork, quietly, unobserved. Could Moe do that? Could he play ball for both the White Sox and his country? Could he finish things out in September and then go into training in October and, probably, be in action by the spring?

Sure he could. Sign me up, he said again to Donovan. And so it was.

But if the plan was to keep it quiet, Moe failed at that. Flush with his new calling, filled with self-confidence, the old Moe faded away into the rainy days of August and a new, bolder, Moe Berg was playing first base now for the Sox. A Moe who was hitting a ton, making the picks at first, running the bases like a madman. Freedom from worry was a wonderful thing and Moe tore the cover off the ball for the last three weeks of the season, hitting .342 and playing great defense. He led the White Sox in a climb from fourth place to third and then to second in the American League. Hell, still five games back at the end of the season but in that last month Moe Berg, baseball player, went from has-been to a hot item. Manager Jimmy Dykes professed loudly that he loved Moe's heart and his determination. General Manager Harry Grabiner praised Moe and swore he wouldn't trade him, and then started trying to make a deal with the Senators.

This was not exactly how Donovan wanted it to go, since it brought attention to Moe, but that was all right, in the off-season most people would forget baseball. There was, after all, a war going on. A hell of a war, what with Rommel revitalized in North Africa taking back Tobruk and knocking on the door of Cairo, and Germany launching those damn rockets at London, and the Luftwaffe's new jet aircraft regaining superiority over Europe. Things were teetering. There were a lot of people, important people, saying it was time for an armistice with Hitler so America could concentrate on the Japanese, where the war was going better since the cakewalk at Tinian.

Wild Bill was not interested in talking peace with Hitler. Wild Bill knew what most Americans didn't: the Nazis were working on a super-bomb, and with jets and rockets and those new, larger U-boats they had a way to deliver one if they got the damn bomb built. If that happened, the Japanese wouldn't matter, Oppy told him time and again. If the Germans got the bomb first, nothing mattered. The war was over and the good guys lost.

Moe Berg, spy, and the key to it all, really, found himself on the fast track.

December 12, 1944Moe got caught in two brief conversations as he worked his way toward the back room, but he had to stay quiet and unobtrusive, blend in, and so he chatted about S-matrix and then about the weather and then, finally, he got to the double doors at the back of the chalet that opened up to the added-on back room. One of the doors was open and he walked through it and there, at the window at the back of the room, the window with the great view of Lake Zurich, was Werner Heisen-berg, chatting with several people, smiling, nodding his head.

One of those people was a woman. Was *the* woman, Moe's mysterious friend from the past two years and the conversation from a couple of hours ago. It was her, he was sure of it, though she was dressed differently now, more elegant and less business, her hair piled up on top and a smart little hat on top of that. There were long earrings and red lipstick and padded shoulders. Putting on the Ritz. Damn, she was a knockout.

He walked toward the little group. The woman saw him coming, smiled, looked at her watch. "Werner, dear, here is the man I was telling you about—the Italian physicist who worked with Fermi?—Mario Antonacci."

Then she turned to Moe, offered her hand. "So good to see you, Mario. I'm so happy you were able to come."

Heisenberg reached out to take Moe's hand in his own. "It is a great pleasure, Herr Professor. As you must know, I am a good friend and a great admirer of your colleague, Professor Fermi. I had hoped he might be able to attend here this weekend."

"I was with him just a few weeks ago, Professor," Moe was able to say truthfully. "He had hoped to attend, but with the political situation as it is ..." Moe shrugged.

Heisenberg nodded. "Of course, Professor. These are difficult times for us all."

Berg felt a hand on his shoulder, that flash of stomach-churning disorientation. It was the woman, and she was putting a hand on Heisenberg's shoulder, as well. "Boys," she said with a little laugh, "time enough for small talk later. Right now I was hoping to take the two of you outside." She took a look at her watch again. "I'm told we're going to see quite a sight in the next few minutes. A very special visit from an old friend of mine. Would you come with me, both of you, please?"

There was nothing to do but follow, as the woman took them both by the hand and walked toward the doors that led out to the backyard of the chalet, where a path led to a wooden walkway that, in turn, led out to a dock. No boats tied up this time of year, but no ice on the water yet, either.

The night was warm for December, well above freezing. They walked out onto the dock, the three of them, alone, the house behind them dimly lit, quiet, as the Scherrers prepared for bed and the servants finished cleaning up the remnants of the small dinner party. A cloudless, moonless night and few wartime lights made for a beautiful sky, the Milky Way arching across in full glory, a reminder, in its own way, of the hell that was nighttime bombing. There was a distant rumble, a rhythmic beat to it, a deep cadence that Berg remembered from a few months ago. Engines. Big twelve hundred horsepower Daimler-Benz diesels, four of them, sixteen-cylinder behemoths, driving the great beast forward. The *Hindenburg*. The *Wilhelm Tell*.

The great dark shadow of it emerged from the east, over the alpine ridges to the back of the lake. Low in the sky, as always, it seemed to take forever to finally clear the ridgeline and establish itself in its full glory.

It came toward them, slowing, slowing and then, no more than one hundred feet above them, a huge thing nearly three football fields long, easing to a stop, the roar of the engines quieting to an idle. Directly above the three of them was the *fuhrergondel*, the control car, where the crew did its work. The passengers and the cargo were inside the envelope.

"She's magnificent, isn't she, Moe?" the woman asked. "I told you that you'd see her again."

"You never mentioned the *Hindenburg*," Moe said, and took his eyes off the huge shape above him and turned to look at the woman.

She was holding a gun. Moe's gun, the Beretta. He reached into his pocket and wasn't surprised to find it wasn't there.

"You know this has to be, Mr. Berg," said Heisenberg, walking over to stand next to her, admitting he knew who Moe really was. "Tomorrow morning, at the Eagle's Nest, Herr Hitler and the others—Göring, Hess, von Braun, Goebbels, Hausser, Messerschmitt, von Ribbentrop, Himmler, and many more—will be gathered to meet with me as I return from Zurich aboard the *Hindenburg*.

"Hitler has an announcement for them. He plans to tell them that the super-bomb is ready, and that Messerschmitt has a plane that can deliver it. He plans to introduce me to them, and I will explain how the bomb works, and the damage it will do to London, and how we are building three more of these super-bombs, these atomic bombs."

"So killing you now is too late. I get that," said Berg.

"No, Moe," the woman said. "In about five minutes they're going to lower a ladder down from that control car. We're going to help Herr Heisenberg get on that ladder and climb up to the control car. Then we're going to watch the *Hindenburg* leave, heading for the border, and then the Eagle's Nest."

"We're not going to stop him?"

Heisenberg shrugged. "No, I don't think so, Mr. Berg. There are no bombs made of the size the Führer thinks they are. There is only one bomb—we have built that—and it's enormous. It weighs nearly twenty of your tons, and it's twice the size of a train car. There is no way for a plane or a rocket to deliver such a weapon."

"It's already built?" Jesus, the game was over, then.

And then it dawned on Moe Berg, spy. The game was nearly over, yes, heading into the ninth. But if that bomb ...

"That bomb is in the *Hindenburg*? It's in there right now?"

The woman and Heisenberg both nodded.

There was a creak from just above, and then a bang as a hatch slammed open and then was tied off. A ladder started inching down from that hatch. The great hulk of the zeppelin was only twenty feet above them now, surreal in its enormity, silver in the darkness, only the single flashlight coming from the control car illuminating the ladder, aluminum, as it cranked slowly down.

"And you're taking it to the Eagle's Nest?"

"Yes, Moe, he is. That's a crew of volunteers in there. The

super-bomb is in the hold, the gas cells filled with hydrogen for extra lift. Tomorrow, before noon, they will reach the Eagle's Nest and tie off at the landing tower. Professor Heisenberg will exit the zeppelin. Herr Hitler and the others will be at the landing pad to meet the creator of the great bomb and then they expect to board the *Hindenburg* and see more of the bombs, brought to them safely through neutral Switzerland."

"Instead ..."

"Instead, the trigger will spring and the enriched uranium will reach critical mass, and this war will come to an end."

"My God."

The ladder touched down on the wooden dock. Werner Heisenberg took Moe Berg's hand to steady himself and then, with Berg's help, got his right foot onto the first rung of the ladder. Berg held the ladder steady and the woman came over to help. Their hands met on the ladder as Heisenberg started climbing and Moe felt that now familiar nausea, the moment of disorientation. He knew to take a look toward the house. The lights were back on, a crowd again visible through the curtains. Did anyone miss Heisenberg? Was there another Heisenberg in there? Was this Heisenberg still here?

Moe looked up and Heisenberg was already at the control car, hands reaching down to help him through the hatchway.

The woman was gone. Moe's Beretta was back in his pocket and he knew that here, now, it had never been taken.

Someone was shouting. Moe felt the ladder being yanked upward, out of his hands, up into the belly of the beast. That was all right. He was sure of it, he was dead certain that it was all right, what Heisenberg had in mind.

The shouts were closer, footsteps crunching through the few inches of snow that now covered the ground. The lake was frozen. It was very cold.

Two men were coming, running, one ahead of the other. The first was Weizsäcker, waving a pistol, a Luger, shouting something in German about stopping, stop the zeppelin, you must stop the zeppelin. Behind him was Paul Scherrer, trying to catch up, yelling something himself: "Carl, don't shoot, do not shoot. The hydrogen! The hydrogen!"

So they knew, or at least Scherrer did. No surprise there. Moe reached into his pocket and pulled out the Beretta. Weizsäcker was a good thirty yards away. It would take a very lucky shot.

Weizsäcker stopped running and stood there, pulling a loaded magazine out of his coat pocket and fumbling with it as he loaded the Luger. There was an audible click as the magazine catch snapped into place.

Scherrer reached him, grabbed his arm, and Weizsäcker turned and shoved him away and then shot him, close range, no more than five feet away. Scherrer spun once and fell.

Moe Berg had taken a first in marksmanship in his training, though that was with the Colt .45. Still, he'd spent two days at Scherrer's house a couple of months ago, standing right near this dock in some other reality a long way from this one, target shooting with the Beretta so he could shoot and kill a Nazi. Okay, here was the chance. He took aim as Weizsäcker turned back around and fumbled with pulling the toggle joint in the rear of the Luger to bring a round into the chamber. That took two seconds and then he started to point the Luger at the *Hindenburg*.

And died there, a hole made by the bullet from Moe Berg's Beretta appearing above the left ear.

Moe walked over briskly, clouds of vapor from his suddenly heavy breathing wreathing him as he reached Weizsäcker, who had fallen to his knees but still seemed to be alive. This man had shot Paul Scherrer. Moe put the second shot into the back of the head and as Weizsäcker fell to his side and then rolled, dead, onto his back, Moe put one more shot, for good measure, into the Nazi's forehead.

And suddenly it was very quiet. Moe could hear the crunching of snow as someone else approached. He looked up and it was, of course, the woman. She knelt over Scherrer, who was moaning.

"The bullet went through the flesh of the forearm. Not much blood. He's very lucky," she said, "but I suppose his pitching career is over, right, Moe?"

Scherrer wasn't wearing a coat, it had all happened too fast for that. She began tearing away the long sleeve of his shirt to get a strip of cloth to tie around the wound.

"You're very funny," Moe said.

She rose to her feet. A number of people were coming, but they had a few seconds before help for Scherrer arrived. "You know, Moe, in some of the scenarios you never get to Europe."

"What?"

"Yes, it's true. Sometimes you're a ballplayer and sometimes you're a lawyer and sometimes you're living at home with your sister, alone, reading your newspapers, afraid of the world."

"Not afraid, really; that's not what it's about."

Behind him, the engines roared to life and the zeppelin moved out over the lake, toward Locarno, and tomorrow to Berchtesgaden and by noon to doing something real, something that mattered.

"It's all very uncertain, Moe," she said, smiling. He shook his head. A moment like this and she's making Heisenberg jokes.

"Moe," she said, "there's a place where you're a catcher for the Senators."

"God forbid."

"But in all these places, all these myriads of possibilities, you're reachable. You move through the frames easily. And you always get the job done."

"You know, I'm not stupid ..."

"Quite the contrary, Moe. Your intelligence, your languages, that and your ability to move through the frames; that's why we need you."

"I got to admit I'm not real sure what's going on here."

The crowd from the party had reached them; people were

kneeling over Scherrer, trying to help, and looking, fascinated and horrified, at the bloody mess that had been Carl Weizsäcker.

"Okay," Moe said, "I get it. Count me in."

She smiled at him, reached out to take him by the arm, and then, after the nausea, after the moment of dizziness, the two of them, Moe Berg and the woman, alone on the lakeshore, walked away into the quiet darkness of a strangely warm December night in Zurich.

This novella appeared in Asimov's Science Fiction *magazine. It is a precursor to the novel,* Alien Morning *(Tor, 2016), which was a finalist for Best Science Fiction Novel of the Year in 2016 (the John W. Campbell Memorial Award). The story was included in the audiotext compilation* The Year's Top Short SF Novels *(AudioText, Inc, 2011) edited by Allan Kaster, which is also available as an ebook on Amazon and elsewhere.*

SEVERAL ITEMS OF INTEREST

"The Earth does not argue, is not pathetic, does not scream, haste, persuade, threaten, promise. The Earth has no conceivable failures."

—Walt Whitman

DANGEROUS COMFORT

I knew from that very first evening at Tommy's house, though it all took some time to finally happen. We'd been chatting, Heather and I, making idle conversation—something about The Ten, no doubt—and I felt myself sliding away. I do not lose myself with women. I do not drift away into imagined passion. I am always in control. But with Heather, oh yes with Heather, I knew the danger and I didn't care. Seeing her. Listening. Imagining. She looked at me, she smiled, and I was lost.

And so, more than a year later, I sat in dangerous comfort, thinking the news from Earth couldn't be good or Twoclicks would never have invited me to meet with him during his afternoon soak.

I knew that he liked to warm himself like this when he was at home; but in the time I'd been on S'hudon not once had he invited me any farther into his personal quarters than that large front room where he keeps his Earthie artifacts: the baseball bat from the Splendid Splinter, the signed first editions by Yeats and Whitman and Wells, the Booth Derringer that fired the shot that killed Abraham Lincoln, the de Koonings and the Rockwells and the two Picassos and the Monet, the top hat from Astaire's movie of the same name, Django Reinhardt's guitar and Stéphane Grappelli's violin from the 1939 Hot Club performances in Paris; all of this accumulation and more tossed onto tables or hung haphazardly on walls cheek-by-jowl, disorganized, incomprehensible, like Twoclicks himself.

I was part of that accumulation, of course, and knew it; though I hadn't been hung on a wall just yet, or tossed onto a table. But the threat of that—or something quite like it—hung over me as I sat in the heat of the fumarole as it bubbled and gurgled in his backyard.

To get there I'd been escorted beyond the front room and on through the private dining area, the private living area, the very private bedrooms, and through the antique stonewood door and down the pumice steps and a hundred paces or more through the cold, soft grass and finally into the first and largest of the hot spring mud baths, where Twoclicks and I sat, up to our necks in the warm goo.

The invitation I'd received was in print—Twoclicks fancies the archaic—on a small embossed card delivered by young Treble, his son and my favorite of the several princelings. The note was written in flowing formal S'hudonni script on the top and then in English, smaller, underneath: "Your presence is requested at soak on the morrow at the home of your mentor for a discussion of a matter of some importance regarding a troublesome situation on your home planet."

That sounded pretty damn ominous, and so once I was admitted to his home, directed to the changing room where I slipped out of my clothes, had a large towel wrapped around me, and then walked over to the hot, muddy spring and climbed in, I thought surely he'd get to the point quickly. But Twoclicks, as always, was indirect and in no particular hurry. Instead, he spent the first half hour talking about various sporting events in the American District on Earth, where his favorite teams all seemed to be doing well. I tried to enjoy the warm muck and the sports talk while I waited for the conversation to get wherever it was really going.

The fog is cold and damp on the coast of S'hudon's southernmost island, and especially so when the wind is from the southwest and has blown over the frigid waters of the Great South Loop current. So the mud bath was a welcome break from the chill and the rain and the general grayness of that winter coast. Twoclicks faced the breeze as he started to talk, giving me the comfort of having my back to the wind. I didn't know if he was being purposefully polite or not. Then he paused and I was thinking this would be the moment when I'd finally hear the news about trouble back home. Riots? Famines? Floods? Plagues? Bombings? An insurrection? All of the above? But he just grew silent, perhaps the chill taking its toll on him or, more likely, he had just hit a lull, having said all he wanted to about the sports interests of the newly occupied minor planet at the edge of the empire.

A long minute or two went by as he stared at me, those round eyes beginning to blink more rapidly until I was sure he finally had something significant to say. Instead of getting on with it, though, he started sliding down into the hot mud, slipping deeper and deeper and slightly backward until, finally, only his mouth and eyes remained visible. He slid the second membrane of the right eye over its pupil and winked with the left eye—that's not a natural act for the S'hudonni and so he'd done this to impress me—and then, finally, he said something new: "Americanos! Conquerors! Libertad! Masses! For you a program of chants." Then, to punctuate whatever the hell the point of that was, he slid down again, disappearing entirely, that falsely closed eye the last thing I saw before he went under, where he could stay for an hour if he wanted.

The quote was from Whitman. Having seen the sexual proclivities of S'hudon's ruling classes, I wasn't surprised to find that Twoclicks had embraced old Walt from among the long readings list I'd offered. Whitman was certainly Twoclicks's kind of Earthie. But why that particular snippet? It must mean something or he wouldn't have said it, but I sure as hell wasn't getting the message. Americanos? Conquerors? Not hardly. Not anymore.

I thought about what once had been and what now remained back home, the old United States gone the way of all empires, reduced to an "economic district." Twoclicks, who'd decided only recently that his title should now be Chancellor of the American District, was in control of most of the old US and Mexico and some of the Caribbean islands. His brother, Whistle, called himself Governor General of the Canadian District, which included old Alaska along with Canada and parts of New England. Other relatives ran other districts and it was all very familial, if not particularly harmonious. The siblings and cousins had their rivalries and their competing districts not only on Earth but on all of The Seven planets that were part of S'hudon's empire.

For parts of conquered humanity, the reality of life under S'hudonni control was not all that different from how it had been before the Arribada. They worked, they played, they made love, they were hired and fired and married and divorced. They had children they loved or were disappointed in, and siblings they admired or loathed. They took vacations. They watched television. They Sweeped and Tweeted and logged on and off as Earth continued to spin.

For these lucky millions, only the leadership had changed. Plus, S'hudon's gifts—the power generators and their grids, the medical tools and drugs, the transportation rails, the nanos for the lucky few—had been parceled out bit by bit in return for the locals' expressions of loyalty to the new order. They were useful gifts, I was sure, in rebuilding a shattered society and getting people back to work and living their lives. Expensive in their own way, but useful.

Others hadn't been so fortunate. Different districts found different profits, some of them consumed locally on Earth, like the poppies that fed a drug-hungry Europe or the entertainment from Japan that kept a whole world's minds off its losses. Others exported their goods offworld. The major grain producers— Canada and the US, Russia, newly irrigated Australia, parts of China and Brazil—these places grew the luxury crops that made money for the ruling classes back on S'hudon who bought cheap from Earthie labor and sold high around The Seven, where alcohol from Earth was all the rage, the tulips of empire.

This meant growing real grain and distilling and brewing real variations on alcohol. Growing a great deal of grain, in fact, some six times the harvest from the time before the Arribada.

There has been, in many places, some considerable disruption. Twoclicks felt bad about that, he'd told me again and again, and he seemed sincere. Of course I am far from perfect at judging S'hudonni sincerity. I'd been on the planet a year and I pretty much hadn't learned a thing, except for what Heather had taught me. That's what was on my mind as I waited for Twoclicks to resurface. Heather. As always, it was Heather.

IN THE LONG RUN

On a typical day in my little Potemkin Village at the edge of the Great Bight I awake with the sunrise, dial up my internal Sweep to get it recording, and then brew some coffee (black, dark) and make some toast, both of these imported from home, as is all my food and drink.

After that I go for a long jog along the path they've paved for me atop the bluffs that overlook the bight. The pavement runs for three kilometers, eventually dropping down onto the Strand for another kilometer, where I can taste the salt spray and pretend, at least for a few minutes, that I am home.

Then I turn and jog home to my faux cottage on my ersatz street in my make-believe village. When the land breeze is blowing out to sea, as it often is, the air is redolent of S'hudon with the rotten-egg smell of sulfur from the inland fumaroles a kilometer or two away and I can hear, in the distance, the sounds of Agitato, the vacation park where the S'hudonni stay when they visit this coast. Along with the sulfur there is a hint of inland marsh in the air, of still water and rotting vegetation and, on a good day, a hint of something nearly cinnamon and, often, the squeals of the S'hudonni children.

I am lucky, I suppose, that my enhanced Sweeper can capture the smells along with the sights and sounds of S'hudon. My current audience back home is around two hundred million, mostly in Twoclicks's district. Since Two has spent a fortune getting me here and constructing an environment for me, it is good to know that my message, and his, has an audience.

THE FAMILY BARGE

Some months ago, Twoclicks invited me to go hunting—for good sport, as he put it—with his son, Treble, his older brother, Whistle, and his younger sister, Octave. They are bitter rivals, those siblings, but on that day they acted as if those rivalries were forgotten. We traveled on the family barge as it slowly wound its way down the main channel toward the sea on a cool summer day, sliding our way through the water plants that grew ambitiously large during the short growing season.

Young Treble and I were on the barge, standing at the side rail and looking out toward the plants as we searched for our prey, a small amphibious creature the size and general shape of a small cat. It reached its juvenile, and tastiest, stage of development only for a week or two each year. Treble whistled and clicked its name and when I asked for a translation he said "bender" would do. Like some animals on Earth, the benders changed gender as needed. At the juvenile stage, they were all females. A few months later, when it was time to reproduce, the larger, more aggressive ones became inedibly male.

Below us, the three S'hudonni were swimming effortlessly a meter deep, their motion so smooth that you couldn't see any ripples from their movement. The water was the color of strong tea.

The animal sat along the edge of one of those plants, serene, as we glided past it, no more than ten meters away. It ignored us, and then as we looked back to watch there was an upwelling from beneath the water plant and the three S'hudonni emerged simultaneously.

The bender never knew what hit it. And then hit it again. And then a third time, Twoclicks and Octave and Whistle each taking turns toying with it for a while before, in unison, they ripped it apart and Twoclicks brought me the still-beating heart so I could take a ritual bite. I'd skinned rabbits in my backwoods youth and Twoclicks had told me he admired that aspect of my childhood. Now I understood why.

There was no question about my response: Twoclicks was my sponsor and my behavior was important. I brought the heart to my lips, opened my mouth, took a small bite and then handed the heart back to Twoclicks. My nanos, I guessed, would neutralize whatever toxicity was in that bite.

Twoclicks smiled and took his own ritual bite, and then they all passed it around and did the same, including little Treble, who finished it off. Somewhere along the line the heart had stopped beating.

How did they know the prey was there, quiet and still on a pad floating atop the warm, muddy water of the slough? Sonar? A sensitive sense of smell? Some sort of infrared sense that can tell a slight heat change through a layer of mud and plant fiber? Some other sense I'm not aware of yet? It could be any or all of those. What I know about the S'hudonni could fill a book—the very book you are reading, in fact, since that's why Twoclicks brought me here: to Sweep back home to all those simple Earthies about the wonders of mighty S'hudon and then to gather all that material into a book and a stemfeed and a linker and, I suspect, a touring minstrel show.

But what you learn in life, if you have half a brain, teaches you as much about what you don't know as what you do, and while what I found out about the S'hudonni could fill a thick, musty old-school book and all the new dorms, too, what I didn't find out about S'hudon could fill a library. Ten libraries. A hundred. The S'hudonni are, by turns, kind and vicious, brilliant and stupid, physically handsome in their own way even while unspeakably ugly, simple and direct and unfathomably obscure. Their world and their empire are filled with these contrasts, rife with these contradictions. That much, at least, I'd come to understand.

SEVERAL ITEMS OF INTEREST ABOUT THE S'HUDONNI

1) There is a small orifice just at the back of the dorsal fin.

2) Placing one of the fragile, small fingers from those delicate hands just at the edge of that small, black hole brings ripples of pleasure.

3) The sleek, taut, olive-colored skin across the flanks of the S'hudonni torso changes colors rapidly and constantly when sexually stimulated, waves of bright orange and yellow coursing over that skin.

4) A one-fingered caress over the thin black line that runs the length of the torso and separates the upper body from the lower also sparks a colorful stimulation, even when it's an Earthie— your faithful correspondent—doing the running of the finger.

5) The female S'hudonni can shiver with pleasure.

6) Assuming Twoclicks and his siblings are typical, the S'hudonni happily embrace sexual activity from any—perhaps all—of their friends and relations who join the party after a hunt is done. The patterns of these embraces struck me as mostly random.

7) Human involvement is oddly welcome. I hadn't realized that this would happen, but then I have a notable history of not knowing when I'm getting involved with strange women.

STORYTELLING

I have spent my life telling stories. My parents were disappointed in this. My mother was in corporate law and hoped I might follow in her capable footsteps and become an attorney. My father was a pediatrician, loved and respected by the families of the hundreds of children he served. The funeral cortege on the day that we buried him in Whispering Oaks was a half mile long and made the local television news. He had been a community activist, raising funds for his favorite charities, vocal in his backing for the politicians he liked and admired. He and his wife were both good, strong, intelligent, caring people and expected their two sons to be the same.

Tommy lived up to those parental expectations. The youngest son, he left high school with enough science credits to start in as a sophomore at Vanderbilt; then he sailed right through his undergrad biology degree before turning to research in grad school as the way to find his truths in life. His doctorate, his tenure at Rice and then at the University of Florida, his research successes: these accomplishments won him respect and love from Mom and Dad, and they told him so often.

As for me, a bachelor's in English literature and a minor in history struck Mom and Dad as foolish and indulgent and my later choices in life confirmed their disappointment. I had been a good high school athlete, wasting my time (as Father put it) playing basketball and baseball for the high school teams and getting some ink in the local papers. I could handle the ball and shoot from outside in basketball, and I understood the game. In baseball I played the infield, second or short, and had good hands and a solid arm if not much of a bat. Ultimately this meant I got to play both sports at a good, small college in a suburb of Orlando. It occupied my time. It made me happy. Father and Tommy were busy, always, and rarely saw me play, in high school or college. Mom, bless her heart, was there often.

Ultimately injuries ended the fun and I turned to my studies, working my way to an MFA by serving as a grad assistant, teaching comp classes, and working for the college paper. I started sending sports profiles to magazines and websites and pretty soon some got published.

That turned out to be my level and, over time, I became a part-time teacher and a writer of magazine articles. I taught at a perfectly nice little liberal arts college in St. Petersburg, Florida, and I was good at that.

It's hard to get published—trust me, the odds are against you —so I was proud of my career, such as it was. But I wasn't published in the *New Yorker* or by Knopf and I wasn't teaching in the Ivy League. I told myself that it didn't matter. Later, when I started Sweeping and millions were paying attention, I came at last to admit something different.

SMOKING

My father smoked cigarettes most of his life: Camels, good, strong stuff that he'd started in on while an undergraduate at Princeton. You might be surprised to hear how many smokers there are in the health field: nurses, doctors, EMTs, even some oncologists here and there. Stress, they will explain, is why they smoke. And, of course, their certain knowledge that as medical people they are immune to the diseases of more common men and women.

Father found out on his sixtieth birthday that the cough he feared was lung cancer was, indeed, small-cell, stage 3B, revised after the first surgery to stage 4. The radiation, the surgery, the chemo: they were all palliative and he knew it and we knew it.

Except for Tommy, the great research scientist, the Great Mind, the Boy Wonder who'd had research published while he was still an undergrad, the man who always Had the Answer.

Tommy kept insisting that Father should try one new trial or another, look for that wonder drug, keep up your hope, stay positive, beat this thing. Tommy, I thought, seemed increasingly angry with Dad for accepting the cancer, embracing it, allowing it entry into his life and death. As the weeks went by, Tommy's calm urgings with Dad turned into strident hectoring about battle and struggles and never giving up.

About a year after he got the news, on the last day of his life, my father walked over to me after yet another angry outburst from Tommy and said this to me: "Son, I do wish you'd done more with that fine mind of yours, but at least you've always been happy."

He shook his head. "Now, your brother, for all his brains and all his publications and all his money and all his awards: that's about the unhappiest guy I know."

Then he coughed, almost politely, and turned away from me.

We were all gathered at Tommy's house that day to share a Sunday meal and celebrate Tommy's being shortlisted for the International Prize for Biology. There were some delicious ironies there, since the prize honors Japan's Emperor Hirohito and while Tommy was on the list for his work in saving the Kemp's ridley sea turtles, the Japanese were still busy slaughtering whales. I mentioned this to Tommy. He just stared at me, shook his head, and turned away to talk to Mom, who was in the kitchen with him, both of them whispering to each other, I knew, over how disappointed dying Dad was that I'd thrown my life away on scribbling when, early on, I'd held such promise. I had, after all, won the countywide science fair in sixth grade.

A couple of hours later Mom and I sat in folding chairs on Tommy's back deck and watched a distant line of storms boil and grow with rumbles of thunder.

"How long does Dad have?" I asked her, holding tight to my beer, some unpronounceable Belgian brand that Tommy liked. Me, I stuck with Corona.

"A month or two," she said.

"He looks better than that," I offered. "And he seems happy enough. I thought maybe things were a little better."

A slight shake of her head, a thin smile. "No, they're not. He accepted it a long time ago, Peter, that's all. The inevitability of it." She chuckled a bit. "I caught him in the backyard a couple of days ago smoking one of those Camels. I couldn't believe it, but he just said it didn't really matter anymore, so what the hell."

I didn't say anything, but looked out toward the distant thunderheads as they lit up the evening sky with half-buried lightning, miles away.

About an hour later I walked over to Dad to say goodbye. He got up off the couch and wouldn't let me stop him from standing. I gave him a firm handshake and his grip was just firm enough in return to be a reminder of who he'd been. I looked at him, gave him a quick, clumsy hug and told him I loved him.

"Thank you," he said. He seemed at peace.

As I got to my car in the driveway that line of thunderstorms was almost to us, but I beat the worst of the rain home. A half hour later, just as I was pulling into my driveway, my parents were getting into their car for their longer drive home across the Sunshine Skyway and down to Sarasota. Dad, despite his health, always insisted on driving, a control freak right to the end. It was pouring by then, the blinding rain, the road across that high bridge. Rain, cancer, control and its lack: these are the things that ended my father's life and put my mother's into ruin.

EMERGING

In the mud pit, some minutes had gone by and I was beginning to worry about when and how Twoclicks might emerge. Would he playfully attack me from underneath? Would he embrace me through the muck or run a thin, fragile finger along my spine? Would he stay down there for an hour or two while I sat like meat in a melting pot? My imagination was getting the better of me, but then I'd seen what I'd seen on S'hudon.

I heard the soft slap of flat, bare feet against the cold stone path that comes from the house to the fumarole. I turned to look and it was Heather: short and stocky, waddling along on those spindly legs, that upright shark shape useful to her when she was on S'hudon. She was smart and funny and strangely wise and I loved her in all her various forms, though I knew she was utterly a lie. I'd taught myself not to worry too much about that, despite the history we shared. Once, not that long ago—looking very different in that place and at that time—she'd broken my brother's heart. For a while after that she enjoyed telling me that she was working on breaking mine. I used to laugh about that.

She stepped carefully down into the fumarole and slipped her body halfway in. She looked at me. She smiled.

"Hi," I said.

"Hi, yourself. You all right?"

"Fine," I said, "just fine."

"He thought it was time for you to know."

"Great," I said. "Know what?"

She stared. "He hasn't told you yet?"

"Told me what?"

"Oh, I can't be the one to say, Peter. This is all his idea; he should break the news to you."

And so I knew, from the way she said it. "It's about Tommy," I said.

"In a way. Mostly, in fact."

"And?"

"And nothing, Peter. I can't say any more. I won't."

On cue, a bubble, round and mottled in the mud, rose across from me, grew larger, tension straining, and then popped. It smelled like cinnamon.

And these creatures, I noted, were the masters of our universe.

The muck began to part underneath the spot where the bubble had burst and I saw Twoclicks's shuttered eyes rising, the nictitating membranes tight over them, the eyeballs visible within. Through the membranes he was looking at me. He rose a bit higher, so that his whole head was clear of the mud. The membranes slid up, disappeared. His eyes were clear.

"There iss trouble on Earth," he said with that annoying lisp that he used as an affectation. Somehow it's terribly condescending. "It iss getting worse."

"There's always trouble on Earth," I answered. "Even before S'hudon arrived there was always trouble on Earth. And it was always getting worse. We Earthies do not play well together."

"*Ah*, but this time iss different."

"Sure," I said. "This time is different."

"Hass to do with your brother," he said, "and iss very trouble-some. Blowing up distilleries and pipelines. Burning crops. Burning a lot of crops."

"And you can't stop that? With your screamships? The hired Canadians? All your technology and all your mercenaries and you can't stop the locals from burning some crops?"

He shrugged. It was an acquired gesture for him, since he doesn't really have much in the way of shoulders. "Guesss not," he said. "No. Certainly not. Cannot. Hass been going on for months now, all over northern areas of my district. Very low tech, friend Peter. Fly below radar ssort of thing, you know?"

Then he dropped what was, for him, the real bombshell. "Is so much trouble that family sayss it threatens profits. My brother says it will spread. He blames me, and thiss is very bad."

And having said that he smiled at me and turned to Heather.

"You explain how brotherss are," he said to her. And then he slid down again, the membranes coming over the eyes, the head sliding down into the muck. A bubble, a smoothing wave: he was gone.

Heather smiled at me. "You know how much Two hates confrontation, Peter. That wasn't easy for him, what he just did."

"Sure," I said, "it couldn't have been easy. So what's really the problem, Heather? It can't be some crops getting burned."

A bubble rose in the muck, popped. We both knew that Twoclicks was listening. Heather gave me a complicated wink, which is hard to do in that body. Right, I thought, just us insiders. Wink, wink.

"The crops *are* a problem," she said, "and the distilleries and breweries and the production and transportation systems; those are problems, too. It must all be handcrafted, you know, Peter. No enhancements, nothing artificial, wooden casks and barrels and the whole lot. The demand for this, this authentic Earthie alcohol in its various forms, is very high on Downtone and Blink right now and doing okay on the other planets. Twoclicks needs to capitalize on that demand while he can, and expand the market before his siblings get in on it. He sees this as the opportunity he's been waiting a very long time for. It's his chance to rise in the hierarchy. His chance to please his father."

"Of course," I said, "he would certainly want to please the old man."

"Don't be snide, Peter, you know how it is."

And I did, in fact, know how that was, trying to please the old man.

It was a typical family squabble, the struggle between Twoclicks and Whistle; a brotherly disagreement over who had the bigger dorsal fin and which one their father loved more. They were both quite willing to spill blood over this.

Heather said, "Peter, the burning of the wheat and corn has meant significant loss for Twoclicks. He has contractual obligations to Whistle that he'll have a hard time meeting now. There are debts between the two of them. Two *has* to meet his obligations."

"Or else?"

"Or else war, I'd guess, Peter. This would be an excuse for Whistle to invade Two's territory. Here it would just be a family spat and the two brothers wouldn't talk to each other at family gatherings...."

She let that thought hang and I picked up on it. "But on Earth?"

"A lot of people would die before it got settled, Peter."

I knew Whistle pretty well and don't like him. He didn't like me, either, and I knew he thought of me as his little brother's Earthie pet. I resented deeply the truth of that.

Heather looked sad. "Understand, Peter, that despite what Two has said to you, this isn't any trouble that he can't fix. There's a screamship waiting in Earth orbit and all Twoclicks has to do is give the word."

"The word."

"The word to take out Tommy and his little band of merry men. De-orbit, a day or two of burns along the Lake Ontario shoreline where they're hiding out—mistakenly thinking we don't know where and how—and that's it. Done. Insurrection suppressed. Trouble over. Back to work on the farm, raising grain for handcrafted alcohol, making Twoclicks richer and more powerful and keeping Whistle at bay. Nothing to it."

"Then why the hell not just get in there...." And it dawned on me what she was saying. "Oh," I said. "Tommy."

She nodded. "Twoclicks wants you to go and talk with Tommy. Twoclicks thinks he owes you both that much. You and your brother helped Two when it mattered. You saved his life once and he recognizes the debt. Talk to Tommy, explain things to him, lay it all out for him."

"And you think I can get Tommy to stop?"

She shrugged. "If you don't stop him, Peter, Two will. He's

just giving you a chance to settle it without bloodshed. He's doing this for you, because he owes you. Because he likes you."

"He doesn't owe me, Heather, I've told him that a hundred times. And hell, even if he did owe me, that debt has been paid twenty times over."

"He doesn't see it that way, Peter. You and your brother saved his life and for him that incurs a deep obligation. He won't forget that. Ever." She stared at me. "But he *will* do what he has to do, Peter, and soon, to maintain control over the colony. Who would you rather have in charge, Two or Whistle?"

There was no question about my answer to that. Twoclicks was an odd character, but he had an interest in things Earthie other than profit. His various collections, his love for Earth's music and literature and art. His interest in me and in my Sweeps to the home world. He was the best of that bad lot by a long shot. "All right," I said, "sure, I'll go."

"Good," she said.

"When am I leaving?"

She smiled. "Right now. You only have a day or two before Whistle acts, I think, so the sooner the better. There's a kelly in a room upstairs in the main house."

"Do I take anything with me?"

"Sure," she said. "Me."

And so we left.

THE ARRIBADA

You have your memories of the first time you heard the news about the Arribada. You remember that the television was on and you were making love to your wife or your husband or your lover; or you sat by your mother's deathbed and the nurse walked in to tell you the news; or you were in your favorite chair reading a book and a frightened neighbor knocked on your door; or you were eating a meal at an inexpensive restaurant and your waiter gave you the news; or you were walking your dog on a crisp, clear winter night and you happened to look up.

My memory of it is this: I was thirty-three years old and felt older as I headed home from the Stagger Inn in the little barrier island town of Rum Point. I'd been playing a little basketball with my friends, Eric and Nick.

On Tuesday nights we played in a half-court league at the local Y, three-on-three, twenty-minute running halves, call your own fouls, make-it-take-it. We weren't too bad. Tommy was on the team but hadn't been playing since our parents' deaths a few months before. He wasn't much of a player and we didn't miss him.

My knees hurt that night like they had since my college days and those three surgeries in five years. My right ankle hurt from the sprain of a month before that I'd never given it time to get over. My neck and right shoulder were sore from a bulging disk that my ortho said would eventually require surgery.

But, stupidly, I suppose, I loved playing basketball even though my playing days were long over and I was reduced to half-court three-on-three with my friends. So I'd taken a couple of ibuprofen an hour before the game and I'd take two more when I got home. In the morning, I'd struggle to get my legs over the side of the bed and stand up on those ankles and knees. But I'd do it, and walk into the bathroom where I'd take two more ibuprofen and then go teach my morning class. By 10:00 AM or so I'd feel all right and I'd have taught my college students nearly everything that I could about nineteenth-century English and Irish writers.

I'd had four or five Flying Bison ales at the Stagger, which was okay because I lived five blocks from there and was walking home, cutting across the ballfield where, in summers, I coached the local town baseball team, most of the players ex-college or high school athletes who still found something worthwhile in sore arms, pulled groins, sprained ankles, and bruised hips from clumsy slides. Every now and then I pitched in relief. I missed my youth.

And I missed my father.

The police gave me details on how he died: A driving rain on the big bridge over Tampa Bay. The pickup truck to their left going much too fast for conditions and trying to change into their lane. The driver—a young guy running his own pool-cleaning business and hurrying home—lost control and started fishtailing. He clipped Dad's Lexus and sent it spinning just after the crest of the bridge where everyone starts heading downhill. The Lexus hit the right-side rail and flipped end over end while climbing the rail and then spinning once or twice as it fell one hundred feet into the water below. Airbags and belts kept Mom and Dad alive through all that, but sinking twenty feet to the bottom of the bay cost Dad his life.

Mom lived through it. She was on her cell phone with Tommy when this all happened. They were talking about me, sharing their disappointment over my career, and then he heard her crying out and heard Dad's angry curse and then nothing more for a few seconds and then an "Oh, sweet Jesus," from Mom as the car started to sink into the warm embrace of Tampa Bay. Mom managed to unclip her belt and the power windows still worked as she hit the button. She'd been a competitive swimmer at Harvard when she'd met Dad, and that background saved her as she got through the window and up to the surface. Only there did she have the time to think about Dad. So she went back down, the car nose down in the sandy bottom. She got back inside, got to her husband who sat there quietly, eyes open. She got to the belt latch, unsnapped it, tried to maneuver her way back out the window she'd come in, tugging and pulling on Dad all the while. Twenty seconds. Thirty. Fifty. Down there with Dad, trying to get him back. Trying very, very hard to get him back.

Months later it was a warm January night, the way it can be in Florida sometimes, and I was thinking I'd get the team together for some batting practice and infield workouts. The grass was green and perfect in the outfield as I walked across in the darkness, away from the town's lights. I stopped to take a deep breath, musing on the usual romantic nonsense about the smell of leather and infield dirt and the sound of cleats on wooden dugout steps and the ping of the bat against the ball.

For no particular reason that I can recall I looked up, and there were ten new satellites drifting slowly by from northwest to southeast as I watched, in a pattern that was a circle slowly turning ovoid as they crossed the sky. I'm the sort of person who pays attention to the news. A launch of something like this would have made it to the science page of the *Times*, which I'd read that morning in hard copy. The news on that page had been about global warming, the volcano in Japan, a new vaccine for Alzheimer's: nothing at all about multiple launches or satellites. I kept looking as I walked, moving faster the more I wondered. I got home. I turned on the TV and a pretty blonde on CNN was telling me about those bright lights in the night sky over North America. The Ten, as we came to call them. A squadron of visitors to our little corner of the universe. They'd arrived undetected and then winked into sight, just like that. And now, serene, they floated above us.

The Arribada, we came to call it, and we marveled and quaked. I'm sure you remember that first night, the next day. The wonder. The fear.

And you remember, I'll guess, the second week, too; and the third month, and the whole quiet year while those ships did nothing but drift overhead, quiet reminders, bright specks in the blackness.

We can get used to anything, as it turns out. The extraordinary, the phenomenal, the outrageous: these things become the new norm and so we cease to notice. Like everyone else, I went back to watching comforting propaganda on television news and reading complacent newsfeeds on my iFeed and paying attention to the American League East standings and the

NBA Finals and the bestseller lists and my own struggle to find something worth writing about. Everything was normal. Everything was fine. Everything was great.

I had started a new part-time job, Sweeping for the local digital feedwork, sending out daily Sweeps about the top personalities of the day and even, every now and then, some actual real news. The quality of the work was ludicrous, so the pay, no surprise, was outstanding. I told myself it was all very F. Scott Fitzgerald.

So it was my words that a few hundred thousand people had in their eyesets and earsets when NASA got some cameras up there and when the Japanese and Chinese sent a joint manned mission and the ESA blew up one unmanned Ariadne on the pad and then launched another within two weeks. That was an exciting couple of months. The cameras showed us what the ships looked like: bulbous spheroids, with a wide girth amidships and one end slightly larger than the other. There was no indication of a propulsion system, no antennae or anything else on the smooth exteriors.

The Asian mission got too close and lost power, then was pushed away and found power, then approached again and lost power and got shoved away a lot harder and got the message. The ESA approached and didn't lose power and so came in closer, and closer, and then disappeared. The NASA platform sent pictures of the small unmanned Holmes explorer disappearing right through the outer hull of one of the ships just as contact was lost.

And that was it. Our various spacecraft took up station at a safe distance and watched and sensed and waited. The Ten did nothing for the longest time. I started Sweeping about Hollywood overdoses and ridiculous sports salaries. It was a good enough living that I could give up teaching and did. My numbers rose into the millions and Tommy, doing real research and important work to save an entire species, just shook his head in wonder at that. I promised him that when the ridleys returned and his research paid off I'd make him famous.

And I did. I made him famous.

THE KELLY

The kelly device is the squirter that gets the S'hudonni around once they've paid their first visit to a place and set things up. You step into one and it disassembles, squeezes, and squirts. At the other end, another kelly unpacks and reassembles. I was told that only a few kellys exist and Twoclicks was lucky to have a couple. I was told the kellys are a remnant technology, but they never fail. I was told they are clean and quick and enormously painful. I was told you don't remember the pain.

When I swam back up to conscious thought I found I could open my eyes, but that was about it. In another minute I could move my head some, side to side. We were in the main room of a small house, the windows closed and shuttered. It looked like a shack, but surely that wasn't so, since it had to be utterly secure or it wouldn't hold a kelly. The warped plank walls and the tarpaper roof were certainly camouflage.

Behind me there were sounds of cracking and tearing as Heather changed. I'd seen her do that too often to want to see more. The sounds eased; there was a slight scuffling noise as she stood.

My strength was returning. I turned to look and there she was, my Earthie Heather, tall, athletic, that beautiful face, those lips that had overwhelmed my common sense a few years before and still did. She was a falsehood and I knew it all too well and somehow it didn't matter.

I was able to sit up as Heather handed me some underwear, a pair of blue jeans, a long-sleeved blue cotton shirt, socks, and hiking boots. She started to put on similar clothing.

"How much did it hurt?" I asked her as I swung my legs over

the side of the bed and started to pull on the jeans. I was thinking about the kelly.

"A lot. You screamed."

I shrugged; that explained my sore throat. I was glad I couldn't remember any of it. Then I finished getting into the clothes, not surprised to find that they fit. Heather always gets it right, as I'd discovered back when she was Tommy's intended. In those days, I used to wonder how and why.

We walked outside, a light mist swirling around us in the cold; fine droplets of rain gathering then freezing on our hair, our jeans, our shirts as we moved out onto an old wooden dock that sat on a rocky beach along the edge of a bend in a river. In front of us, the water swirled in a wide whirlpool before working its way out of the bend and heading downstream. I turned to look and behind us rose the sidewall of a deep gorge, disappearing into the gray fog above. The sidewall was covered in bushes and small, bare trees. A few taller oaks and maples jutted out from the wall and then angled to grow upward toward what light could reach this far into the gorge.

"Where are we?" I asked.

Heather listened to her data feed. "Niagara River gorge," she said, "below the Falls a few miles. On the American side." She pointed upstream. "The Falls are up around that bend." She pointed the other way. "And Lake Ontario is that way, not far."

She listened again to the data feed, pointed downstream. "I'm told we'll find Tommy over there, but there's some confusion about just where." And I followed as she walked over toward the sidewall of the gorge where she found a path and we began climbing, the slippery clay making the going tricky for me in the mist and freezing rain. Heather had no trouble.

Confusion about just where? I was walking along behind her when that finally sank in. Heather, confused about where Tommy was? It wasn't possible. Heather could locate anything. She was deeply a part of the data wash that is everywhere, courtesy of our Masters of the Universe. Everyone on Earth—just like every being on each of The Seven Planets—was traceable instantly. It wasn't possible for those senses of hers to fail. Ever. But apparently they had, and I had no idea how that could happen.

It started to snow and the wind rose as we hiked up the steep gorge path. The flakes were big and heavy and in a few minutes they began to stick, slippery, to the stones and cold mud beneath our feet. I wondered what in God's name Tommy was doing here. Growing up, we'd only seen snow once or twice on visits to the grandparents and then, later, every now and again as adults. It wasn't something we missed. Tommy was a Florida boy, the kind of kid you could find knee-deep in a mangrove swamp looking for snakes and heron feathers and alligators. He loved the heat and the humidity. He loved the sunshine and the beach at low tide. He loved the thunderstorms in summer and he embraced September's hurricanes. He loved to body surf the waves that would kick up when a storm went by out to our west, heading toward the Panhandle.

Here there was none of that. Here there was nothing, I guessed, but lake-effect snow and cold summer rain. It didn't fit, not for the Tommy I'd known all my life. Not for my brother Tommy, the smart one, the scientist who'd made a career out of tropical seas and beaches and endangered turtles.

We didn't get more than two hundred meters down the gravel path before Heather held up a hand to stop us and then turned to look at me. I looked at her as she shook her head, even used the heel of her palm to slap her forehead. "I'm blocked," she said in a tone of voice I'd never heard before.

"Blocked?"

"My feed is gone."

"Your feed?"

She stared at me and I saw puzzlement on her face. "My data stream, the wash, the flow. It's gone."

"And that doesn't happen often?"

"Peter, the data stream is never gone. Never."

"Except now. Here. How's that possible?"

"I don't know," she said, and that was the first time I'd ever heard her say those words about anything. And then she tapped her forehead again. She seemed to be trying to focus on something. I was wondering what this all meant when I heard the first rattle of gunfire and the leafless tree next to me seemed to come alive, its bark exploding and branches flying. For a very long second or two I didn't know what was happening, then I saw the back of her head explode in a suddenly slowed time that allowed me to see the small bits of her hair and skin as they flew toward me, seemed to surround me, and I was turning to see her collapsing next to me as I felt a hard punch in my right shoulder blade—there was no pain at all—and then another punch, like I'd been hit by a baseball, in my lower back and then another in the back of my right knee and then something hit me hard in the back of my head and I felt just the barest fraction of anger before things got strangely quiet and I was staring up at a wet, brown leaf on a low branch above me as a single huge snowflake landed on its edge and hung there ready to drop while I watched the world get darker and then darker still and then there was nothing.

DISAPPOINTMENT

Tommy was the smart one, growing up, the one who knew the real facts about things while I was the hazy dreamer who wanted to do nothing but play sports, read books and daydream. I was into religion and was going to be a priest. He was into science. We were altar boys together for one year when I was twelve and he was ten. There's a moment in the Catholic Mass when the priest holds the host—a little wafer of bread not much bigger than a quarter—up high with both hands and says "This is my body," and then, a bit later, "This is my blood." At that moment, Catholic belief says, the host becomes the body and blood of Christ. Not *like* the body and blood, but the actual, real thing.

It's called Transubstantiation, and I'd believed it, firmly, from the time I was seven until that year when Tommy became an altar boy.

Tommy and I were kneeling on the cold marble of the altar in St. Thomas Aquinas church as the priest raised that host up high. Tommy shook his head. I saw him do that and wondered if the church walls would collapse in a great roar of godlike anger. Mom and Dad were in the front pew, watching us. They didn't notice that disbelieving shake, but I did. After Mass, he sneaked a host home and put it under the microscope so we both could peer at it. Just bread, he concluded. Then he took snippets of it and ran it through his chemistry set to see what it really was.

"It's bread, Peter," he told me at the end, as he tore off a piece of that host and popped it into his mouth. I expected lightning to strike. "It's just bread, with some esters and carbonyl compounds maybe for flavor. Basically just bread," and he chewed on it.

Then he looked at me, grinning. "You can believe whatever you want to believe, Peter; it's a free country. But me? I'll take science."

That was it for him, and even then I knew better than to argue, even though, for a long while, I didn't stop believing otherwise.

THE WET OF HER EMBRACE

I was dreaming of making love to Heather, the wet of her embrace, the urgency of her lips, when I heard arguing, whistles and clicks between two S'hudonni, the conversation much too fast for me to follow, even after a year of studying the language. Something about failure.

I came awake, the dream fading. I was naked, lying on my back on a cold, metallic table. How the hell had I gotten in here? I had no idea. My last memory was of me and Heather stepping into the kelly to be squirted to Earth so I could do what I had to do with poor Tommy. The kelly must have failed. I was lucky to be alive.

The whistles and clicks slowed, stopped, and then Heather waddled in the door on those short, thin legs. She came over to me, touched my arm. "What do you remember?"

"Everything," I said, "Tommy, the crops. We were getting squirted to Earth. Home. I remember walking into the portal right behind you. What happened?"

"Nothing, really. A minor malfunction in the kelly. We're still on S'hudon."

Later, I found out the truth about the kelly, about life and about death and originals and copies and about my own personal reality. That knowledge cost me my life. Several times.

But at that moment I believed her, having no reason yet to think otherwise.

"Was that Twoclicks you were talking to?"

She nodded, shrugged. "He wasn't all that happy with the malfunction."

"And?"

She reached down to take my hand and helped me stand. I was a little shaky for a moment or two for some reason, and she waited. I nodded and she led me off, me holding her hand and following behind, her loyal puppy, as we walked out the door, turned right, walked right back through another door and there, ominously humming, was the kelly. We stepped in.

CHANGES

The first time I saw Heather change, Tommy and I were waist-deep in the shallows off Egmont Key, a little island at the mouth of Tampa Bay. It was my thirty-fourth birthday and we celebrated by staring at the sea through our polarized sunglasses, hoping that a few of his Kemp's ridley turtles might come in to lay eggs. Tommy had spent eight long years working to save the Kemp's ridleys from themselves and that day, at that small island, would tell us whether he'd succeeded or not. I'd promised him fame if they came and I intended to live up to that bargain. My audience was normally about thirty million, but I'd been promoting this moment for a couple of weeks and it was close to forty million who were watching through my eyes and hearing through my ears and listening to my commentary.

For at least fifteen thousand years the Kemp's ridleys had come ashore and laid their eggs on one particular beach in a few weeks of frenzy on the Gulf Coast of Mexico north of Veracruz. It's an isolated spot and safe from most predators, though the local raccoons must certainly have had their fill of eggs once a year. When the mother ridleys arrived by the thousands to lay up to one hundred eggs each, the overwhelming number of those eggs more than made up for a few raccoons and the enjoyment of the locals, who ate more turtle meat than normal for a few weeks a year.

Then, in 1948, a local fishing guide who'd received an eight-millimeter movie camera as a present from a rich gringo took movies of the egg-laying frenzy and the word got out. It wasn't the eggs that people wanted so much as the mother turtles. The ridleys' meat is sweet and tender and the mothers are helpless when they lay their eggs. For the sake of turtle steak and turtle soup, the mothers died by the thousands each year. In ten years the annual arrival of the mother turtles was mostly a memory on a scratchy home movie. The Mexican government banned the harvest but years too late and the few remaining ridleys struggled for survival for decades before Tommy Holman came along with a plan.

Tommy figured that if he could find the right beaches and the right tides and the right water and the right climate he could take the eggs from Mexico to safer beaches on an isolated barrier island in Florida. When the hatchlings emerged they'd scramble for the water and in doing that they'd imprint on the beach where Tommy had planted the seeds of their future.

On Egmont Key he placed six hundred eggs deep into nests

and watched, six weeks later, when the babies emerged and made their way to the water. Then he waited. Maturity and the urgent desire to mate and lay eggs takes eight years, so doctoral candidate Tommy Holman became assistant professor and then associate professor Tommy Holman before the big day came and he and I stood there waiting for the turtles to return. One returning turtle would be all right, ten would be better, one hundred would be an excellent sign, and more than that would be miraculous, the mortality of turtle hatchlings being high. Tommy had his tenure, but a few turtles showing up would, no doubt, get him the full professorship he wanted.

The ridleys did come, a few and then a dozen and then they came by unlikely hundreds. Tommy's research had panned out and I was there to see it, proud of my little brother, proud that he'd saved an entire species from certain oblivion. We were standing in calf-deep water watching the turtles come in, and Tommy was so happy that he came splashing over to me in joy and gave me a wet, triumphant high five with his open palm before turning right around to wade back onto shore so he could watch his turtles arrive to lay their eggs.

That was the last time I ever saw him happy.

CRACKING AND TEARING

When I swam back up to conscious thought I could see we were in the main room of a small house, the windows closed and shuttered. It looked like a shack; but that, surely, wasn't so, since it had to be utterly secure or it wouldn't hold a kelly. The warped plank walls and the tarpaper roof were certainly camouflage.

Behind me there were sounds of cracking and tearing as Heather changed. I'd seen her do that too often to want to see more. I loved her, God knows, whether she looked like the girl I'd known in St. Pete or the waddly porpoise I knew in S'hudon or anything else of the right weight and mass. But loving her didn't mean I had to watch the changing as it took place.

The sounds eased; there was a slight scuffling noise as she stood.

My strength was returning. I turned to look and there she was, my Earthie Heather, tall, athletic, that beautiful face, those lips that had overwhelmed me before and still did here. She was a falsehood and I knew it all too well and somehow it didn't matter.

I was able to sit up as Heather handed me some underwear, a pair of ski pants, a long-sleeved T-shirt that read "Niagara Falls" across the front, an orange and blue hooded sweatshirt, and a pair of thin gloves. She had cotton socks and high-cut shoes for me to wear, a kind of athletic shoe, padded, with a hard, plastic extra length in the sole that extended an inch or more out in front of the toe of the shoe. She was wearing the same shoes.

"How much did it hurt?" I asked her, thinking about the kelly.

She smiled. "Quite a bit, I think. You were screaming as you formed up." I shrugged; that explained my sore throat. Then I got into the clothes, not surprised to find that they fit. Heather always gets it right.

The shoes felt better than I'd thought they would. We opened the door to walk outside and it was snowing hard, a foot of the stuff on the ground already and more coming to add to it. It would be a difficult slog, walking through this mess.

But we weren't walking. There was a rattle from behind me and Heather came through the door carrying two pairs of skis and poles. The skis were long and narrow. She set two of them down in front of me. "Step into them like this," she said, and showed me how the front edge of the shoes snapped into the bindings, leaving the heel free.

"Cross-country," I said. "I've never done this."

"It's easy. If you can walk, you can cross-country ski, Peter. Trust me."

I did trust her. Mostly. I clipped into the bindings. "We'll go slow, right?"

"Absolutely. It's not complicated, Peter. No sweat."

She'd lied about that last part. There was, in fact, a lot of sweat as we pushed down a narrow trail that edged along the riverbank. Heather went first. Her skis were shorter and wider, meant to cut tracks in the new snow, and so I followed in her trail. We were in a deep gorge, with a cliff wall rising up to our right just a dozen yards away or so and a swift river to our left another dozen yards away. Part of the path went up, climbing the side wall of the gorge. We stayed on the other, smoother, part that wound through the trees. It must have been a hiking trail in older, better days. It was all very scenic, I'm sure, but I was so busy trying to stay upright as I kept up with Heather that I barely had time—or energy—to notice anything to either side. Instead, I focused on keeping my skis inside the grooves she cut into the snow with hers. When I stayed there, I did fine. When I let my skis slip out of the grooves she'd cut, I slid or, twice, fell. It was no damn fun at all.

But we made progress for a good half hour, staying down in the river gorge, sliding along toward wherever we were going. Twice Heather stopped and seemed to take her bearings, though I couldn't see any option other than straight ahead or straight back. Then, a third time, she stopped and tapped the side of her head. I stood behind her, breathing hard, my breath a cloud of wet vapor in the cold air, the steam rising from me as I slowly cooled down a bit.

She tapped her head again, nodded to herself, turned around to face me. "Out of the skis, Peter, quickly."

She used the sharp end of her poles to hit a button and step out of her skis while I fumbled to do the same. Seconds later she was next to me, using her pole to press down hard on the release of my right ski and then my left. I stepped out and then nearly fell as she tugged me into the foliage to the side of the trail.

"Down," she hissed at me, "and be quiet."

I knelt. And shut up.

Heather reached into a pocket in her ski pants and pulled out a small device the size of a deck of cards. This was a remarkable act, since as far as I knew all her electronics were deeply internal and constantly upgraded. I couldn't imagine a use for an external, but there it was.

She looked at the screen on the device and frowned. "Nothing," she said. "No energy, no metal, a few mammals. Damn." And she tapped the screen and then reached up to tap her head.

She turned to stare at me. "Your brother has better equipment than I thought, Peter. He's out there, maybe with some friends, but I can't read any signatures, even with this external."

"You're sure it's him? How would he know we're coming?"

She shook her head and smiled at the same time. "Oh, Peter," she said and was about to explain things to me when I heard a kind of blowing noise, a slight rushing of wind, and an arrow appeared, buried deep into that beautiful neck, the shaft vibrating as she fell back into the snow, gasping and gurgling as blood began to spurt from the wound.

I was reaching out to her when I heard another blowing noise and then felt something punch me in my lower back, and then in the left arm. I turned to look and felt another in my chest and thought I might take a look at that to see what the hell was going on but then it was getting curiously dark out and then there was nothing.

DEEP WATER

After Dad's death Mom faded away from us. Tommy and I knew how hard it would be for her, not just the moving on without Dad, but also the memory of those final ghastly moments, struggling with the belt, struggling in the warm water of Tampa Bay. Struggling. And failing.

She couldn't talk about it, no surprise, and we didn't push her, thinking it would all come out when it was time. The psychologist urged patience on us and, slowly, the quiet became the norm. We didn't ask, and Mom didn't tell.

She took an indefinite leave from the law firm and then hibernated, insisting on staying in the old family home. We thought she might want to put the place on the market and move into something smaller, something with fewer memories, but she refused to even consider that. Instead, she mostly sat in the same living room where she'd spent her adult life with Dad, sitting there on her couch and reading, and waiting.

Tommy would visit with her on Mondays and I did Fridays every week. She had her friends, too, who came by often. We wanted to find that difficult balance between not enough and too much for her, but it was hard to tell how we were doing at it. The strong, vital woman she'd been was gone. This new, more frail version of her was opaque to us. Was she fine? Was she tired? Was she interested in whatever we offered? It was hard to tell. This went on for months.

And then, one Friday in the winter, some seven months after Dad's death, I found her packing. She and a friend, she said, were going on a cruise, a four-night Caribbean jaunt out of Port of Tampa: a day at sea, a day in Grand Cayman, another in Cozumel, and then back to Tampa.

To me, and to Tommy, that sounded perfect. Safe, calm, confined, scenic. Lots of fresh air and sunshine. It might revive her, it might help bring back the mother we both remembered.

There was no friend with her, we found out later. And her clothes weren't unpacked in her stateroom. All we know is that as the good ship *Scenic Seas* passed under the Sunshine Skyway on its way out of Tampa Bay and into the wide open Gulf of Mexico, Annette Holman, age fifty-nine, climbed over the side railing and dived toward the warm embrace some seventy feet below her. She never surfaced and the ship's tenders, the Coast Guard cutter, the big Coast Guard helicopter, the Tampa police boat, the half-dozen fishermen in their boats not far away: they all converged and ultimately, an hour too late, one of them found her.

We buried her right next to Dad. Tommy blamed me for her

death. Not enough attention, too much attention, didn't see the signs, let her go so easily, didn't check on that friend, didn't ask the psychologist about it, didn't do this or did do that or should have should have should have.

I didn't argue, and eventually he calmed down and we papered things over and got on with our lives.

THE SHIPS

The ships showed up at about the same time that Tommy and I had started to patch things up. He was at the university's department of marine science and I was a successful freelancer, making a living off adjunct teaching at the local college campus while I wrote sports and entertainment profile books (*Johnny Harvest, MVP: as told to Peter Holman*) and joined the newest social media fad, Sweeping, where some cam-glasses turned me into a camera crew as I chatted with celebrities and jocks. At first, it was a living, the books doing pretty well and the Sweeping helped me promote the Peter Holman brand name.

Meanwhile, the ships kept watch over us, sometimes changing formations for reasons we couldn't begin to divine, but usually just up there. Orbiting. Normal.

Sweeping got competitive quickly, though the equipment was pricey. Before long some of the most daring Sweepers were getting the cams as implants and were Sweeping anonymously. It did tend to make one nervous, never knowing for sure if the girl you were chatting up at the bar had one eye doing double-duty so everything you said to her was reaching an unintended audience. Me? As a matter of ethics I kept wearing the glasses and even kept the tiny glowlight that let you know I was Sweeping.

At first, I just Sweeped my work, so the interviews I was doing for the books and some webzines could be watched live or from the recordings. Then I started using it to Sweep myself before and after the interviews as I chatted with myself about the personality and merit of the interview. Then, within a few weeks, I left it on during some parties and other social occasions and things started to get busier.

For the first month I hadn't been getting much out of the Sweep thing: you couldn't sell ads if you had just a few thousand viewers. But then, when I start getting personal with it, my numbers began to rise into the tens of thousands and then the hundreds of thousands and then, one January day, over the one million mark. I figured my natural talent was reeling them in.

Tommy and I hung out some when we could and for those times, of course, the Sweep was off. Tommy seemed settled and less angry. After Mom died we'd each received a little over a million dollars from our parents' will and our father's life insurance. We both put most of that into real estate. Tommy had a nice house down at the south end of town, overlooking the bay and with the Skyway Bridge arching across in the distance. He liked to sit out on his dock at night, smoke his cigarettes, and look at the water and the stars and the distant lights of that bridge.

My own place was a nice twelfth-floor condo right downtown, with an impressive view of the city's waterfront and, in the distance, the lights of Tampa ten miles away across that part of the bay. The women I brought home were always impressed with that view.

Tommy called me one day to say he had a surprise to show me and asked me to bring someone along and come to his place for a classic Florida dinner—grouper out on the grill, some sweet corn in the boiler, a few Ybor Gold beers, some Buffett on the sound system. That sounded pretty good to me, and Danni, my current friend, would like it just fine. I didn't kid myself that we had a future, Danni and I, but she was a joy to look at, didn't have any Sweep implants I had to worry about, and was perfectly good in the sack. I'd learned the hard way that that was all I should expect.

We got there about seven, and Tommy was grinning as he opened the door. Behind him, standing shyly, was Heather.

She was plain enough. Short, straight blonde hair framed a round, pleasant face with dark eyebrows, brown eyes, no lipstick, thin lips, a nice smile. She folded her arms a lot, was a little stoop-shouldered and meek, but must have looked wonderful to Tommy, who stood proudly next to her.

"Pete, this is Heather," Tommy said, and put his arm around her as he brought her forward.

I wondered, shaking her hand and saying hello, how long Tommy had known her, since they were acting like a couple that had been together for a while. As we headed through the house and out to the back porch and that nice view of the Skyway, she made her way to the kitchen for drinks, acting at home, comfortable, like she knew her way around.

Tommy might as well have read my mind. He followed out right behind me as we walked onto the wooden decking that edged out from the screened porch. He lit a Camel, blew out a cloud of contentment. "We've been seeing each other for a week, Petey. Can you believe it?"

"No," I answered truthfully.

He laughed. "It's like I've known her all my life. I didn't know it could be like that."

"True love, you mean?"

"Hell, I guess so." He shrugged his shoulders, took another pull on the cigarette. "What else would you call it? It's like we're perfectly made for each other. Fate, I guess."

"Am I hearing you right, Mr. Scientist? Fate? You were *meant* for each other?"

He laughed. "It's really something, huh?"

"Yeah," I said, "it's really something."

Later, when Tommy came out on the deck to explain to Danni about how that Skyway Bridge was the longest concrete suspension bridge in the cosmos, I wandered back inside and sat down next to Heather. She looked at me and smiled.

"So you're the famous writer and Sweeper," she said. "Tommy

talks about you all the time. He says you're very good at what you do."

"He's too generous," I said, though the truth was that I was proud of the fact that Tommy had copies of all five of my books on display. I didn't think he even knew what Sweeping was.

"No, he's not. I read one of your books last night, the one on the quarterback with the autistic child. It's very good. You're honest but fair, and that's hard to do."

"Thanks."

"And I've started tuning in to your Sweep. It's good, too. That's a whole different sort of editing and writing skill involved, but you seem to have a gift for it. And, of course, while it's deeply personal, it, too, seems to be honest and fair."

"Maybe," I said, smiling, "or at least sometimes."

She laughed. "The way you Sweep on just about everything, girls like Danni must worry about hanging around with you."

"Girls like Danni are hoping I'll say something about them. Anything."

"I wonder, are you going to Sweep about me? Should I be careful about what I say?"

"Yep, I probably will. If I were you I wouldn't talk to me at all." I almost wasn't kidding, since I was feeling a kind of vibe from her that I liked. And yet she was my brother's new girlfriend.

She smiled. "I guess I'll just have to be very careful, then. In more ways than one, actually."

I laughed, maybe a little nervously.

"What a strange thing it is to be the kind of writer that you are. I've wondered about that, about what it's like, making a living off the lives of others."

I shook my head. "It's not about the money. I think of it as finding out the truth about things. I'd like to think I'd do it for free."

"You love it that much?"

"Yes, I do," I said, but I was thinking as I said it that I

wouldn't have answered that way a few months back, when not many people were viewing my Sweeps. Now that there were millions, I'd found a new affinity for Sweeping.

"And you think telling the truth is that important?"

"Yes, very. Plus, it's all I know how to do. That's all there is. Hell, it's who I am." And as I said that I realized I was contradicting myself. Lying. *Ah*, well.

She laughed at me. "Mr. Truthfinder? Well, it's been working for you, I'll admit that. I see this week that your numbers are up again, nearly two million now. How's that feel, that kind of success?"

I shrugged my shoulders. Maybe gave her a little smile.

"You know," she said, "my guess is that what you really want is the biggest audience you can find."

I laughed it off, but she stared at me, dead serious for the moment. "Here's my prediction, Peter. You and your brother are a lot more alike than either of you know, and you both want success. Tommy's going to find it with his turtles; he's going to make it work, you know. He's going to save that whole species. He'll pay any price he has to for that to happen.

"And you. Someday very soon the right story will come along and you'll realize the price of telling the whole world the truth is worth all the risk and you'll go for it, too. Bingo, you'll be a Big Star. Capital 'B' and 'S.'"

"Well," I said, "'B' and 'S,' for sure, anyway."

She was still staring at me: those eyes, those eyes. "You'll get a chance to go global, and you'll take it. And Tommy, he'll get his chance, too." She raised her glass to me. "And you know what else? Both of you will find out that some things are worth almost any price."

I was going to shake my head no, but I didn't. I just looked right back into those eyes and felt something I couldn't quite place.

She broke the spell with a chuckle, and looked away. "Well, I guess we'll see then, won't we? The turtles, Tommy says, are supposed to come back to nest this summer and that will be his time."

"And me? When's my time coming?"

She laughed again. I liked that laugh. She put her fingertips on her temples, acting the mystic. "I sense it coming soon. Fame. Fortune. Difficult decisions."

I smiled and shook my head. I meant to ask her then what she did for a living, and why she was in St. Pete. But Tommy and Danni came in to get out of the humidity and we all wound up talking about the Rays, who were on a winning streak. I kept looking at Heather as the evening wore on. She was all subtleties with her looks, I decided, in contrast to her conversation, where she seemed to delight in saying exactly what was on her mind. Tommy seemed to find that charming.

The more I saw of Heather as the days went by, the more I liked her. She wore almost no makeup and didn't seem to care about her looks in general. But every time I'd be at Tommy's or he would bring her by my place over the next few weeks, I'd find myself seeing, as if for the first time, how natural and honest she was. I watched her walk, watched her talk, watched how she moved around, marveled at how her face came alive when she cared about something—and she cared about a lot: politics, the environment and plenty more—and how she had ideas on how to fix them all.

And I watched her as she watched me. Little smiles. Little messages in those blue eyes, those full lips as they slightly parted. Eventually, that all got the better of me.

We never got a chance to talk our way out of it, talk about how it was happening between us, before it all got so crazy. As far as Tommy knew, one day she was there for him and the next day she was gone. All she left behind was a polite little note saying goodbye. And right about then the Ships arrived and the whole world got a little crazy. Everything, in fact, got a little crazy.

EARTHIE FORMS

I was dreaming of making love to Heather in her Earthie form. She was on top, looking down at me as she rose and fell, smiling at me, eyes half closed, murmuring something in the sibilant clicks and whistles of S'hudon, a message I could almost understand, was just about to understand, was nearly there in several ways, in fact, when the dream slipped away and I was flat on my back on a cold slab and the clicks and whistles were very loud and insistent and right next to me. I turned to look and it was Heather in her S'hudonni form, engaged in a heated discussion with Twoclicks, their faces close together as they argued.

Twoclicks was not happy. I sat up, wondering how I'd gotten here. My last memory was of stepping into the kelly to be squirted to Earth so I could do what I had to do with poor Tommy. The kelly must have failed. I was lucky to be alive.

The whistles and clicks slowed, stopped, and then Twoclicks looked at me for long seconds with that inscrutable face of his before he turned and waddled away.

Heather came over and stood in front of me. "What do you remember?"

"Everything," I said, "Tommy, the crops. We were getting squirted to Earth. I remember walking into the portal right behind you. What happened?"

Heather gave me a necessary lie. "A malfunction. Something wrong in the data stream. I couldn't figure it out or fix it, so we're still on S'hudon."

"That's what Twoclicks was yelling at you about?"

She nodded. "He's not very happy with me at the moment."

"And?"

"And he's sending someone along to help me with the stream, someone with special equipment." She wasn't pleased.

The door at the far end of the room slid open with a sigh and I could hear a quick *pad pad pad* as someone came our way. I knew that sound; only one of the S'hudonni I knew walked like that, with small quick happy-feet steps.

He rounded the corner and came in the door. It was chubby little Treble, Twoclicks's son and my favorite of all the various princelings. "Hey, Peter!" he yelled to me, and came hurrying over for a quick hug. "I get to go! I get to go!" The folds of excess flesh on his belly were jiggling.

I hugged him back. I liked the kid. And his English was getting very good, I thought.

Heather shook her head, looked at me and smiled, and then, resigned to taking the princeling along, she reached out to take his hand and turned to head out the door and down the hallway to the room where the kelly waited for us.

I stood there for a few seconds. Obviously there were a lot of things going on that I didn't understand. Wheels within wheels, in typical S'hudonni fashion. But it wasn't as if I had any choice. Nowhere to go but forward, I told myself, and so I came along behind my two companions. Off we go into the wild blue marble.

I reached the kelly room and walked in to see Heather and Treble inside the framework, starting to lie back down onto their transfer beds. I'd been told the transfer process was a painful one, but that I wouldn't remember it. I'd lie down, I'd slip away into oblivion, and then I'd wake up. On Earth. Ready to go talk with my brother Tommy.

And I was supposed to stop him? Well, okay, how bad could it be if Twoclicks was sending his one son along to help? A walk in the park, I hoped. No big deal. I lay back onto the warm transfer bed. There was a slight hum and I was suddenly very tired. I closed my eyes.

ENERGETIC

It was past midnight when I pulled into Tommy's driveway. I'd been at a reading at the Miami Book Fair, four long hours' drive away from St. Pete. Chapter Four of my book on quarterback

Daniel Davies and his autistic son had been reprinted in an anthology of essays on children with special needs and I'd been invited to read my piece to a crowd at the book fair. I'd enjoyed it. It wasn't the couple of million or so reading my Sweep, but it was nice to actually see my audience, and know they could read, and that they seemed to like what I'd written.

I had a text message from Tommy asking me to stop in and say hi on my way home. I'd replied that I would and then my cell phone ran out of battery and I hadn't thought to bring along the charger that worked from the car.

Tommy wasn't there. Heather opened the front door before I got to it. She was wearing blue jeans, a short-sleeved blouse, no bra. Her hair, longer, I realized, than I'd thought, was pulled back into a ponytail.

"We figured your phone was off," she said. "Tommy texted you. He got a call that there are two Kemp's ridleys nesting down on Marco Island. He doesn't think they're really Kemp's, but he has to check those out. He said he'd be back tomorrow around noon."

Heather had been spending most nights at his place for a few weeks by then. There'd been rumblings from Tommy about asking her to marry him. I'd told him I thought it was a great idea. I'd told him she was smart and nice looking and seemed in love with him and what more could you possibly ask than that?

I stood there and took it all in for a moment. She smelled like the energy in the air right before a summer downpour. I looked at her and she looked back, not saying anything. She smiled, leaned up a bit and kissed me. Those lips, full, soft. My brother's girl, the one he was talking about marrying.

We went very slowly. She didn't say a thing at first, stepping back so I could undo those buttons, one by one, from top down to bottom. Then I reached up inside the blouse to push it back off her shoulders as she let it slip to the floor.

I'd never seen her breasts before, though God knows I'd fantasized about them. They were round and firm and perfect, the areolas a thin dark band around the deep red of the nipples. I stared at them.

"They're yours, Peter. I've wanted you to see them. Kiss them for me, please."

I did. Later, after, in bed, I did again, kissing those breasts, her lips, her belly, and then entering her one more time while she brought me to her, the electricity crackling as if for the first time.

We fit together. It was perfection. I didn't want it to be, but there it was. Making love with her was the best thing I'd ever done, the only true story I'd ever written, the best truth I'd ever discovered, a weird and welcome transcendence from what I'd thought, with so many women, was love.

But there was Tommy to think of. Jesus, there'd be hell to pay. I wondered if that's what she'd been getting at that first night we met when she talked about paying the price. Had she known then that we'd wind up in bed, in love?

Was I in love? I sure thought so. One of the things I'd finally learned after a hundred girlfriends was that great sex and true love aren't in the same neighborhood. And this was so different, so not-what-I'd-known, that I had to think it was something real. Looking back, I can see that at the time I was so full of myself that I never got around to wondering if Heather felt the same way. I assumed she did, but never asked and she never offered.

So, finally, burdened and torn between these truths, my head whirling over what we'd done, I left. Went home to my own house. Climbed into bed but couldn't sleep. Got back up, slipped into shorts and a T-shirt and sat on the couch, waiting for the phone to ring or for the pounding on the front door from Tommy's hurt and angry fists. Finally, around 7:00 AM, the phone jangled. I picked it up.

"Hello."

"Petey." He sounded so terribly hurt.

"Yeah, Tom."

"Pete. She's gone. Heather's gone."

"Gone?"

"There's a note here. She loves me, but she has to leave. She's gone."

And that was that. As the weeks went by Tommy seemed to get used to it. Some more Kemp's ridleys sightings helped him with that. Me? I couldn't believe, at first, that she'd chosen that path, but eventually you have to face the facts. And maybe, I thought, she'd done the right thing for us both. With her gone, I never told Tommy what had happened. If she'd been around, all that would have gone differently.

A QUANTUM HISS

I opened my eyes and tried to focus. It took a few seconds before the ceiling came into view: rough-cut wood slats set into place. To the right an open space. We were in some kind of wooden shack. How could that be secure enough to hold a kelly device? If we were on Earth like we were supposed to be, then the kelly would be proscribed technology and completely secure, wouldn't it?

Another half minute passed and I could turn my head some side to side. We were in the main room of what seemed to be a hunting cabin or shack, the windows closed and shuttered. The warped plank walls and the tarpaper roof were certainly camouflage.

Behind me I began to hear the uncomfortable sounds of Heather changing: cartilage and muscle and skin and bones all breaking and snapping at once. I'd seen her do that too often to want to see it again. I waited and the sounds died down.

There was a slight scuffling noise as she stood. I heard the door to the shack opening, too, and looked that way. Treble walked in, almost bouncing along on those spindly little legs, happy as he could be.

"Peter!" he said when he saw me looking. He ran over and stood next to me. "How do you feel?"

"Yes, Peter, how do you feel?" It was Heather, my Earthie Heather, walking into view. "You should be getting stronger very rapidly now."

My strength *was* returning. "I feel good, guys, thanks," I said as I sat up and, a little cautiously, swung my legs over the side. Heather reached out to take my right hand and steady me, and little Treble came over to take my left.

Heather was a blonde this time, her hair cut short, her body short and stocky. I'd never seen this human form before, but it was her, I'd know that face anywhere. That she was so change-able should have worried me, it was further proof of the artificial nature of who or what she was. But I knew that, and it had never mattered before and it didn't now.

Treble whistled his excitement and Heather whistled back as I stood up. I felt better, a whole lot better, my nanos kicking in.

Heather let go, so that only Treble held hands with me. On a bench at the far side of the room was a small stack of clothing. Heather grabbed a few things and returned, handing me some underwear, a pair of ski pants, some insulated gloves, a long-sleeved T-shirt and a hooded sweatshirt, socks, and a pair of low-cut boots with odd soles that had an inch of material coming out the front of the shoe. She handed Treble some other clothes and then began putting on her own clothes, an outfit like mine. Treble slipped into a brown coverall complete with a hood over his head so that he looked like a tiny monk: Brother Treble from S'hudon ready to meet the aborigines of this strange planet.

I finished getting into the clothes, not surprised to find that they fit. Heather always gets it right, as I'd discovered back when she was Tommy's intended. In those days, I used to wonder how and why.

We finished dressing, each of us, and then walked to the front door of the shack. There were two pairs of skis and poles there and a small sled with a seat on it and a front harness attached to it.

The weather on S'hudon—at least the part where I lived—is

generally damp and cool. I hadn't seen more than a light snow flurry in my time there, and I'd lived mostly in Florida before my sojourn to S'hudon, so I was a long way from being an Alpine skier.

"I take it there's snow outside?" I said to Heather and Treble as we reached the door. "And I'm supposed to know how to ski?"

Heather smiled at me. "These are cross-country skis, Peter. If you can walk you can ski in them. It's easy. It's even kind of fun."

"Sure," I said. "It's fun."

Heather spent five minutes getting us ready, showing me how that front edge of my boot clipped into the ski binding, leaving the heel free. Then she gave me a thirty-second lesson in cross-country skiing. Use the poles for balance, slide the right ski forward while pushing with the left pole. Repeat with the other ski and pole. Voila, you're a skier.

When she pronounced me ready we all grabbed one piece of equipment or another and she opened the door.

It was my first time home since the day I'd walked into a screamship and headed for S'hudon two years before. The kelly machines took enormous power to work and there weren't very many of them, I'd been told, so their use was rare. For most travelers, the long voyage by screamship was how it was done.

I remembered leaving Earth in the middle of a torrential thunderstorm in coastal Florida, lightning flashing all around as Heather, Twoclicks, and I walked across the wide sand of the beach at Rum Point and then up the ramp and into the ship. That first trip from Earth to S'hudon took two months and I'd thought I might be leaving forever. Now, in a heartbeat, I was back.

Wherever we were now was a very different place. A bright one, for one thing. A low winter sun in a cloudless sky glared off the ice and snow. It took a few seconds for my nanoed eyes to adjust and then a frozen Earth came into view. We were in a deep river gorge, standing on a wide shoreline that edged along between a towering rock wall behind us and the river in front.

The shoreline was bouldered and wooded and a couple of hundred meters wide. The river was in a hurry, water rushing over rapids just visible upstream. There was no ice in the river. Thick woods ran deep along both sides of us on our shoreline and there were more woods visible across the river. Those woods ended at another steep rock wall that rose to form that side of the gorge. The gorge was a couple of hundred meters deep and I thought I saw houses along the top of the far side. I turned to look behind me and on this side the top of the gorge over-whelmed the view: the rock ended abruptly and then there was blue sky.

We stood in a clearing with the shack just behind us, the rock wall behind that, woods to both sides. A path wound its way out of the woods to the left, weaved through the boulders to pass near where we stood and then weaved away again through the boulders to the right and on into the woods.

"That way," said Heather and pointed toward the right as she stepped into her bindings and took the harness onto her shoulders. She started skiing and the sled came along behind her, Treble sitting upright in the contraption looking very happy about it. I stepped into my bindings and followed along behind. The snow was a foot deep, but Heather cut right through it and the sled's runners fit perfectly into the twin grooves she cut into the snow. I kept my skis in the same ruts as I followed along. In five minutes we'd made it to the edge of the clearing and into the woods. We headed downriver, the tumbling water to our left as we slid along. I had some questions—a lot of questions, in fact—but Heather was in a hurry to get us somewhere and I couldn't hold to the pace she was setting and talk at the same time, so I shut up and skied.

The temperature was below freezing, with icicles hanging from the lower branches of the trees that overhung the river to our left and the snow glaring in the sunshine. There was a light breeze in our face and for the first few minutes I enjoyed the skiing. I discovered the trick was to slide the feet forward rather than step, and I discovered, too, that staying warm wasn't a problem when one is cross-country skiing. As soon as we were in the woods and out of the breeze, in fact, I could feel the sweat break out on my face.

By that time Heather and little Treble were thirty meters ahead of me and so I tried to quicken the pace, which turned out to be a mistake. There was a fallen branch in the path, and while it was covered with as much snow as the rest of the trail it still meant I had to either stop, turn sideways and carefully step over the branch, or go ahead and try to ski right over it. Heather's tracks made it clear she'd gone right over it, and so I tried to ski it, too. I fell.

Cross-country skis don't have quick-release bindings, so when one falls, one ends up in a tangle of skis, poles, arms, and legs. And, in my case, some pain.

Pain is more interesting than you perhaps know. Sometimes it's real, sometimes it's phantom pain that your brain—confused by amputation or other systemic shock—invents for you as it tries to cope. Sometimes there's more pain than the injury should be producing as the brain amplifies the signal. Sometimes there's no pain at all even when the signals are being sent; the brain simply chooses to ignore them.

In my case, I hadn't felt any pain in a couple of years. I'd had two knee surgeries and a battered right ankle that were reminders of my time spent playing basketball. Those injuries used to ache pretty much constantly before I met up with Twoclicks and was brought to S'hudon, where I'd been injected with nanos that did their work admirably. Since the day I'd had the nanos introduced I'd nearly forgotten what it was like to not feel good, and so as I lay there in the snow and wondered whether my ankle was sprained or broken I marveled at the pain—electric jabs of it that shot up from my ankle through my calf, along with a nauseating deep ache that was centered just above the ankle.

I tried to move my body around enough that I could reach

down and touch the ankle, as if that would help somehow; but the movement sent more sharp jabs up through the calf. I decided that I needed to lie there for another few minutes and rest, thinking surely Heather would come back for me soon.

And then I realized the implications of the pain. What the hell had happened to my nanos? They should have instantly dampened the pain and started the healing process. I'd twisted ankles during my daily jogs a few times on S'hudon and the pain of that had lasted for seconds, no more.

I heard the sound of boots crunching through the snowy underbrush behind me and well off the path. I managed to turn my head up enough to look, wondering why Heather was off the path and off her skis, and there was my brother Tommy, walking toward me, stepping through the snow to stand over me and shake his head and say, in that same tone of voice he used the very day I left Earth: "You always were clumsy, Peter."

EGMONT KEY

On that day at Egmont Key, I stood there in the waist-deep water and Sweeped the scene like crazy as turtles by the hundreds, by the thousands, swam past me, bumping my legs and then moving on, driven to lay those eggs and ignoring anything that lay in their way. Tommy would be famous, I thought. All those years of work had paid off.

I looked for him. He'd been next to me for a while and then he'd left to move toward the beach so he could video the mothers arriving and digging. I stayed in the water and did a Sweep of him heading into the beach. It was astounding footage, watching him wade through a thick throng of turtles all heading to shore with him. You could see their plate-sized shells all scrambling along in a hurry, bumping up against each other and him as the turtles fought to reach the shore, find a patch of sand, scratch a deep hole and then deposit one hundred eggs or more.

I zoomed in, I pulled back, I panned, I came in tight. Every shot was better than the last.

Tommy, I was sure, would be a global household name within a day. I was happy for him, happy to have a small part in making it happen.

And then there came my way a shape, sharklike, a shadow in the water. Near it, another shadow, thicker, surfacing and then down again rolling in the warm sea, a porpoise, I guessed. Around these two visitors there were ridleys everywhere by the hundreds, serving-plate-sized little sea turtles, swimming hard, driven by the need to lay those eggs on the beach just a few dozen yards away from where Tommy stood, triumphant.

The shark form circled and then came to a stop, the thicker porpoise next to it. They were dead still in the water as the ridleys swam on by. And then the porpoise sank at the rear end and I could see in the clear Gulf water that there were short legs and it planted them and stood, rising from the water to stare at me, nictitating membranes blinking in the sun. This was how I met Twoclicks.

The shark was blurring and there were terrible changes taking place there in the water. I could hear tearing and cracking sounds as cartilage and bone and skin suffered and altered and then the shark shape, no longer anything like a shark at all, of course, stood on its own legs and it was Heather rising from the water to brush back her wet hair and smile at me. I knew her well. Much too well, and I was ashamed of our history; but then she smiled and shook her hair out a bit and said, "Hello, Peter. I'm back," and I was, once again, lost.

TANGLED UP

"Let's see what we can do to get you out of that tangle, Peter," Tommy said, kneeling down beside me and working on the bindings to my skis.

In a few seconds he had clicked open the bindings and, very

gently, pulled the skis and poles away from where I lay there. Then he helped me sit up.

As he pulled me up, I looked around and Heather and Treble were nowhere to be seen. I hadn't thought they were that far ahead, and in any case Heather's senses are remarkable: hearing, eyesight, touch, taste, smell, all are enhanced dramatically. She is a construct, after all, a mechanical creature; and she had demonstrated to me emphatically any number of times that her creator had endowed her with inalienable rights that were blindingly superior to yours and mine.

And yet she wasn't here.

"We'll meet up with Heather and that little prince in a bit, Peter, don't you worry," said Tommy, smiling. "And this time we'll keep you all alive for a while, too."

This time? I didn't know what he meant by that.

I also didn't know what the hell had happened to Tommy. I took my first good look at him and couldn't believe what I was seeing. He was on snowshoes, dressed in jeans and a ski jacket with a pea cap on his head. He leaned on a staff for support, standing crookedly as if he might fall right over without that staff for support.

His clothing hung on him loosely, his face gray with illness. He looked like he was dying, and yet I knew that couldn't be so. I'd made a deal with Twoclicks more than a year ago that I'd trail along to S'hudon, a polite Earthie pet to entertain Twoclicks and his aristocratic friends. I'd send my Sweep home and keep the Earthies entertained. I'd take notes and write a book. I'd play nice. I'd willingly suspend my disbelief about Heather and make love with her in the most public of ways while S'hudon and the six worlds of The Seven other than Earth watched and commented. That was the insanity that was my life on S'hudon.

And in return my nanos kept me healthy and what I saw and what I said and what I heard and what I felt and tasted and smelled: it was all being watched and heard back home. By hundreds of millions, Heather told me. On a good day, when something as exciting as the hunt with Twoclicks and his siblings occurred, nearly a billion.

And there was this:

One month to the day after Twoclicks and Heather showed up at the beach, we were all out on the Gulf, the four of us, beyond sight of land where Twoclicks could swim in the warm Gulf in peace, while we three watched. He had dampened his nanos so the screens were down. He wanted to feel the water, breathe the air, revel in the warmth without protection. He liked the sense of danger, knowing, always, that in seconds he could re-engage and that, always, Heather was there to protect him.

Tommy, watching from the aft deck of *Serapis*, wasn't saying much. He looked tired. It had been a difficult month for him. First, the realization that somehow—he couldn't figure out how, but it had to be true—Twoclicks and Heather had brought those thousands of turtles to that beach. No test could prove that was so: Tommy and his colleagues had done everything they could to analyze the turtles and their eggs and couldn't find anything. But Tommy knew, he knew. And in that knowing he knew more. These first tentative appearances by the S'hudonni had been made: Twoclicks in Florida, Whistle in Toronto, Octave in Paris. They said they were curious, that was all. And then, a week later, that they had seen some areas where they might help us. And then, a week later, they voiced a certain insistence on helping.

And so it went, and Tommy knew what it meant. Science. Our science. Our understanding of Things as They Are and our efforts to understand more: all that was gone. We knew, essentially, nothing. As Yeats once said: All had changed, changed utterly. And yes, a terrible beauty was born.

Tommy told me, a few days before we agreed to take Twoclicks and Heather out on the *Serapis*, that he felt like he'd been thrown back to the Stone Age. Everything he knew was obsolete. Science itself was obsolete. The S'hudonni knew everything, could go anywhere, could do anything.

If, of course, they wanted to. And that turned out to be a very large "if," as we came to realize.

But all that was yet to come. For now, I joined Tommy on the aft deck while *Serapis* lay at anchor over the Boca Banks, the water just twenty feet deep though we were ten miles out.

We watched Twoclicks swimming, those small arms folded back, that stubby body suddenly looking suited to its environment as he sped by, then surfaced and looked our way, then went back underwater and sped away at a pace that was astonishing. He so obviously belonged in that medium; all the clumsiness we saw in him when he walked on land was gone.

Tommy lit up a Camel, blew out the smoke, looked out toward Twoclicks as he said quietly, "You do know I hate these sons of bitches, right?"

"They're just a few hundred years ahead of us, Tommy, that's all. And they happened to come now, and happened to find you and me."

"You think it's all coincidence, Petey?" He took another drag, then flicked the cigarette out into the water. "You think they came and just stumbled onto you and me? That seems pretty damn unlikely to me."

I shrugged my shoulders. "Lots of things look unlikely if you think of them that way, Tommy. I think they were looking for some people, some humans, to do certain things for them and we just happened to be in the right place at the right time."

"Yeah, right place, right time," he said. He nodded toward Heather, who was up on the flying deck keeping an eye on Twoclicks's cavorting. "And what about her? God, I thought I loved her."

"Yeah," I admitted, "that's a puzzle, why she did what she did." Then I jabbed him in the shoulder. "But hey pal, you never could figure out women."

He didn't laugh.

We heard a distant rumble, deep, the throaty growl of a cigarette boat. In those days the shock of the Arribada had worn off and the big changes hadn't started yet, so life for most people was going on as it always had. Your typical American doesn't know much about science, or care. As long as the car starts, the wireless and cell phones work, the planes fly, the stores are open, the bars sell beer: everything seems fine.

That was *Tempest* headed our way, the big cigarette boat of the Jensen brothers, a couple of bubbas that we'd known since childhood, when they'd been the high school bullies. These days, they lived on a barrier island in some luxury and with a very fast boat, but with no discernible source of income. You figure it out.

I nodded toward *Tempest* and the brothers. "Coming back in from a pickup, you think?"

Tommy lit another Camel. "In broad daylight? I doubt it."

"So they're just out for a little fishing?" But I didn't see any poles and *Tempest* wasn't rigged for fishing. They were four or five hundred meters away, but I thought I saw the Jensens standing on deck together, looking our way, maybe pointing.

There was a puff of smoke from where they stood, and then, a half second later, a sharp crack of sound. They were shooting at us. No, they were shooting at Twoclicks; I heard more shots fired and saw the splash where the bullets were hitting the water around Twoclicks.

Tommy saw all this the same way I did, and both of us were running for the flying deck at the same moment. We had a rifle up there somewhere, and we could gun the engines and get *Serapis* moving, but it was really futile and I knew it even as we ran. *Tempest* was three or four times faster than *Serapis* and those boys knew how to shoot and Tommy and I didn't.

Still, we had to try something, and so Tommy grabbed the unloaded rifle and started pulling open drawers and lockers, searching for some ammunition. I pushed the throttle forward.

I heard Heather behind us, coming up the steps to the flying deck. "Can you buy us a few minutes' time, Peter?"

I looked over at *Tempest*, which hadn't bothered to react yet to our slow turn to move away. More shots were fired. Twoclicks was under water, presumably swimming our way.

"Five minutes is probably all we have if they decide to come after us," I said.

Heather smiled. She was very calm. "Two minutes will do it," she said, and she started back down the steps. I heard a splash over port side and there was Twoclicks, just his face above water as another shot was fired. Nothing splashed nearby.

Instead of running I turned us to starboard and put us between *Tempest* and Twoclicks. I could hear the bullets slapping into the water, then my front glass shattered as a slug hit it and pieces of wood sprayed all around me as another shot hit the railing next to me. I felt a bee sting in my right cheek, another in my forehead, and realized I'd been hit by the shattered shards of wood.

We were, by then, blocking the aim of the Jensens and Heather went in over the side and helped Twoclicks get to the boat. I'd pulled the throttle back while they got that done and as the engine noise died down I heard a curious distant scream in the air, catlike, a yowl. Tommy helped pull them aboard and as they lay there, Heather tending to Twoclicks, I pushed the throttle all the way and headed away, *Serapis*'s engines drowning out that high scream. But I knew something was coming. Something did come. The world changed.

Afterward, with *Tempest* burned to the waterline and the Jensen brothers dead, with Twoclicks nursing a flesh wound where one slug had nicked him, with me putting alcohol on the cuts on my face from where I'd pulled out the wooden splinters, with the screamship that had saved us all back in orbit and circling peacefully, with me and Heather standing there on the aft deck as Tommy took the helm and *Serapis* headed toward the Boca pass and home: a lot of things cleared up for me, a lot of realities emerged.

For starters, Heather told me I was right about everything, much to my sorrow. My brother was dying, a tumor in the brain:

a glioblastoma multiforme astrocytoma. Grade IV, as deadly as it gets. He had ninety days to live if we didn't do anything, maybe a year if we went for the surgery and full chemo. Twelve months. Maybe.

The S'hudonni could fix what was killing Tommy, Heather said. They had med nanos that could do the job, and Tommy's humanity didn't matter. They were proscribed for Earthies, these nanos, but Twoclicks could manage it if I was willing.

"Willing?" I asked her. "Willing to do what?"

And she told me the plan. I would leave Earth and travel to the home planet with Twoclicks and herself. I could Sweep a journal and send it home. I could write a book or two about it all. I'd be well paid and I'd be comfortable. And I'd have her.

But I'd be leaving Tommy and everything else behind. For two years, she said, or maybe more. I said I'd think about it.

When we got *Serapis* back to the marina there were no officials anywhere. The only indication that anything had happened was a Coast Guard helicopter that had trailed us politely from about five miles out to the boat slip and now hovered as we tied *Serapis* off and disembarked. Then the Coasties left us to ourselves and we went our separate ways. And I chose what I had to choose, as you must know, though it all got a lot more complicated right there at the end.

AGGRESSIVE

And now here was Tommy, dying, and all bets were off.

Tommy saw the look on my face. "I look like crap, *eh*, Peter? Well, I should look like crap. I'm dying. The cancer's back and aggressive and I've got another couple of months, maybe, say the medics."

"I'm sorry, Tommy. I thought the cancer was in remission."

"Yeah, well, it was, until I figured out what was going on. And why. And that you were behind it all."

"Oh, Tommy." I tried to stand and managed to get to my

feet; the pain seemed to be easing. "I don't know what you think is happening, but I can tell you it's a whole lot more complicated than you know."

"Sure it is, Peter. And you've got it sussed, right?"

He put his fingers to his mouth and whistled, a long, crisp single note. It echoed sharply in the gorge and then died away. A few seconds after that there was an answering whistle: two short notes and then nothing.

"Your girlfriend and that S'hudonni princeling are waiting for us up ahead, Peter. We have to get moving."

"I don't think I can put any pressure on this ankle, Tommy."

He smiled. "I think you'll be surprised at how good that ankle starts to feel, Peter, at least for a few minutes." He walked over into the underbrush, pushed the snow away from a pile of branches, found one he liked, and brought it back. "Here, use this like a crutch for the first few minutes and then see what happens. It's only a half mile or so downriver to the cave and there we can talk a little more and I can clue you in on how things really are."

"Thanks," I said, and grabbed the branch. It was a long way from being a crutch, but it would help. "Maybe we can talk a bit while we walk?"

"I doubt it," Tommy said, and walked away while two others dressed in winter jackets came in from the woods to stand by me. Tommy turned back once to glance at me. "Meg and Andy will help you get there, Peter, but they're not very talkative with people like you, so I suspect you'll do best to just focus on your walking. I'll be up ahead, getting things ready. See you in a bit." And he melted away into the winter woods. It was interesting that as he disappeared into a thick stand of trees near the river-bank, the pain began to ease considerably in my ankle. And as I walked along with the very quiet Meg and Andy, the sprained ankle felt better and better. By the time we reached a pile of large boulders that had fallen to block the path, I was able to follow my guides as they scrambled over the boulders, down the other side, and then to the right and onto a narrow path that wound through more boulders, some spindly trees and, finally, to a spot where I could see, perhaps one hundred meters ahead, the mouth of a large cave at the base of the gorge wall.

Just outside the cave mouth I saw Heather and Treble, standing there, waiting for me. I'm not great with body language when it comes to the S'hudonni, but it looked to me like Treble was sad. Couldn't say I blamed him much.

SUPPRESSION

"I'm sorry I didn't see this coming, Peter," Heather said to me as I walked up to her.

"Yes, Peter, we're sorry," said Treble, who was holding Heather's hand.

Tommy wasn't around and Meg and Andy stayed behind, keeping an eye on me but not interrupting otherwise. My ankle felt sore again as I stepped inside the cave.

Heather looked ... odd. Displaced somehow. Treble looked excited. I gave both of them a quick hug. It was good to see them alive and well.

"How did this happen, Heather?" I asked her.

"Your brother seems to have a suppressor."

"A suppressor?" I had a crazy image of one of those things the doctor uses to hold your tongue down while she looks at your throat.

"Suppressors put out a field that stops everything generated by S'hudon's technology. All the power generated, all the data feeds, the whole stream. And so everything quits working, including the nanos. Or that's what I'm told. I've never actually seen one."

"You've never seen one?" That didn't seem possible. As far as I was concerned Heather knew everything or could find it out in fractions of a second.

"I wasn't sure such a thing existed, Peter. It's said to be a

First Empire artifact, something from the days before the families came to power."

I'd heard something from Heather before about the First Empire, but I'd never followed up on it. In the great flood of information I'd been wallowing in for months, the First Empire was just one more impenetrable piece of history. When was it? What was it? Obviously I needed to know.

Heather was still talking. "It's just the same as with the kelly devices, Peter. There are only a very few and no one talks about who has them or who doesn't or how they got them or even how they work.

"There are always rumors. Maybe one family or another has one; or maybe there's one for each ruling family; or, some say, the reason the families go to war so often isn't for profit, it's to get the one suppressor that's said to exist or to take a kelly away from another family."

"And Twoclicks hasn't told you exactly where the truth is in all this?"

"Two doesn't know any more than I do, I think. Or at least I thought that until today." She reached up to touch her left ear, shook her head. "I can tell you this: I'm isolated. My feed is gone. My access to the wash. It's a terrible feeling."

I could see she looked frightened by it, and I'd never seen Heather look frightened. Ever. "Where would Tommy get something like that?"

Treble had been listening quietly. At that question he piped up with a quick low, sibilant hiss and a few clicks. Then he said in English so I could understand: "Uncle Whistle."

Heather nodded, patted him on the head. "Well, that would make sense, though it's hard to imagine Whistle having such a thing and parting with it, much less giving it to an Earthie."

I wanted to ask her about that and it might have changed some things if I'd been able to, but that was when I heard, "Peter!" And it was Tommy, walking over toward us. He was smiling. "You and Heather get the little princeling ready for some travel. We're leaving in thirty minutes, on skis. The three of you are going to watch all the fun."

And that we most certainly did.

SEVERAL MORE ITEMS OF INTEREST

Here are some more things I have learned during my time with Twoclicks and Heather.

1) When Heather changes from one form to another the sounds are unfortunate, the smells disturbing, the sights unbearable. On a good day, the end result is pleasant, even too pleasant. On a bad day, the end result is terrifying.

2) Prostitution sneaks up on you. You think your job is to write the truth of a thing and then you realize it is actually something quite different. You think you are a Cronkite and realize you're a Tokyo Rose. It's shameful, but the pay is very, very good. The deal was that I would live a very long and very healthy life thanks to S'hudon. My brother's cancer would be gone, eradicated. My sex life with Heather would be amazing. Many millions would view my Sweep on a regular basis. I would be important, trusted, loved. I would not be a one-hit wonder. I would be a success.

3) Blood is thinner than the water of the Great Loop Current. Blood is angry and guilty and venomous. Blood is deadly. Blood is brothers. And brothers lie.

RELEASE

I hit the release button on the bindings with the tip of my left pole and then stepped out of the skis to walk over to the edge of the bluff and look out over the winter waters of Lake Ontario. My ankle felt weak, but okay. Straight ahead, a couple of kilometers across the lake, rose the Futures of Man, enormous and spindly towers more than four hundred meters tall. These towers and a dozen more sets of them dotted around North America propagated the wash of energy, and so the prosperity that had purchased the loyalty of most of the population. Built in a week by the nanos, "Free Power for a Free World" was how the S'hudonni styled it when the Futures first went up, long after I was already on S'hudon. Yes, "Free" came up twice in those six words. No ironies there, right?

All one had to do to enjoy this energy was buy the receiving units and play by the new rules. Most everyone had, but not my brother Tommy and his little crew of dissidents.

We had hiked and skied to get to the shoreline. I was tired after reaching the shore, Tommy's suppressor hiding us and denying us at the same time.

Tommy showed me the suppressor, such a small thing, the size of a deck of playing cards. Black, with a small touch screen on one side, its range adjustable and directional, from a few meters to several kilometers. He claimed he'd acquired it through a dissident cell on the old Canadian side: people who still loved their freedom, who hadn't been seduced by the S'hudonni. There were thousands of dissident cells all over North America, he promised me, ready to take their own action once they knew the moment had arrived and the Futures of Man had fallen. And there were tens of millions of people, he was sure, ready to rise up and join them when the moment came, when freedom came, when the towers came tumbling down. They'd give up all those creature comforts that had been bestowed by the S'hudonni: the medical gifts, the high-speed rails, the internal comlinks that every kid had or wanted to have, the prosperity that came from a firm hand on the controls of government, of economy, of life. They'd give that all up to be free.

Me? I had my doubts. I don't know much about anything, I'll admit. But I'd spent enough time in America to know comfort mattered, and prosperity trumped trouble every time. Most

Americans had spent their comfortable lives ignoring anything that hinted at discomfort, physical or emotional. In this case, given S'hudon's might, that American attitude might just be the right route to take.

Behind me, Heather and Treble were standing behind some trees, trying to stay out of the wind that came in off the lake. Just behind them were our guards, Meg and Andy. It was very cold.

I watched Heather as she slapped her arms against her chest a few times for warmth. It was unthinkable that Heather—the perfect construct, the complete package—could be cold, but there she was, shivering.

Treble, though, was smiling, enjoying himself, unaffected by the weather. Since the nanos weren't working inside the suppressor field I supposed that his warmth was natural for him. The S'hudonni were comfortable in cold water, their body fat protecting them from hypothermia. Treble probably liked it here.

I turned around again to look back over the lake and to the Futures of Man. To my right, a pair of funnel clouds edged along the back side of a squall line of lake-effect snow that was moving south and east. I hadn't realized that waterspouts could happen like that over cold water, but then that was just one of many things I was coming to realize that I didn't know.

The snow might eventually drift our way. Treble would enjoy that, I guessed, depending on what happened here at this shore.

HEATHER

After the turtles, after the Arribada, after the Jensen brothers, Tommy disappeared and Heather reappeared and life got very interesting for me.

I didn't worry about Tommy for the first few days. He was a big boy and he'd been through a lot. If he wanted to go find a place to walk on the beach and think it all through that was fine with me. I hoped he was doing a lot of drinking and staring at a lot of sunsets and finding some people to talk about the weather with.

For me, I came to think I was done with Heather and Twoclicks after the day I saw the Jensen brothers die and then she offered me that future out among the stars. After we got *Serapis* back to the Sea Horse Pier and tied her off, after Tommy went his way and a limousine took Twoclicks and Heather away behind tinted glass, I was alone.

I expected a call or an email or a knock on the door within the day but that didn't happen. And then a second day passed and I started to think it had all been a mirage, a shining image of a distant city that would always be just out of reach. I decided that it was for the best. It was too outrageous to be real, healing Tommy and sending me on such a journey to such a place. It was unthinkable and I'd been smart to not even hint to Tommy what the offer was, the heartbreak of offering a cure and then yanking it away would have been horrendous. He was already shattered by the Death of Science, which I'd already started to Sweep and blog about. We were the natives, the aborigines, and mighty S'hudon and its Six Planets (we'd be the Seventh) had probably forgotten more about the sciences than we could ever learn.

I had just blogged on that and was thinking of heading back to the Sea Horse Pier to do a Sweep follow-up when there was a knock at the door and there, when I opened it, stood Heather.

"Where's Tommy?" I asked her, angry that she was here and suspecting that she and Twoclicks knew where he was.

She walked in past me and went over to the bar, poured herself a glass of water, took a sip. "He's all right, Peter. And hello, it's nice to see you again, too."

"Tommy's been gone since we all left the boat, Heather. No phone calls, no texts, no emails, no nothing."

"We're keeping an eye on him. He's on Caladesi Island, alone, camping, smoking his cigarettes. There are several turtle nests there, leatherbacks, and he's camped right next to them. He keeps trying to go for walks on the beach."

"Trying?"

"He's dying, Peter. He doesn't know that yet, but his cancer is very aggressive. For now, he has a headache that won't quit, and he's dizzy and disoriented much of the time. There's some nausea. In another week that will all get worse. In six more weeks he'll be dead."

"Unless?"

"Yes, Peter. Unless you come with us. And Twoclicks promises he'll make it very comfortable for you there. Just like home."

I laughed. "Sure, all my friends will be there, and when I'm in the mood I'll head over to the Harp and Thistle for a shepherd's pie and a pint of imported Guinness, right? And there's always some basketball on the high-def and the latest movies to watch, too, right? And plenty of half-court hoops with my friends?"

"Close," she said, smiling. "You'll be the only human, but otherwise, sure, there will be plenty of home cooking, and you'll get televised sports and all the rest, Peter, including plenty of exercise. We'll make you comfortable, I promise."

"Two years? That's it, and then I come home."

"Two years, Peter, and then home if you want it. Or you can stay longer if you want that. That's not long, Peter; just a couple of years and you'll return as one of the richest—and healthiest—men on Earth."

"Healthy? Those nanos?"

She nodded. "We're not sure how you'll age, Peter. You're the first human to get this kind of full treatment. But you are definitely going to be one very healthy guy."

"And Tommy will live?"

"Tommy's cancer could be in remission by tomorrow, Peter, and gone, eradicated completely, a day or two after that. All he'll know is that he feels a lot better. He'll figure it was a virus and he's thrown it off at last."

So it was all pretty obvious, except for one thing: "Why me, Heather?"

She walked over to me, stood close, her face a foot away from mine. Those lips, those eyes. She leaned up to kiss me and I sank into the embrace. The smell of her, the feel of her; these mattered as much as anything. I was lost. Utterly.

We pulled apart a few inches. "Okay?" she asked. And I nodded, picked her up, and walked her back to the bar, set her atop it, started, slowly, deliberately, pulling her T-shirt over her head. Those perfect breasts. My God. I kissed the nipple on the right breast. The left. Still kissing the breasts, then her lips, then back to the breasts, the side of the neck; each kiss a light touch as her breath caught. The smell of her was perfection. Perfection. I reached to her shorts and was undoing the front button as she leaned over me, her hair falling over me as she kissed the top of my head, her hands on my cheeks. The button loosened.

And I heard the door behind me open. Heard a cry of anger and anguish and disgust and pain. I turned. It was Tommy. Standing there. Watching us.

Tommy turned and fled. And me? I went to S'hudon.

IN THE WATER

There was an object out in the water, working its way toward the shore. That would be Tommy, I was certain. He'd kayaked away from the cold stone beach a couple of hours ago, heading out toward the Futures in an old small Swifty kayak with an electrical trolling motor attached to the back, its footprint blocked from S'hudon's detection by Tommy's suppressor set to cover him, even as it still covered us. He carried a half-dozen bangers, their signatures blocked by the same suppressor. The bangers were small things, no bigger than a loaf of bread; but they would bring down the Futures of Man, no question about it.

His plan was to attach the bangers to the central tower and head back to meet us on the shoreline before he sent the signal to ignite the bangers. Then we could all watch as Everything Changed, as he said to me just before climbing into the kayak.

Well, here he was, heading toward us. Great, just great.

Heather walked up to me. She held Treble by the hand, that thin arm of his reaching up to Heather and all three of those short, stubby S'hudonni fingers buried in Heather's hand.

The three of us stood on the bluff and watched Tommy motor in the last two hundred meters to the shore. We could hear the scraping of the bottom of the kayak as it hit the shoreline rocks. Tommy got out, looked up at us, and walked our way, up the narrow switchback path that climbed the bluff from rocky beach to where we stood. We watched him climb, going slowly. I was guessing he was very tired.

Finally he began to near the top of the bluff.

Heather's other hand found mine and she squeezed. "I want you to know something, Peter."

I looked at her.

"Whatever happens in the next few minutes, I want you to know this: I care for you. As much as I'm capable, I do. I always have."

Treble giggled and reached up with his other hand to grab mine, so the three of us all held hands there while Tommy climbed up to us. "I care for you, too, Uncle Peter. Can I call you 'Uncle Peter'? I *will* call you 'Uncle Peter.' And you're the very best Earthie that ever was!" And he hugged me, those arms not quite making it around my waist.

Good grief. I admit to a certain confusion. Love and hugs?

"Heather," I said, "what the hell is going on?"

But Tommy got to the top of the bluff before she could answer.

He stood there, catching his breath, panting as he leaned over to put his hands on his knees and recover from the climb.

Then he stood up straight. He looked terrible: pale, gaunt, his eyes feverish and sunken. "Well, Peter," he said, struggling to say it through that troubled breathing as he reached into a jacket pocket and pulled out the suppressor. "Well, here we go, brother. This is it. First, I turn this off," and he thumbed it. I could actually feel the difference. I felt better, stronger. He tossed the suppressor to Andy, who caught it and held it in his hand as he walked over with Meg and each of them took a side and helped Tommy stand up straight. It occurred to me that Tommy might have been exaggerating about the number of people he had in his little group of dissidents. He might have been exaggerating about a lot of things, in fact. But the three of them were all that was needed at the moment. Meg reached into a pocket and pulled out a small device the size and shape of an old-fashioned pen. She handed it to Tommy. So that meant the remote that would start this war had been right here by me for hours. I could have fought for it. I could have tried.

Treble let go of my hand and so did Heather. They backed away to stand alone. Tommy was busy using both hands to pull down on one side of the device, then press on the opposite side. On the top side a round, phallic segment emerged and grew to six or seven centimeters in height. Tommy held the device in his hand and looked out toward the Futures of Man.

"Tommy," I said, "you know this doesn't have to happen. All hell is going to break loose. A lot of people, a lot of humans, are going to die. Please, Tommy, think about it. Heather can talk to Twoclicks back on S'hudon. You can negotiate. You can get what you want and no one has to die. Including you, Tommy. You can live. The nanos can heal you."

He turned to look at me. "You're so stupid, Peter. You really think that's what this is about?"

"Tommy. You know we can't let you do this." It was Heather.

"That's right," Treble piped in. "We can't allow this."

I turned to pat the cute little princeling on his head, wondering if he—if any of us—would survive the next few minutes.

But Treble didn't need any comfort from his Uncle Peter. Instead, Treble's right hand was buried in the folds of his fleshy gut and he was pulling something from those folds. The small little antique derringer from Twoclicks's collection. How had he hidden it there? I had no idea.

Treble stood taller than I'd have thought he could. He aimed the pistol at Tommy, who wasn't more than two meters away. "I'm sorry," he said.

Meg and Andy had weapons out now, some kind of handguns, aimed at Treble. Tommy waved at them to hold their fire, then shook his head and spoke to Treble. "That old thing can't possibly fire, little princeling." And then he laughed. "And, hell, I'm dead anyway soon." He pulled his thumb down on the remote and there was a bright flash behind us, out in the lake. He tossed the remote down onto the ground, shoved the suppressor into his pocket.

"Yes," said Treble, "my father told me you'd think that." And he pulled the trigger and the derringer fired. The force of the slug striking his chest staggered Tommy and sent him reeling. In a kind of terrible slow-motion I saw Meg and Andy begin firing their weapons and the bullets hit Treble as he fired again and this one, too, caught Tommy in the chest and sent him backward, flailing, as he went over the edge of the bluff.

The sound of the explosion from the Futures of Man caught up with the light from the blast and I felt a concussion as I heard a low, rumbling boom. Treble was falling, hit by multiple shots fired by Meg and Andy. Heather was turning toward them —heroics in mind, I suppose—as they changed aim to fire at her. She didn't make it more than a few steps toward them before she fell.

I thought about doing something heroic myself, but by now it should be clear to you that I am no hero; I am, rather, a struggler, a striver, a drudge.

So I turned to run, thinking I might jump over the edge of the bluff and hope to catch enough scrub brush on the way down to survive the fall.

"Uncle Peter," I heard from behind as I turned.

I turned back. It was little Treble, bleeding and dying but still holding the derringer. He raised the gun to aim it at me.

"I don't understand," I said, wondering if the weapon was real or a clever fake, capable of anything. Could it fire another shot?

It could. "I'm sorry, Uncle," he said as he pulled the trigger. I felt a horrible blow against the center of my chest and had a moment or two to think about why he'd done that to me— weren't we pals, little Treble and I?—as I felt my legs give way beneath me and I collapsed toward the ground. I kneeled there, shocked. Treble seemed to be healing, and that weapon was no antique. He turned and fired at Meg and Andy, and as they fell the suppressor fell free onto the ground. Heather was rising, smiling at me as she picked up the suppressor, thumbed it to make some adjustment, and then, at least, came pain but also a sort of peace as it all began to recede from there and then it was getting very dark and there was a welcome, quiet calm and then there was darkness and a most profound peace at last.

THINGS EMERGE

A bubble emerged from the muck, slowly cleared as it rose, and then abruptly popped. It smelled of cinnamon and apple. It smelled like winter in Racine at Grandma's house and my brother Tommy and I were just in from sledding and there were a lot of complicated things to do for two Florida kids visiting Grandma up north: taking off the mittens, taking off the knit caps, taking off the bulky down coats, undoing a long row of clasps on each rubber boot, shucking the boots, getting out of the snow pants, hanging all this up to dry on various nails in the snow room before we could finally sit down. And all that time we could smell the hot cider and it was so incredibly appealing that we could barely stand being patient and waiting for Grandma to pour it into the cups for us and set it down in front of us.

But that was long ago, in another reality.

Here, in this reality, I was waking up from a deep sleep, and doing it while sitting in the hot muck of a backyard fumarole with Twoclicks. As my head slowly cleared I saw his smiling face emerge from the mud, eyes open as they cleared the muck, their membranes sliding back, then that porpoise smile of his emerging.

"Good memoriess?" Twoclicks asked me with that lisp of his.

They were. "How did you know I was thinking of home?"

He just smiled, then laughed. He was happy about something. Then he disappeared again beneath the bubbling mud and water and a final cinnamon bubble rose and popped.

I heard the sound of bare feet over the rock path that led to the fumarole from the house and I turned to see who it was.

Heather. Beautiful Heather. In her S'hudonni form, waddling toward me. I could see beneath or through or past that form, and I chose to think of the human form as her truest self, knowing it was a lie.

"Hello, Peter," she said. "Looks like you're finally really awake."

She looked at the spot where Twoclicks had just disappeared; the mud was smoother there in a small circle of calm. "And Twoclicks was just chatting with you, I'm guessing?"

"He was, but he didn't really say much. What the hell happened, Heather? I thought I'd wake up on Earth and we'd go find Tommy."

"It's a rather long story, Peter, but the simplest truth is that you've been there now several times and we all did what we had to do. You just don't remember any of it."

"Been there? To Earth?"

She held out a thin hand at the end of a frail arm and I took it. I heard the patter of smaller feet against the stones and turned to see little Treble, Twoclicks's heir and my favorite of the various princelings. He smiled and took Heather's other hand.

"Peter," Heather said, "we have some terrible news for you."

"Terrible news?" I was, after all, barely awake.

"Terrible," said Treble, looking very somber.

I needed to get out of that fumarole. Only on S'hudon would they think it perfectly normal for someone to return to conscious thought to find himself in hot mud. I started to rise, but Heather put a hand on my shoulder to stop me.

"Tommy is dead, Peter. I'm sorry."

I sat back down into the muck. I didn't know what to say. My job had been to go to Earth and keep Tommy alive and calm things down. Tommy? Dead?

"Apparently I didn't do a very good job on Earth," I said.

"You did just fine, Uncle Peter," said Treble, "it wasn't really your fault."

Wasn't really my fault? What the hell did that mean? Treble reached out to take my hand. "You did really, really good, Uncle Peter. Honest. You'll realize it once you see the memory feeds."

"That's true, Peter," said Heather, "it was all very necessary and you were something of a hero." There was a disturbance over on the other side of the fumarole and Twoclicks's head emerged. I'd forgotten he was in there.

"Yess," he said, "you did fine, friend Peter. Tommy chose death."

Oh, my God.

Heather spoke. "He was killed on the first day of fighting, Peter. He's a great hero to millions of people now, but he paid a terrible price for it. You'll get the details later."

"There was fighting?"

"A kind of civil war has broken out."

"But the fighting goesss well," said Twoclicks. "Our side prossperss."

Heather patted my hand. "You'll see, Peter. Twoclicks' territory on Earth looks like it's going to double. All of North America will be his. Whistle will have to capitulate soon." She smiled. "Poor Whistle's technology keeps failing at critical moments. There's a little device we obtained because of your help that gives us the tool to win this war."

Treble giggled.

"And meanwhile," Heather was saying, "Two has plans for you. Right, Two?"

"Yess. Big planss for Peter." And he disappeared again into the mud.

Great, I thought. Big plans. But Tommy was dead? How did it happen? I needed to know the hows and whys of his death. I needed to mourn.

Heather held out her hand to help me out of the mud, and I stepped up and out.

Treble handed me a towel. "You were great, Uncle Peter. Wait till I tell you the whole story. You were very brave!"

"Yes, Peter, wait until we tell you the story," Heather said. "But first," and she smiled, "let's get you inside and cleaned up."

And she took my hand and waddled toward the door. I had questions, a lot of them. About Tommy. About life and death and myself. About those plans.

But later, while I was in the shower, there was a crackling and some groans from the bed in the other room as Heather changed. And so I finished the shower knowing that she would be there for me, my Heather. I stepped out of the shower and patted myself dry and then walked from the shower room into the bedroom. I took a deep breath and set aside my worries as she reached out to me and she pulled me to her. The questions, there were so many questions, would have to wait.

I've visited Edinburgh, Scotland, many times, often staying with friends and relations. The first faint hint of this ghost story came to me on a visit there when I climbed the tall hill called Arthur's Seat in Holyrood Park during a time when I was much caught up in the general moodiness of Edinburgh's climate. The story appeared in Adventures in the Twilight Zone *(Daw Books, 1995, ed. Carol Serling) and was a preliminary nominee for the Stoker Award.*

HOPE AS AN ELEMENT OF COLD, DARK MATTER

Annie Lindsay watches out the tired glass of the classroom window as a mountain peak emerges and then is hidden again in the gray clouds of drizzle.

Hope, she thinks, would have loved a day like this. Hope always loved the rain.

Annie leans forward to look around the corner of the building and can see the long line of rowan trees that line the path she walked along earlier from her room in the hostel. The trees look very tired; they drip with the moisture, wet and gray day, official Scottish weather just like her mother promised.

Annie tries to pay attention to the welcoming lecture; she can't allow herself to fall behind right away. This is astronomy and she's not sure her math is up to it, so she'll have to bear down. Annie knows she's bright enough; her PSAT showed it, and she's always made As in high school, but she hates science generally and would rather be writing poetry or playing some basketball. Still, this is the course that's paid for, so she's stuck with it.

She's trying hard to concentrate, but she can't think of anything but Hope. Thoughts that Annie wanted to leave behind keep intruding. It's been nearly six months now and Annie still thinks about it all the time.

There were no warnings, that was the hardest part. They were supposed to be best friends, supposed to tell each other everything. Everything. And then that.

Annie was the one who found her. Walked across the street to see why her phone was turned off and kept going straight to leave a message.

Hope's parents were gone every Saturday morning, playing tennis. Really nice people, Hope's parents. Annie liked them, especially her father. Annie envied Hope on that score, having a father around who was all tanned and handsome, full of friendly smiles.

The front door was unlocked. The door to Hope's room was open. There was no warning, no hint, there was just her father's gun and that awful smell. Hope and Annie had laughed about when they first found it out in the garage, poking fun at a big guy like her father having a little tiny gun like this.

It looked like a toy, lying there next to Hope, who was sitting cross-legged, back against the wall, in the corner of her room, a grimace on face, her eyes open. The hole in her chest really wasn't very big, but there was blood everywhere in the corner behind her.

Hope hadn't said anything, anything at all about this to Annie. No hints. She'd been fine the night before at the basketball game, the season opener. Hope had scored ten points; Annie had scored eighteen. They'd won.

They'd both been happy. Pizza afterward, talking about boys, about school, about the basketball team.

Little parts of the orientation lecture drift through to Annie, snatches of information about Edinburgh's landmarks and some famous Scots. There's a place called Arthur's Seat, a Scot monument, some writers like Burns and Stevenson, some old hero named Bruce, some bonnie dog named Bobby. It's all boring, they haven't started on the real work yet.

Two months ago Annie actually managed to agree with spacey Beth, her mother, about coming on this study trip. A proud moment there, mother and daughter both quite reasonable about something for a change. Annie thought it might actually be fun and at least it meant getting away, finding some distance from Hope.

Scotland, after all, is half of her heritage, as Annie and Beth discussed, and Annie hasn't seen her father in ten years, not since he and Beth divorced. Since he was willing to pay Annie's airfare and tuition for the college prep classes she'll take, well, why not go? It means early college credit, a chance to see the country of her birth and visit London and Paris while she is at it.

The price is the Big Meeting with Duncan, who, except for a vague childhood memory or two, is a distant voice on the phone to her once or twice a year. But that's okay, no biggie, really. It is quite an opportunity.

Hope would have loved it here, all gray stone and wet green grass. Together, Annie and Hope would have had a blast. Hope always knew how to make the best of bad weather by just ignoring it. During the summers back home it was Hope who went jogging right in the blazing heat of the middle of the day and Hope who liked walking on the beach in the middle of the thunderstorm, laughing at the crack of the lightning out over the water.

But Annie is alone in this cold rain, and despite all the warnings about the weather she hadn't really realized it would be this damp and miserable. It poured in London as she started the tour that preceded the class. Drizzled in York. Poured again in Glasgow.

And now she is here, with people she doesn't know and with two months to go of what looks like a long, wet summer in this tired city of old stone, gray skies, and pale people.

There is a general shuffling of feet. The opening orientation lecture is over and Annie hasn't taken a note, hasn't really heard most of it. She sighs, rises; the rest of the American students are already pairing up and making plans for the day, but Annie has only a couple of hours and then Duncan is stopping by to pick her up. The Big Meeting, Day One: Getting to Know You. She says no thanks to two girls who ask her to come along and shop on Prince's Street and instead opts for a walk on her own.

The rain is easing off as she walks up a steep street toward Edinburgh Castle, all stark and moody, very Robin Hood and Middle Ages and longbows and stuff. It seems to grow right out of the little mountain of rock it is built on. The mist, she thinks, looks perfect, swirling around the battlements.

What a weird place to live. She wonders how Duncan can bear it, rainy like this all the time.

Duncan—she can't call him Dad—is a scientist. She's never really figured that out. How could her mother—weird and all New Age and all that—ever have fallen in love with an astronomer, for Christ's sake?

You'd expect Beth, with her out-of-body experiences and her pyramids and breathing sessions and channeling and all that, to be miles away (light-years away, she thinks and laughs at her own little joke) from a nerdy science type like Duncan.

But fall in love they did, when Beth was a student on a one-year stay at the University of Edinburgh. The marriage lasted a few years, long enough for Annie to crawl into the world, and then slowly started to fall apart. By the time Annie was six, the long decline had ended in anger and disappointment and it was over, mother and daughter leaving for the hot and humid Florida sunshine, about as far away from Scotland as Beth could take them.

Annie and Duncan talked on the phone for a good fifteen minutes just a few weeks ago, when her tickets showed up in the mail. It was a clumsy, hesitant conversation, Duncan trying to explain what he did after she asked, telling her about looking for something that isn't there, searching for cold, dark matter.

Annie talked about basketball and she said she was looking forward to coming over for the summer, and then, both of them out of words, lost for conversation, they hung up. Later, Annie had googled dark matter and found out a few things about the search for the stuff. Now, at least, she had some better questions to ask Duncan, something worth saying. Maybe this afternoon's conversation wouldn't be so stupid.

Annie has a tickle of recognition as she reaches the High Street and looks downhill from the Castle to Holyrood Palace. From her vantage point the street looks long and dull, full of rickety old shops and pubs and tourist traps, selling trinkets and that warm, dark beer to the summer visitors.

Boredom city, but somehow it all looks pretty familiar, too. She can almost see a five-year-old version of herself walking into the Camera Obscura building, and come to think of it, she remembers the place pretty well, how the big white bowl under the lens shows what's going on outside. She remembers standing at the rail that circles the bowl watching the tiny images of the people outside walk up and down the street.

She's surprised by the memory, wonders how often that's going to happen here as she wanders around, and decides to check it out. She has nearly two hours to kill. She needs the exercise anyway, and so starts walking hard, almost turning it into a jog, threading her way through the sidewalks filled with shoppers who showed up as soon the rain slacked off.

Annie misses working out. Back home it was jogging on the beach, and basketball and volleyball at school. There was always something. Here, in a week in Britain, all she's managed to do is walk. She promised Coach K that she would run a few miles every day just to stay in shape for her senior year. Coach has high hopes for her and for the team.

Things ended kind of poorly last season, after Hope's death. Coach gave Annie the standard We All Understand and added the Anytime You Need to Talk Just Stop By chat, but nothing really seemed to help. Annie saw ghosts every game.

She'd be fine in practice, usually, but every game she saw Hope wearing that grimace, standing underneath the basket, waiting patiently for something as Annie hustled up the court, setting up just outside the paint, ready for a pick-and-roll or a backdoor move or a drive into the lane or a jumper from the corner or whatever.

Of course, she wasn't there, not really. Annie would blink, or look away and look back, and everything would be back to normal. Still, it kind of got in the way, to be honest.

The Barons had a chance to take the district title last year before it all fell apart, and they can do it this year if they can find a guard to replace Hope, someone who can bring the ball up the court and run the plays, someone who can shoot a little bit or get the ball to an open Annie on the wing. And if Annie Lives Up to Her Potential, as Coach put it.

On the one hand, walking down the wet bricks of the High Street, Annie hopes she won't get too rusty with two months away from the game. She's always loved it. No one has ever had to force her to play.

On the other hand, it feels good, really good, to not have practice, not have any summer league games. To generally get away from it for a while feels fine, all things considered. This will be the most time she's spent away from basketball since the third grade.

She wonders, as she walks, if she should have a few things ready to talk about with Duncan. Maybe that would help her be less nervous. Maybe she could ask him the history that's all around here? She didn't hear much of it during the orientation, after all. When was the castle built and all that kind of stuff?

Or maybe she'll just keep it simple. Hello, Duncan, how nice to see you. A handshake, a polite hug. And she'll call him Duncan, that she's sure of.

Annie hasn't really had a father and frankly hasn't missed the experience. She and Beth have done just fine, thanks. Annie always gets along well with Beth's various boyfriends, the Toms and Phils and Davids and even the one French guy from Canada, Claude with the attitude.

There's always that first wave of excitement from Beth about someone, and then the Period of Closeness when the boyfriend tries to get know Annie better, then the Big Break-up when Beth cools off and it all falls apart. It's all very dependable. Annie has learned to keep a certain safe distance. Smiles, handshakes, nice chat, and then walk away. This happens about twice a year.

Annie and Hope always had a great time making fun of Beth's boyfriends, the poor guys, giving them nicknames like the Jogging Suit for Phil, and Yoda for the first David, since he sort of said everything backward.

Hope never really liked any of them, even the second David, a lawyer—a really nice guy, handsome in a soft kind of way—that Annie got along with pretty well.

Hope said the good-looking nice ones were the ones you had to watch out for the most. The nicer they seemed, she said, the worse they were, trust her. Hope knew that Annie wondered what Hope meant by that, worse in what way? But Hope wouldn't explain it.

Annie tries to picture Duncan but can't. The pictures she's seen online are all stiff, formal headshots or pictures of him at a podium from conferences or universities. They don't look at all like the images she has from her memory. Can he be balding now, as the photos show? Can he have put on that kind of weight?

He was a good athlete when he was young. Beth told Annie about that, about watching him play soccer—football they call it here—at the university, about how he used to be a serious runner, dashing around on the hilltops near the city, peak to peak in the rain and scattered sunshine.

Beth has talked about how glamorous it was at first; Duncan at nineteen was the star of the soccer team and already doing doctoral work in cosmology. He'd presented a paper on gravitational fields at a graduate seminar down at Oxford and Beth had gone to listen. She didn't understand any of the details, but watched in awe as Duncan talked about how there was mass hidden from view out there in the universe and how better detectors would allow science to prove it, not by seeing it, really, but by seeing how much the dark mass bent light.

Beth told Annie she'd found it all very metaphysical and mysterious, and, at first, the science had been so amazing and so appealing and Duncan so famous in certain high circles that she'd been happy and proud to be his girlfriend and then his wife. Finally, though, a kind of sad understanding had come Beth's way when she'd realized that the gravity and darkness of Duncan's universe didn't leave any room for her and her little girl.

Annie wanders off the High Street and finds herself standing by a statue of a dog. Greyfriars Bobby, it says on the plaque, and talks about how the dog was loyal to its owner and stood by his grave for years. Annie recalls hearing about it during the orientation lecture, but she can't recall the details.

There's a bench there, and the sun is shining for the moment. Annie sits, leans back against the cold stone of the bench and closes her eyes to soak up the thin sun. It's good, warm on the face.

There is a rustling like somebody else sitting and Annie opens her eyes. Hope is sitting on the far end of the bench, legs folded under as usual, that grimace on her face, just staring at Annie. There is a hole in her blouse, in her chest, right between the too tiny breasts that she always complained about. Annie starts to raise her right hand in a greeting, is going to say something but then she blinks, long and hard, and Hope is gone.

Annie wonders if she's going crazy. There was a shrink who came as part of the crisis team at the high school after Hope's death. Annie tried to tell her about Hope, about seeing her all the time, about how Hope's grimace seemed to carry a message. Maybe, Annie said, Hope was trying to say why.

But the shrink just said Annie's mind was playing a few tricks with her, trying to cope. The why of it wasn't something they'd necessarily ever find out. In time, the shrink said, these things would fade, Annie would get used to Hope being gone.

That chat was six long months ago. Annie gets up, starts walking again, looking down at her feet mostly, afraid of who she might see in the crowds on the street, who might be there.

There is a roundabout, cars whizzing by, and she walks around it to find herself near the old palace at the bottom of the High Street. The lecturer said there was something important about the place—Mary, Queen of Scots, maybe? Some murder?—but Annie can't recall it.

She starts to walk around the palace and hears the incongruous sound of a basketball against pavement. A rim rattles, players shout instructions to each other.

She rounds a corner and there, wedged into a parking lot, is a half-court and five players—all of them about her age. She didn't know the Scots played the game.

Annie watches them. The small mountain that she saw out her classroom window serves as the backdrop here, rising in the middle of a park across the street from the courts.

The lecturer called the little mountain Arthur's Seat and said it was really just a steep hill, not even a thousand feet tall, and that people walked up it all the time. Annie thinks maybe she has memories of being carried up it as a kid.

She doesn't think she'd like to climb it now, though. Annie gets a little dizzy when she's up high. Nothing serious, but she has a little bit of a problem with heights, including her own. There aren't a lot of boys interested in dating the tallest girl in the school. And basketball, which makes a boy all the more attractive, does the opposite for her. Too intimidating. Tall, red hair, nice features, green eyes. She knows she looks all right. Hey, looks good, even. But not to the boys at RFK. Her straight As don't help.

Hope, all curly blonde and cute, now there was a girl that was popular with the boys. Too popular maybe. She had a reputation for that, but she just laughed it off when she told Annie about her dates, the groping, the boys' clumsy kisses. Hope and Annie giggled together for an hour, sides hurting from it, when she told Annie about her one date with the Barons' quarterback, Donny Pascal, and how hilarious it was when he took her out to dinner at L'Auberge. He tried to order wine and got carded, then tried to read the menu to her and got it all messed up. The whole evening, right up to the panicky goodnight kiss, was a stitch. Hope was so funny when she told that story.

Annie watches the Scottish girls play. Two of them, she thinks, are pretty good. Two others are passable. The fifth is an athlete but just doesn't seem to know the game. As Annie watches, that girl rolls off a screen and tries a clumsy jump shot, all air, that misses the rim by a good foot or more.

Annie laughs out loud and the game stops.

They all turn to look at her. There is an embarrassing moment of total silence.

"I'm sorry," she manages to blurt out. The first time she's been to Edinburgh since she was a little kid, and right away she acts nasty to the locals. She shouldn't have laughed, but that shot was pretty awful.

"You think you could better, do you?" the girl who shot the air ball says.

Annie shrugs, says, "I said I was sorry."

"Come on out here, then, Yank, and show us your game," the girl says back to her. And then she smiles. "Look," she says, "we need one more to even sides for three-on-three, right? So join us." And she tosses Annie the ball.

Annie thinks for a moment about saying no; she's really not in the mood, and these girls aren't really at her level and she'll have to play down just to keep them in the game. But it is hoops, and despite what she's been telling herself about having some time off, now that the moment is here, well. She smiles, takes off her jacket and watch and friendship ring from Hope and sets them on the grass.

And plays the game.

It feels good. It feels great. She cuts backdoor for an easy layup, hits a pair of fifteen-footers, and a three from down in the corner, makes two sharp passes that turn into easy baskets for her teammates—the flow, the joy is all there. It feels good. It feels great.

She loses track of time as she gets into the rhythm of the play. They have an odd way of doing things, playing brief but intense games to five instead of the usual game to fifteen that Annie plays back home. And they switch possession of the ball every time instead of playing make it/take it.

But these are minor details. The point is, it's basketball. She is easily the best player on the court and knows it, enjoys it, enjoys being good and being comfortable in herself. She's been lonely and homesick and insecure and out of place for days, and here at last is a chance to do something familiar and fun. In fact, truth be told she hotdogs it some; a behind-the-back pass or two, an extra head fake to leave the defender hanging up there useless, a bounce pass to a teammate that turns into an easy jumper.

It's in the fifth game, with the score tied at four, that Annie is out at the head of the key, takes a pass from a teammate, looks underneath, and sees Hope standing there, starting to raise her hand in greeting, that deadly frown on her face, that stare.

Damn. Why here? Why now? Annie, in that moment, angry, is fed up with this. She throws the ball at Hope, trying to knock it right through her, knock the ghost her off the court, out of Annie's mind, out of her life.

A teammate, a girl named Eve, has pulled a beautiful spin move on her defender and gone backdoor toward the hoop. She reaches out to grab the ball as if it were meant to go that way all along, a perfect pass. The game ends with Eve's lay-in. Annie blinks, looks, and Hope is gone, was never there.

They take a break, the local girls gathering around the best player of their age they've ever seen. There's Eve, Caroline, Rachel, Alice, and Kat. They start chatting with Annie, finding out about her plans for the summer, about basketball back in the States, laughing about Edinburgh's weather, about their schools.

Three of the girls are a little older, in their first year at university. The other two are in their version of high school. There's some talk about your Highers that Annie doesn't quite understand, but that doesn't matter, these are nice people, Annie decides. Not great basketball players, maybe, but nice people.

When they find out Annie will be in town for the next eight weeks, they immediately ask her to play on a team they have in a summer league. Three games a week for six weeks, then the play-offs. Not great talent, but loads of fun.

Annie begs off. She's not ready for that, not yet. They play pretty scraggly ball, she tells herself, and she doesn't want to mess up her game. But that isn't the reason, not really. The real reason is Hope. She was there again, big as life, staring at her.

Still, they trade phone numbers and Annie promises to play some more half-court, for sure. And then, when the girls want to play another few games, Annie starts to say yes but then thinks of the time, grabs her backpack, and discovers it's nearly noon. She has to get back to the dorms, clean up, change and be ready by 12:30 PM.

As the girls get back to playing, Annie jogs off to the dorms. They were nice, she thinks. It would have been fun to play on their team. She probably should have said yes. Only then, as she runs back toward her hostel, does realize how she must have sounded. What an ego. She must have sounded really full of herself. But how can she explain about Hope?

She can't. Instead, she'll try and focus on the afternoon with Duncan. Getting to know her father is important. Maybe that will go better.

But it doesn't. An hour and a half later, Annie sits in a puddle in the mud with the rain pouring down on her. She is soaked to the skin, and when she looks up to see where her father is, the only person there in the rain is Hope, six feet away, staring at Annie. Hope's face is tight in that death grimace. There's that hole in her chest. It's so terrible.

Duncan has tried hard enough. He seems like a nice enough guy, if a little spacey and distracted. It started out okay, really. They talked about the good times they'd shared when she was a little girl, and the memories started flooding back to her. She remembers a lot more than she thought she would.

But it didn't take long for things to start going wrong. Duncan wanted her to see the city from the top of Arthur's Seat; he had packed a picnic lunch so they could walk to the top and see the city while they ate their sandwiches.

There is a car park on the back side of the little mountain. They parked there and started the long walk up to the top, which seemed easy enough at first.

The sun had come out and was warm on Annie's face as she climbed, her legs complaining some after the earlier basketball games and the week of no exercise that had gone before. But there were others making the same climb and all seemed to be doing fine. A few young couples, several school-age boys, one older couple, maybe in their seventies. It just couldn't be that tough, Annie thought.

She stayed right in the middle of the path, away from any risky edges, and she didn't allow herself to take in the view. Instead she stayed focused on the path and her footing, upward and upward, step by step.

Then, about halfway up, the sun disappeared behind dark clouds and the sky opened up and a cold rain poured down, light at first and then harder and then harder still.

The others all around her seemed prepared, with rain jackets and caps and sturdy boots, but Annie was in sneakers and a thin Barons hoodie and was soaked inside a couple of minutes. With the wet wind in her face, the footing getting slipperier by the second, and Duncan a good twenty yards ahead and paying no attention to her, Annie was miserable.

Then she slipped and fell onto her rear, smack into a puddle. It might have been comic under better circumstances, but as it is, sitting in the puddle, Annie is a long way from laughing.

She puts her hands down to push off a small boulder and stand up, and then, after she rises to stand and take a deep breath, that's when she sees Hope, sitting there, frowning at her, shaking her head.

Behind Hope, their backs to Annie, the other people on the walk are all happily moving on, the older couple with umbrellas, others with their rain gear on. Annie looks down at her muddy feet and starts to cry.

Great, she thinks. Just great. She looks up again. Hope is gone. But then, just like that, in a flash, the whole weight of all that's happened comes crashing in on Annie. She is five thousand miles from her family and her friends, trying to ignore a ghost that won't go away, trying nervously to get along with a father she barely remembers and can hardly understand with his thick accent, while they walk together up a slippery slope in the driving rain with eight weeks to go before she can go home; and it just all seems too much, just way too much.

But Annie is not a quitter. In basketball when the game is on the line for the Barons, Annie is the one they go to. They have an inbounds play that starts—well, started—with Hope and ends with Annie taking a ten-foot jumper. They use the play late in close games. Hope always finds a way to get the ball in to Annie, and Annie always gets the shot to fall.

Annie always finds a way. Annie's never been a crybaby, not even when Hope died.

She stands up straight and takes a look around. Even through the rain she can see the great view of the Firth of Forth out there, and the city below them.

"Annie? Are you all right, then?" she hears from behind. It's Duncan, who's finally realized what has happened and made his way back to her.

She is smiling when he gets there, and she laughs as she brushes the wet dirt and grass off her rear end and he helps do the same with her back. She gladly takes his offered rain slicker and tosses it over her shoulders. Side by side, they give up the foolishness and trudge back down the little mountain.

A couple of hours later Annie is warm and dry in the front room of her father's house. She feels better but is embarrassed about the mountain, though Duncan seems to have forgotten it. The two of them have been trying to talk, but it seems impossible to really say anything. His wife, Jane, should be home in a few minutes. She's been out getting the messages.

Annie has no idea what that means, except that she'll be home soon, and Annie dreads that, too. This whole thing is even tougher than she thought it would be.

Annie and Duncan have avoided all the really troublesome topics, like why he never comes to the States to visit, or why after ten years of nothing more than occasional phone calls he's sent the money for this summer's stay. Annie wonders if he even knows about Hope. She supposes not, since he doesn't bring it up.

They hear a car. Jane has pulled her Toyota into the driveway, and Annie watches out the front window as Duncan goes out to help. There are bags of groceries in the boot that he grabs, and Jane works her way out of the tiny car on the driver's side, then goes around to the other side to open that door, push the seat forward and reach into the back seat. When she pulls back out of the car, she holds a baby in her arms.

The baby is one year old. Her name is Sarah. She has Down syndrome. She's cute as she can be, with a goofy smile in that round face, and with all the appropriate drool and coo, but when Annie holds her she seems droopier than Coach K's little girl that she sits for back home.

The baby reaches out to hug Annie and smile, and Annie wants to cry for the second time in one day, which sets some kind of record. The baby is so sweet, and Jane loves her so much.

At one point little Sarah tries to stand, pulling hard on a chair, but she's too weak to manage it and never does get to her feet. Instead, a few minutes later she struggles onto her hands and knees and crawls for a few feet.

Jane sees the crawl and yells out to Duncan, who'd left the room to get Annie a glass of water. He hurries back in to watch. The three of them laugh and clap, all for the baby who's just crawled for the first time and Annie was there to see it.

Back home, the baby that Annie sits for is about a year old, too. And is walking. Crawled at five months. Stood at seven. Annie thinks about that and supposes she ought to feel sad for Duncan and Jane, and sad for the baby, too, the poor little thing. But she can't just then, there's too much delight in seeing her crawl.

The afternoon goes by and things get better, Annie playing with little Sarah and getting to know Duncan and Jane. They seem interested in Annie's life, her basketball skills and her grades, her boyfriends or girlfriends or lack thereof, plans for her future. It's all pretty warm, really, and after a while Annie, rolling a little ball toward Sarah, begins to forget about all the problems —hers and the baby's both—and starts to see Sarah for herself, a happy little girl, all smiles and giggles.

Duncan and Jane are great with Sarah. Duncan's face lights up when he holds her and Jane glows with parental joy. They seem to ignore the problems, as if the Down syndrome wasn't there at all.

A bit later, after dinner and while Jane is off changing Sarah's nappy, Annie gets up the nerve to ask Duncan about how they manage to be so great about it. He just looks at her for a second or two, thinking it over, and then says, "I don't know, Annie, but somewhere along the line I finally realized that you can't figure out a reason for everything. Sometimes you just have to accept things and get on with it, that's all. Just do the best you can with what you have."

He sips his coffee, looks at his oldest daughter. "Annie, I'm so sorry that I haven't been the father to you that I should have been. I was wrong about so much, maybe about everything. I was filled with anger when your mother left, and I couldn't let it go." He stumbles over his words for a moment, tries to add, "I was just. It was. Annie. I don't know."

He can't find the words, Annie thinks, and maybe there aren't any.

"All right," she says to him, and reaches over to pat his hand. "It's all right. Let's, you know, work on it, okay?"

He looks relieved. "Yes," he said. "We'll work on it. I'll work on it. I'll do better."

Jane walks back into the room, carrying a happy Sarah. "Don't go in that room for a few minutes," she says, waving her hand dramatically to fan away the fumes. "Whew, what comes out of this wee wain. It's amazing."

Duncan laughs and Annie with him. Little Sarah smiles and waves her own arms around and coos and burbles.

"Can I hold her?" Annie asks, and Jane passes Sarah to her. "Hey, little sis," says Annie, and Sarah burps in response.

Duncan smiles. "She's great, really, isn't she, Annie?"

"She is," Annie says, and makes a face at Sarah, who giggles. They're pals, Annie thinks, and how cool is that?

A few minutes later, Jane calls Duncan into the kitchen for some help making tea, and he rises, says he'll back in a minute or two, and asks if Annie's okay with Sarah. "Absolutely," she says.

With Sarah drifting off to sleep in her arms, Annie idly looks through the magazine rack that is next to the chair where she sits. There's a copy of the local paper on top, the *Scotsman*. It's folded to the Personalities page, and when she looks at the bottom of the page, she sees there's a picture of Duncan, all serious-faced, standing in some drab hallways with his arms folded.

The story is an interview with Duncan, and he's explaining in the story about the search for cold, dark matter. The latest thing is that a NASA satellite has picked up fluctuations in microwave backgrounds, he says, sort of ripples. The data seem to show that the ripples acted together with other forces as part of the Big Bang. Duncan thinks it's the cold, dark matter that added some push.

"It seems to follow quite logically that cold, dark matter is required for us to see this kind of push," Duncan says in the story. And then the reporter adds that Duncan Lindsay, her own father, the man in there helping make the tea, is "one of the top cosmologists in the world in the study of dark matter."

Whew. Annie knew he was important, and she's read about his dark matter stuff. But famous? One of the best in the world? Her father?

What's spooky is how close this all seems to come to the stuff Beth talks about with her New Age friends: the unknowable cosmos, the invisible reality, the ripples in the fabric of time and space.

Duncan comes back into the room, sees Annie reading the papers and laughs it off. "Rather overstates my importance, really. It was Smoot and Silk at Berkeley who did the actual work on this."

And he reaches down to take Sarah and holds her up high, all clean and smiley and giggly. "Hey, you," he says to the baby and rubs his nose into her and blows on her stomach. She squeals with delight. Annie laughs.

"You know," Duncan says to Annie, sitting down and bouncing Sarah on his knee while Jane brings in a tray with tea and coffee and some scones on it, "she's a great wee baby in her way. We just want to help her make everything she can of her life. Like any parents would, with any baby."

He looks at Annie, and shakes his head, "As I should have done with you, Annie. As I will, from now on." The tea and scones are great.

Later, as Duncan drives her back to her dorm rooms, Annie thinks about the day, thinks maybe she's beginning to understand a little bit why Duncan has paid for her to come to Scotland. That part he said about helping her be everything she can. Like any parent would. With any child.

The baby has changed things for him, and so for her. Duncan —better late than never—is trying to reach out to Annie, trying to earn his way back into her life a bit, back where he belongs, back where he should have been all along.

The next morning, Annie gets up, walks to class. It's a cool, sunny morning. She didn't get much sleep, thinking about things. This whole trip is a challenge, she realizes. Like a tough game in basketball. Like tournament time.

She thinks about cold, dark matter and Hope and that little baby. Just get on with it, Duncan said.

The rowan trees have blossomed overnight and there are white blossoms everywhere lining the path she takes. A few of them fall in the breeze to soften her path as she walks across The Meadows.

The lecturer talks about some basics, outlining the material they'll cover over the next few weeks. The Big Bang is the title on the handout he gives to all forty students. Annie, reading that, smiles. She knows a great tutor who'll help her through the tough spots.

By noon Annie is walking in bright sunshine back to the outdoor courts down by the park. By half past she is back at the courts. The girls are there again. Annie asks the girls if she's still invited to play with them in their summer league and they laugh and say something that sounds a lot like och aye, and then grin. Then they split up for some three-on-three. Annie's passing is perfect, her shooting is fine. Hope never shows.

A bit later Duncan comes by the courts as he'd promised the night before, and an hour later Annie and her father are at the top of Arthur's Seat, the two of them looking out over the city. The sun shined through the whole climb, but now the weather is turning yet again, and gray clouds are spitting rain. Duncan sits down to rustle through a backpack and pull out their rain slickers.

Annie smiles; she's prepared for it this time. She turns away from one gust of wind while he pulls the slickers out and there, standing on a rock outcrop is Hope, that frown on her face, those eyes in their frozen stare, that hand coming up to wave hello.

Annie is worried for a moment, but then her eyes slowly blink and the frown fades, becomes a slight hesitant smile. The hand waves once, a goodbye, and Annie watches as Hope turns to walk away, steps down the slope, pivots once to wave again, and then disappears into the mist.

"Who was that?" Duncan asks her as Annie turns back to face her father. "One of your new basketball friends?"

"Yes," Annie says, "yes. She was a friend."

In 2002 I was the primary caregiver for my father and mother, who were living in an assisted-living facility near our Florida home. After my father's death in 2003, I began work on a memoir, My Father's Game: Life, Death, Baseball *(McFarland Press, 2008), about the stress and turmoil of the caregiving role. This story is a work of fiction related to my writing of that memoir, which was called by Philadelphia's* Broad Street Review *a work "that may well become a classic in the literature." The story first appeared in* Gulf Stream Literary Review, *the literary magazine of Florida International University, in 2005.*

PRICES

T he red digital image on the clock face reads 3:14 AM. I'm sitting up in bed, wide-awake, waiting. It's quiet, the thunderstorms are done with us for the night.

The phone rings. I don't want my wife to wake up, so I reach across her and pick up before the first ring ends.

"Hello."

"When are you coming to get me for breakfast?" It's Dad.

"Dad," I say, "it's three fifteen in the morning."

"I know. I was just making sure I'd reach you."

"You have to stop calling like this, Dad. It's too much. It's way too much."

He clears his throat with a deep, choking rumble. All those Marlboros that went along with all the Jack Daniels. Lung cancer was one of the things that killed him. That and prostate cancer. Parkinson's. Hell, he had cataracts, too, and an artificial hip that gave him fits. He was in bad shape. He was very unhappy. He died a year ago.

"Yeah, I know," he says, "but breakfast at the Seahorse would be great. Two eggs over easy, some bacon, toast, a cup of coffee."

"Dad, listen now. You have to stop calling, all right? We miss you, but you have to stop this. You understand?"

"Goddamn it," he says, and hangs up.

I'm feeling pretty good about the call. I'm thinking I really let him have it that time. I told him off at last. Maybe that will end it. Then the light on the side desk comes on. My wife, awake, sits up and looks at me. She shakes her head.

"It was Dad again," I say. "Sorry it woke you."

"The phone didn't ring, Tom. Your father died last year. He's not calling you anymore."

"Sure," I say, "sure, you're right." And I reach over to give her a kiss on the forehead, place the phone in the cradle, turn off the light, and try to get some sleep.

Dad was a baseball player, a major-leaguer. A pitcher, a middle reliever mostly, but a spot starter here and there. He was traded often, and his lifetime stats aren't all that impressive. Over the course of eight seasons he played for six different teams and accumulated about two season's worth of decent numbers. He pitched in fifty-four games, he won a total of fifteen and lost eighteen. He had a pretty good fastball but had trouble with his control. He struck out 135 hitters during his time in the big leagues, but he walked nearly two hundred. These kinds of statistics do not get you into the Hall of Fame.

But in August of 1951, pitching for the Phillies in Shibe Park in the second game of a Sunday double-header, he struck out the first four hitters he faced, got the fifth one on a groundball to second, the sixth on a lazy fly to left, and it went on from there. He faced twenty-seven hitters and he got them all, including a couple of more strikeouts to end the game: no runs, no hits, and no errors in a three–nothing win. A perfect game.

He thought he'd arrived, really arrived, at last, and sure enough he pitched pretty well for two more games, winning one of them. Then his hitting got him into trouble when he slid into second trying to stretch a single into his only double of the year. He felt a twinge in his pitching shoulder, tried to get back on the mound for the next inning, but there was too much pain, and the next day he was on the disabled list. By the following April his pitching days were done, and he turned to coaching and scouting with various teams. Baseball was all he knew, and he spent his whole life in the game, right up to a few years before he died, coaching third base for the White Sox for all those years, and then scouting for the Tigers after that.

Those jobs might have sounded good to a lot of men, but to Dad they were just a paycheck. They were a long way from perfect.

Dad called the north side of Chicago his home; a good, solid Midwest place. Dependable. Polite. Friendly. On-time. He liked it fine there. Once he got into his seventies he became a bit of an institution, with a nice circle of admirers, baseball fans, who would sit around at Sally's Café over coffee and doughnuts and listen to the old pro tell his stories about that golden age of the game; about the time he struck out Stan Musial in the seventh inning of an important game and then gave up a huge home run in the ninth or how he walked in the tying run for the Pirates in 1950 and then on the very next pitch hit Ralph Kiner in the hip to lose the game. Dad always played it humble in those stories, but you got the point, Chicago knows its baseball, and Chicago liked him as much as he liked living there.

But while he liked Chicago okay, he downright loved Florida. From the middle of February to the start of April each year from 1946 until last year, he never missed a spring training. He came alive in Florida and told me so toward the end when he knew he was dying. He loved the smell of salt in the air, the sandy soil that was perfect under his cleats, the humidity, the seafood, the sense of promise each spring, like anything was possible.

After Mom's troubles became clear and she couldn't take care of him the way she always had, he said he wanted to move to St. Pete so he could be in the sunshine year around, so it would always be spring training. I reminded him that the real Florida and his spring training version weren't quite the same, but he didn't care. There was no family, no one to help him, in Chicago, and he needed someone to take care of things. That someone was me, the classic middle son, Mr. Dutiful. So I smiled and agreed and helped him make the move, which was a lot more complex and difficult than I'd imagined, though we finally got it done and got Dad and Mom settled in.

Both of my brothers played minor-league ball. One might have made it to the bigs if Vietnam hadn't gotten in his way. The other had a major-leaguer's arm but couldn't hit when it mattered and never got past class-A ball, despite considerable help from Dad, who made the right phone calls to get his son a second and third chance. Baseball likes to take care of its own. That brother lives in San Jose now, the other lives in Boston. Nice towns, both of them, but they're not Florida.

Me, I didn't have the talent for even a first chance to play ball professionally, never mind any phone calls. I managed to relief pitch some in college, but I had to leave hardball behind and get a real job after I graduated. I drifted into teaching, got a couple of graduate degrees, and now I'm walking across to Merwin Hall to meet with the big lecture class: Intro to Mass Media. Today I'm lecturing to two hundred students about a few of the Big Names in early radio history: Marconi and Tesla and Fessenden and Armstrong and Sarnoff and Edward R. Murrow. They all made significant contributions, I'll tell the students. They all helped create a global medium that changed how we know our world.

None of them, however, could throw a baseball ninety-two miles an hour to a particular spot in a very small strike zone.

As I enter the lecture hall my cell phone rings. Stupidly, I've left it on. Stupidly, I answer: "Hello?"

"Nice day today," he says.

"A little humid," I say. Truth is, I've lived in Florida for twenty-five years now, and I've had it with the heat and the sweat, with the cockroaches the size of mice and the constant summer storms, with the politics and the greed and the general insanity of an unreal life in an unreal state. Spring is nice, but the price you pay for that is summer, when the humidity and the temperature race to see which can climb faster each day, and the summer rains are blinding in their intensity.

"I like the humidity," he says. "And I need a bacon cheeseburger. Now."

"I can't get you a cheeseburger, Dad," I say, "for a lot of reasons." That throat clearing sound: *Harrumph.*

"I'd like that burger. Now," he says. "And some of those Walgreens diapers, too. I don't like the ones they give me here. Bring some over right away."

He was never very good at listening. When he was alive I nicknamed him the Black Hole for the way he expected everything and everyone to come his way, including the adult diapers that he had stacked up in the closet, dozens of them, ready for whenever he might decide he needed them. He wanted. Often.

And Now.

"I'm sorry. I can't do it anymore," I say.

"Goddamn it," he says, and hangs up.

I tell my students this story about Edwin Howard Armstrong, the father of FM radio. He spent a lifetime telling everyone that FM was better than AM, but no one would listen. He explained again and again how, in the words of Steely Dan, there was no static at all and the signal was clear. He couldn't have made it more obvious, but no one was listening. Finally, on January 31, 1954, worn down, broken by the losing battle, he put on his hat and coat, wrapped a scarf around his neck, and walked right out the front window of his thirteenth-floor apartment in Manhattan.

A few years later FM radio began its rise to dominance.

I'm driving south on the interstate, heading home after class.

231

The road takes a broad, sweeping curve here as it goes under the Crosstown Expressway. Dad was plenty hard to deal with when he was alive, but I knew it wasn't forever, and that helped. Then, in February, a couple of months after he died, he called me. Just the one call, and it was in the middle of the night, and I thought I'd dreamed it. Then came another call a week later, then two a week, then six. We're into late March now, and there are several a day. I'm on my fourth cell phone, a new number each time. Eve changed the number at home, too. But he wants his cheeseburgers. He wants those damn diapers. He wants to go out for breakfast. He wants to talk about that perfect game, about how if he hadn't hurt his arm a couple of weeks later it would all have been different.

My wife laughed at first, then she asked me to see the doctor. He's a good friend, a family-practice guy. He laughed at first, too, but when the calls kept coming he sent me to a psychologist—a nice woman, calm, understanding. She didn't laugh, but the phones kept ringing. The phones never stop ringing.

So now I'm driving along, steering a bit left to take the curve. The abutment to the Crosstown's overpass is right over there. Tons of concrete. Seventy miles an hour. There'd be no more phone calls. No more demands. I'd be done with this.

My cell phone rings. Shit. I answer.

"You don't need to think about crap like that," Dad says. The signal seems very clear.

"Sure," I say, "thanks."

"I can't help it, Son. I wish I could," he says.

"Sure," I say again, "thanks."

"You know I threw a perfect game in 1951?"

"Yeah," I say. "You won, three–zip."

"I had good stuff, by God," he says. "I mean, I not only had my heater that day, I had a curveball that Koufax would have envied, you know?"

"Yeah, I know, Dad," I say.

"That was the only perfect game ever pitched in Shibe, you know. And the first one in the National League since 1880."

"Yeah," I say, "I knew all that."

"You better now?"

"Yeah," I say. The abutment is behind me now. The road ahead is clear.

"Okay," he says, and hangs up.

So I keep driving. Up ahead is my daughter. My son. My patient wife.

Dad couldn't say please to me. I tried asking him once or twice when the demands got to be too much, and I actually thought a little Midwestern politeness might help us both. But then I had to watch him struggle with it, the spittle flying as he couldn't get past "P,p,p ..." before he'd quit and shrug, both of us humiliated at the effort.

He did, however, face twenty-seven hitters in August of 1951 and got them all out, one by one, in perfect order.

I'm walking into the Boca Ciega Towers with my son. He's a Down syndrome kid who worked hard in his life to make liars out of a lot of experts. He holds down a good job at McDonald's. He has his own apartment and has, like his grandpa had, a nice group of friends. He fixes his own meals and has me over to watch baseball on television. He knows how to say please and thank you. He calls all this "My good life."

We're visiting his grandmother, Dad's widow, who lives on the Alzheimer's floor of the Towers. She likes it there. Every morning she wakes up thinking she's in a nice hotel on the bay and it's the start of a Florida vacation. She loved the Florida she knew from fifty spring trainings, so each new day makes sense to her.

My son punches in the secret code on the wall unit and the

closed door swings open. We walk down to Mom's room. He knocks, and we walk in.

Mom recognizes him, and they hug. She fakes it with me. She can't come up with my name, but she knows I must be someone she knows if I'm with the grandson she loves. Close enough.

"Hi, Mom," I say, "I'm your son, Tom."

"Oh?" she says, and smiles, the light bulb coming on. She gives me a hug.

"Where's your father?" she asks. "I've been looking for him all day."

"He stepped out," I say.

"Well," she says, "you'd think he'd leave me a note, at least."

"Yeah," I say, "you'd think."

The phone in her room rings. I ask my son to answer it. He looks at me like I'm crazy. He can't hear it, but he walks over to the phone anyway and picks it up, listens, shakes his head and hands the phone to me. It's Dad.

"Where's that bacon cheeseburger?" he asks.

"Dad," I say, "I'm sorry. I can't."

"Let me talk to your mother," he says.

I hand the phone to Mom. She listens. Her face brightens. "Where are you?" she asks Dad.

She listens some more. "Well, take care of yourself," she says, and walks over to hang up the phone. She turns to me. "He's at spring training right now," she says. "He won't be home for a while. He said he'd stay in touch, though."

"Sure," I say, "spring training."

My boy, my good boy, my always boy, just looks at her, then looks at me, then smiles.

Twenty percent of the population of Florida is over sixty-five years of age. That works out to about three and a half million Floridians. Almost all of these citizens are happy to have found their place in the sun. Almost all of them live with dignity and a sense of self-worth that's admirable. Some of them have health problems, cancer or heart troubles or dementia creeping up on them as they pay the price for their youthful mistakes: smoking, mostly, and drinking. There's always a price, and Florida is where it gets paid.

I'm home at the computer, answering student emails. "Do i really haf 2 take the m/term on tuesday? How many Xtra-credit book reports can i rite? Do i need 2 read the textbook? i missed the last 2 classes, did u say anything importent?"

I sigh and sit back, then crack my knuckles. They're paying, too, these college students, for their youthful mistakes. This is how they write, and this is how they think, and I am their teacher. This is my good life.

Spring training in Florida began in 1911, though it didn't really become a serious thing until after the Great War, when the Yankees came south in 1919 and other teams followed. My dad's first spring training in the sun was in 1946, when he earned his way onto the big-league roster for the Phillies. He'd done well in Columbus, Georgia, in 1941 and might have made the big club the next spring; but then came Pearl Harbor and five years of stateside duty, mostly playing baseball for the Army Air Force. After that he finally got that chance for the big leagues, where he wasn't spectacular or anything except for that one day. But how many guys his age would have given just about anything to play in the major leagues at all?

You know, Dad did all right. He played, he coached, he scouted. He made a life of it, heading to Florida each spring from 1946 until right near the end, driving or taking the train or, later, flying south out of the slush and snow of Chicago in February and into the sunshine. Renewal, every year. A fresh start, every year. It was a hell of a way to live a narrow life. And in August of 1951 he had that perfect game. Twenty-seven up, twenty-seven down. Hugs from his catcher, his back pounded by Richie Ashburn and Eddie Waitkus and Del Ennis and a lot of other Whiz Kids from that good era of Phillies baseball.

I spent my whole life hearing about that game in considerable detail, how in the fifth inning Ashburn made a diving catch on a soft, looping liner to center, how in the eighth Dick Sisler did the same in left, how in the top of the ninth Dad struck out the last two hitters on six straight fastballs, all of them swings and misses. I was proud of Dad, proud of his life, proud of my childhood inside his game. I used to talk about him all the time. I made a lot out of being his son. But then there's always that price.

I'm sitting at my computer, trying to write this all down. On the wall to my left I've taped up a scorecard from Dad's big game. It came in the mail from a fan who wanted Dad to sign it and hadn't heard he'd died. The scorecard is filled in by whoever the fan was who was there that day. Sure enough, there's that long line of zeroes. No runs, no hits, no errors. I need to send the scorecard back to the fan with an apologetic note; but for now it's there for all to see. Students and colleagues come into my office and see it and marvel. That's your father? He played in the big leagues? He was a pitcher? He threw a perfect game? Man, that must have been a great way to grow up.

Yes, I say, yes it was. And then, in my pocket, the new cell phone rings.

This story first appeared in Alien Sex *(Dutton, 1990), an anthology of original fiction edited by Ellen Datlow. The anthology has been reprinted in many languages, but this is the first time this story has been reprinted on its own. "War Bride" is a precursor to my long-running series of S'hudonni Empire stories, including the novel* Alien Morning *(Tor, 2016) and its sequel,* Alien Day: Notes from Holmanville *(Tor, forthcoming).*

WAR BRIDE

J ames packs his bag.

Ahab, Huck, Yossarian, Emma Wodehouse, even Horn-blower goes in it, along with six toothbrushes, a handful of postcards with various sunsets and palm trees, and four new baseballs. He would like to pack his basketball, but it just won't fit.

He needs them—the books, the cards, the baseballs. He won't be coming back, and he's picked the things that will last the longest, and serve him the best. But no clothes. Whistle made that perfectly clear. The Pashi can't stand those Earthie clothes, and James won't need them where he's going. Whistle will take care of his attire, as she takes care of most everything else he needs.

He does pack his prosthetic lengthener. Whistle has promised him an operation once they reach the home world, and then he won't need the lengthener anymore. But the trip will take months, James has been told, so the lengthener comes along.

James stands, his head nearly touching the light fixture in the apartment's living area. James is very tall, nearly seven foot three. The Pashi are even taller, and thin, but James is about as big as

Earthies get, and Whistle has developed a real fondness for him. That's why Whistle has decided to bring him along, now that the Pashi are leaving.

James looks out the sliding glass doors toward the Gulf of Mexico. The Pashi landing rigs and comm relays are just visible on the horizon line. That's why Whistle bought James this apartment on the seventh floor, Gulf Boulevard, Madeira Beach, so they could see the rigs and towers against the setting sun when Whistle came to play with her American pet.

Whistle is beautiful, in her own damp Pashi way. James knows he is lucky to have been chosen by her, lucky to be able to pack his one small bag with anything he can think of that will last forever on another world. Lucky guy, he tells himself forcefully, trying to make the sentiment stick. Lucky guy.

James has not always felt so lucky, so wanted. For most of his life, James has felt alone. He thinks about his loneliness as he looks out the sliding glass doors. All the years of it. Too tall, too many books or too much basketball, too many stares and too many expectations and too many needs.

Only Tom, of all the people James has known, found the way through all the incongruities, all the implausibilities, to be his friend. In all of James's twenty-eight years, only Tom has been willing to think of James as a friend instead of a marketable product with a few esoteric quirks.

James tries to staunch his thoughts of Tom, his one true and good friend Tom, who will die tomorrow with the rest of them, with everyone, when the Pashi leave.

Whistle has explained it to him, explained that the rest of humanity, all the Earthies here who don't have Pashi lovers ready to whisk them away, are going to die tomorrow. It will be about lunchtime in St. Petersburg, and Tom will be having a grouper sandwich and order of fries about then if he can afford it. James tries not to think about that.

Tonight the Pashi leave. The great benevolent Pashi who brought so much to the world, who opened wide the doors to all those cosmic possibilities and the promise of trade with a hundred Pashi worlds strung like pearls through the whole spiral arm of the galaxy.

Of course it wouldn't happen too quickly, the Pashi explained. The Earthies would have to be patient as the details were worked out. And there were certain adjustments that would have to be made to accommodate the Pashi presence on Earth. Economic adjustments. Military adjustments.

Whistle had explained it all to James just last night. She was very sorry about it all. The promises hadn't worked out. If only the Bendies hadn't come quite so soon.

But the Bendies are coming. The Pashi comm towers have done their job, detecting the approaching enemy. So now the Pashi have to leave. This small planet, this little place where they have built their advance base, has done its job, and now the Pashi have to go. There aren't nearly enough Pashi to defend this outpost against the Bendies. To stay would be suicidal.

So tonight the landing rigs will send the ships home from their bases around the planet. And tomorrow the Bendies will arrive.

There is a knock at the door: James thinks it must be Whistle, a good two hours early. Very unlike Whistle to be early.

But it isn't Whistle, it's Tom.

James tries to smile as Tom walks in. His best friend, Tom.

High school, state champs, college, final four, two years in the NBA—best of friends, the quick guard with the uncanny passes and the giant with the hard slam and soft hook.

And then came the Pashi and there was no more play for pay now that there was work to be done for the benevolent Pashi. Tom had found a job waiting tables. James found Whistle.

Tom doesn't say anything at first. He just looks at James and then walks past him into the room where he notices the nearly packed bag.

He looks, reaches into the bag to grab a paperback. Laughs.

"Books and baseballs?" he asks, and turns to look at his best friend. "Whistle want to get to know all about our way of life or something?"

Tom chooses to ignore the sight of the lengthener, its tip just visible, crowded in with the baseballs.

James doesn't know how to answer this. Whistle has made it very clear that James is to tell no one about the Pashi leaving. If James told Tom, Whistle would know. Whistle always knows. And then James wouldn't get to go himself.

James doesn't want to die tomorrow when the Bendies destroy the landing rigs and comm towers. Whistle has told James about the Bendies and the struggle the Pashi have been involved in for generations. The Bendies are very thorough, Whistle said. James got the message.

Tom walks away from the bag and over toward the kitchen nook, where he opens the refrigerator door, takes out a bottle of Harp, opens it, and takes one long gulp. "*Ah*," he says, "the privileges of prostitution."

James doesn't protest for a change. There have been certain advantages to being the lover of a Pashi diplomat, imported beer in these hard times has been among the least of them. James doesn't even drink the Harp anymore, anyway. He just keeps it here for Tom. James has acquired a taste for the salty, thick ooze the Pashi drink.

James can't whistle the tune that names the stuff, he just calls it ooze. Whistle laughs at her pet for that, and then strokes his head for being so cute, and then tells him to get out the lengthener, and then ...

Tom is talking. "So what's the bag packed for, Jimmy? Seriously, is your Pashi trying to catch up on some American classics?"

"Some of the books are British," says James.

Tom laughs, drinks, says, "Damn, boy, you're taking all of this a little too seriously, aren't you? They're going to leave someday, you know, and you'll get left behind. That'll be that."

He points his Harp at James, says, "Listen to old Tommy,

now. You've got to keep your head on straight, Jimmy. Don't dive off the deep end on me here, all right? Remember who you are. Remember what you are."

"Tom," James says. "Tommy." And he takes one step toward his friend, one step toward him and away from the door and the view of the rigs.

But Tom turns away to open a wood veneer cupboard door and find some Mexican peanuts, right there where they sit next to the Brazilian breakfast cereal and the Venezuelan pretzels. Most things are imported these days.

"Listen to me, Jimmy," Tom goes on to say through the crunch of the nuts. "It's tough times right now, and you've found a way to get through them. That's great. I understand. Hell, I even stand up for you when people talk. I understand, I really do." And he takes another drink of the Harp, finishing off the bottle in one long pull, setting the empty down on the counter and pointing a finger at his friend.

"But there's a big 'but' here, pal. I've been watching this happen for six months now, and you've gone from making the best of a bad thing to ..." He searches for the right word while he fishes another Harp out of the refrigerator. "... to, I don't know, something really strange. It's like you really like the big blue webbers."

James can't stand to hear the Pashi called that. He admits that there is that bluish tint to their fair skin, and that there is a webbing between the toes and fingers. "But what would you expect of an amphibious race?" he's said to Tom in the past, letting his friend know that he's offended by the nicknames that Earthies use for the Pashi, especially the American Earthies who had so much to look forward to for having helped the Pashi. That's all changed now, so James doesn't say anything.

Tom just laughed at that sort of thinking. He knows James will be angry for the names, and so Tom uses them anyway, trying purposefully to shock his friend, the recipient of those high, arcing passes that led to all those stuffs and happy screams and TV time.

James turns away from Tom and walks over to the window that is to the left of the sliding glass doors. It will be sunset in another couple of hours and Whistle will come, just before the sun goes down.

Whistle will come and then the two of them will watch the orange sky and Whistle will talk of home. The sun will seem to flatten a bit as it enters the water, and then it will quickly sink. If they are lucky, very lucky, they will see a quick bright flash of green. And then it will be gone. And then they will leave, the chauffeured floater taking them out to the rigs where they'll board, lift off, and leave. Whistle said it would only take about an hour. Sunset will be about 8:20 PM. By 10:00 PM, James figures, he will be on his way. Gone forever.

James turns from the window and shakes his head, says, "You've got to go, Tommy. Whistle will be here soon. You know she doesn't like you."

"I know," says Tom, smiling. He walks over to his best friend and reaches up to touch his shoulder. Tom nods his head a bit, shakes it ruefully, squeezes the broad, hard collarbone, and adds, "I just had to come by and say something, all right? I just had to say it. You mean too much to me, you know. You understand? You mean too much to me."

James can only look at him. There's too much to say. There's nothing to say. Tom shrugs, smiles, turns and leaves.

James cries, gets over it, gets back to packing. No electronics allowed, so it's the paperback versions of the *Oxford Guide to English Literature* and his old *Norton Anthology* and a couple of others. He'll have *Prufrock* and *The Red Badge* and some Cather and some Walter Miller and some Karen Joy Fowler and some Le Guin and some Updike and some time to sit back down and cry a bit more. Hard tears. So alone. So very alone.

He stops that nonsense. He rises and looks down at the bag. Quite full.

If he can only get the air out of the ball, he reasons, he can collapse it and take it along. He knows they've got air where he's going, the Pashi breathe it. He can always build a rim and fix up some sort of net. He can always find ten feet high.

He gets the needle in and the air hisses out. He looks at the ball. Tom's signature is right there where he's looking, right under James's own name and the scrawl that says "Kennedy Hawks, State Champs, 2016."

The ball doesn't flatten the way James hoped it would. Funny, but then he's never deflated a basketball before, so how was he to know?

He pushes, squeezes, even stands on the ball, but it doesn't seem to help much. The ball clearly won't fit into the bag unless he takes out a lot of the books, and he can't do that.

Finally, he takes the obstinate ball and places it on top of the bag, hoping that Whistle will let him bring it along anyway. Surely when he tells her what it means to him she'll let him bring that one extra thing. Surely.

But, later, she doesn't. She insists, and he leaves it behind, leaves it on the table, partially collapsed, so that it seems to flatten against the glass tabletop the way the sun does as it sets. Under the flattened part, hard against the glass, are the two signatures.

The Bendies arrived the next day. About noon.

ABOUT THE AUTHOR

Novelist and editor Rick Wilber has published several novels and short story collections, several college textbooks on writing and the mass media, a memoir about his father's life in baseball, and more than fifty short stories in major markets, including the Sidewise Award-winning "Something Real," and the poignant "Today is Today," reprinted in the *Best Science Fiction of 2019* (Prime Books, 2019) edited by Rich Horton. Both stories and seven more tales of determination are in this collection.

Wilber is the editor of several reprint anthologies, including *Field of Fantasies: Baseball Stories of the Strange and Supernatural*, *Future Media*, and *Making History: Classic Alternate History Stories*, among others.

Wilber's novel, *Alien Morning* (Tor, 2016), was a finalist for the John W. Campbell Memorial Award for Best Science Fiction Novel of 2016, and the sequel, *Alien Day: Notes from Holmanville*, will be out in 2021, also from Tor.

The son of a major-league baseball player and coach, and a three-sport college scholarship athlete himself, Wilber often incorporates sports into his fiction. He is the father of a Down syndrome son and often incorporates the disabled in his fiction, as well. He is a Visiting Professor in the Genre Fiction track of the low-residency MFA in Creative Writing at Western Colorado

University, and he is the co-founder and co-judge, with *Asimov's Science Fiction* magazine editor Sheila Williams, of the Dell Magazines Award for Undergraduate Excellence in Science Fiction and Fantasy Writing, awarded annually at the International Conference on the Fantastic in Orlando, Florida.

IF YOU LIKED ...

IF YOU LIKED RAMBUNCTIOUS, YOU MIGHT ALSO ENJOY:

Selected Stories: Science Fiction, Volume 1
by Kevin J Anderson

Infinite Fantastika
by Paul di Filippo

Dangerous Worlds
by Brian Herbert

OTHER WORDFIRE PRESS TITLES BY RICK WILBER

The Wandering Warriors

with Alan Smale

Our list of other WordFire Press authors and titles is always growing.
To find out more and to see our selection of titles, visit us at:

wordfirepress.com